MRS. ROSSI'S DREAM

MRS. ROSSI'S DREAM

KHANH HA

THE PERMANENT PRESS
Sag Harbor, NY 11963

Portions of this novel have previously appeared in somewhat different form in the following magazines: "A Far Place Called Home" (*Artful Dodge*); "The Yin-Yang Market" (*Lunch Ticket*); "The Snake Catcher's Son" (*Mobius*); "One Wish" (*Quarterly Literary Review Singapore*); "The Red-Devil Tattoo" (*storySouth*); "Mother" (*Sugar Mule*); "Size-Twelve Boots" (*VietNow National Magazine*); "The Drifter, The Hooker, and The Girl Photographer" (*Outside in Literary & Travel Magazine*); "Sleeping Beauty" (*Verdad*); "The Orphan Child" (*Belletrist Magazine*); "All the Pretty Little Horses" (*Wilderness House Literary Review*); "In a Far Country" (*Waccamaw Journal*); "The American Prisoner" (*Permafrost Magazine*); "Heartbreak Grass" (*Greensboro Review*); "The River of White Water Lilies" (*Moon City Review*); "A Mother's Tale" (*Louisiana Literature Journal*).

For information, address:
    The Permanent Press
    4170 Noyac Road
    Sag Harbor, NY 11963
    www.thepermanentpress.com

Library of Congress Cataloging-in-Publication Data

    Ha, Khanh, author.
        Mrs. Rossi's dream / Khanh Ha.
        Sag Harbor, NY: The Permanent Press, [2019]
        ISBN: 978-1-57962-568-9

    PS3558.A13 M77 2019
    813'.54—dc23   2018049569

Printed in the United States of America

*In memory of my father, whose indomitable spirit—
anti-dictatorship, anti-communism—was forever
with the deprived;*

*For my mother, whose compassion and guidance has been
the mainstay of my life;*

*For Nguyen Phuong Thuy, Ha Thuc Khoa, and Ha Thuc Duy,
who give me love and joy;*

and

To Dan Pope, with gratitude for your vision.

now
something so sad
has hold of us
that
the breath leaves
and we can't even
cry.

—CHARLES BUKOWSKI

1987
Le Giang

I live in a coastal town in the deep south of the Mekong Delta. During the war this was the territory of IV Corps, which saw many savage fights.

I work at a roadside inn. The owners are a couple in their late sixties. The old woman runs the inn and cooks meals for the guests. I often drive to Ông Doc, twenty kilometers south, to pick up customers when they arrive on buses, boats, or barges. Most of them come to visit the Lower U Minh National Reserve, twenty kilometers north.

I seldom see the old man. He stays mostly holed up in his room. Sometimes when his door isn't locked, I glimpse him wandering like a specter. He and his wife had a son who served in the Army of the Republic of Vietnam. One morning I looked out the window to see the old man digging near a star fruit tree, a small figure, clad in white pajamas and a black trilby on his head. The grassy ground was dotted with bluebells, and hibiscus bled in mounds on the grass. After digging down a foot or so, he stopped. From the pocket of his pajamas he pulled out a bone. It looked like a wrist bone. He sat on his haunches and placed the bone in the hole and scooped dirt over it. After a while the old woman came out, grabbed him by the arm, and dragged him inside. The next morning, he was out there digging again. The same spot. I could hear the sound of his spade hitting the bone and saw him stop. He picked up the bone, smeared with brown dirt, and dragged his spade to the lemon tree. There were fallen lemons on the ground, deep yellow and wrinkled, and they sank with the fresh loam into the earth. He fretted about the placement of the bone, turning it this and that way.

I had to ask the old woman, and she told me that their son was killed in action somewhere in IV Corps in 1967—exactly twenty years ago. They never found his body.

One afternoon the old woman tells me to drive into town to pick up new guests at the ferry. As I ease their old Peugeot into first gear, the old woman runs out and yells, "Have you seen my husband?"

"No, ma'am." I let the car idle.

"Can you drive down the road and look for him?"

"He could be anywhere."

"He went down that way before." She points toward the town beyond the tree crowns and a patch of pale blue sky.

"I'll look for him."

The road is empty and quiet, and I can hear the hoarse cries of storks flying overhead. I know the road well—the houses dotting the road, the dwellers' faces as they stand in the dark doorways. Alongside the road, hummingbird flowers burst in white, their fruits long and pendulous like green beans.

Ahead I see him walking in his white pajamas. He wears the same trilby pulled down over his eyes, a brown bag clutched in his hand. He looks back nervously.

I pull up and he glances toward me, then looks the other way. I get out and take him by the elbow toward the car. He follows meekly, cradling the brown bag against his chest. The rustle of paper makes me curious. "What do you have in there, sir?"

"Where is a safe place?" he asks in his southern accent.

"For what, sir?"

He opens the top of the bag. Inside is the bone. An ox bone, I see.

The barge arrives very late, the rain falling in gray sheets across the quay.

I wipe my face and pull my raincoat tight around me. I cough. My throat hurts. People are coming onto the quay. Bicycles and motor scooters rev in tandem in their lanes. The air smells of gasoline fumes. The wet dusk glows with the scooters' headlights. I watch for the next wave of passengers, those on foot. Waiting behind them are the big, blue trucks. Rain slants and pops on the quay, on the gray-steel hatch of the barge's liftgate. I scan the blurred faces of the passengers hurrying up the quay, nylon bags, pink, blue, in hands, jute bags slung across shoulders. They stream past me, rustling in their nylon raincoats. Here, the locals bring them along after checking the color of the sky and shapes of the clouds.

Then I see them: a girl and a white woman, both wearing wide-brimmed straw hats but no raincoats, lugging their suitcases down the hatch. They are coming toward me, as I stand to one side, hunched, on the quay's slope. I raise my hand. "Mrs. Rossi?"

The woman turns toward me. "Hello!" she says, half smiling, half wincing from the pelting rain.

I extend my hand to help her with the suitcase. Instead her hand comes up to shake mine.

"Please, let me help," I say, reaching for her suitcase.

"Are you from the inn?" she says.

"Yes, ma'am."

"I'm terribly sorry about the delay. I thought you must've left. I'm awfully glad to see you still here."

"Yes, ma'am. May I take you and your daughter to the car?"

"Yes, of course." She smiles, wrinkling the corners of her blue eyes. She takes the girl's hand and both of them follow me to the Peugeot, parked on the ramp. She talks to the girl about getting raincoats for their stay, for monsoon season has arrived. Although wrinkled and gray, perhaps in her late sixties, Mrs. Rossi has a clear, cheerful voice.

I open the rear door. The girl says, "Thank you," as she slides onto the seat. She must be Vietnamese, slender, rather tall. Her blue jeans are notched above the ankles, and her light skin blends perfectly with her scarlet blouse, collarless, fringed white. Mrs. Rossi takes off her wet straw hat, shaking it against her leg, and says, "No one here carries an umbrella."

"People here wear raincoats when it rains," I say as she clears a wet lock of white hair from her brow.

"In Ho Chi Minh City too?" Mrs. Rossi asks.

"Yes, everywhere."

I put their suitcases in the trunk and close it. The rain smears the windshield as I drive through the town. Shop lights flicker. Water is rising on the main street and motor scooters sloshing through standing water kick up fantails in light-colored spouts. Ho Chi Minh City. The old name is Saigon. I hunch forward to look through the smeary windshield. Rain drums the car roof. From the ferry comes the sound of a horn. Another barge is arriving.

"This looks like a badly crowded Chinese quarter," Mrs. Rossi says from the back seat.

"Very crowded, ma'am. You never see the sun when you walk the streets here."

A surge of running water against the tires shakes the steering wheel. Water is rising to the shops' thresholds; store awnings flap like wings of some wet fowl.

"Are you from here by any chance?" Mrs. Rossi asks me.

"No. Most townspeople here come from somewhere else. Drifters, ma'am."

"You too?" Mrs. Rossi asks with a chuckle.

"Me too," I say, coughing, my throat dry as sand.

"I didn't catch your name."

"Giang, ma'am."

She repeats my name. "Can you spell it for me?" Then, hearing it spelled, she says, "So it's Zhang, like the Chinese name."

"Yes, ma'am."

"I'm Catherine Rossi. My daughter is Chi Lan."

The girl offers a hello from the back seat. I simply nod. Mrs. Rossi says, "My daughter understands Vietnamese. Only she can't speak it very well."

"She must not have lived here long."

"No, she didn't. She became my daughter when she was five years old. She's eighteen now."

"You adopted her, ma'am?" I glance again at the rear-view mirror and meet the girl's eyes. I feel odd asking her mother about her in her presence.

"Yes, I adopted her in 1974. Just a year before the collapse of South Vietnam. How fortunate for us!"

"You came here that year?"

"Yes." Mrs. Rossi clears her throat. "And what were you doing in '74?"

I give her question some thought, then say, "I was in the South Vietnamese Army."

"Were you an interpreter?"

"No, ma'am."

"Then you must excuse my assumption. You speak English very well. And I'm glad you do. Otherwise we'd be making sign language now."

She laughs and the girl smiles. Her oval face, framed by raven, shoulder-length hair, is fresh. Her eyebrows curve gracefully, like crayoned black. I remember a face like that from my past.

"Were you an army lifer?" asks Mrs. Rossi.

"What is that?" I ask.

"Did you spend a lifetime career in the army?"

"No, ma'am. Only a few years."

"Did you teach school before that?"

These curious Americans. "I was on the other side. A soldier of the North Vietnamese Army."

"Were you born in the North?"

"Yes."

"And then you defected to the South and joined the South Vietnamese Army?"

"Yes, ma'am."

"They have a name for those. I'm trying to remember."

Then I hear the girl say it for her: a *hoi chánh*.

Mrs. Rossi seems to be deep in thought as we leave the town, following the one-lane road north toward the U Minh district. The headlights pick up windblown rain in sprays, blurring the blacktop. There is no lane divider. Along the road drenched palms toss in the wind. Wet leaves and white cajeput flowers fall onto the windshield, and the wipers sweep over them, pressing them to the glass.

"Your victors, the North communists, didn't like the *hoi chánh* very much. So I heard."

"That's true, ma'am."

"Did they treat you any differently than the regular ARVN soldiers?"

"Sometimes worse, ma'am. I was one of those."

"What happened to those like you?"

"The North communists sent us to reform camps. Very far from here."

"For how long?"

"Ten years, ma'am. Where nobody saw us."

"Atrocious," she says. "So you were released just two years ago? 1985? Why so long?"

"Perhaps we were not reformed well enough."

The road bends around a banana grove and on the other side golden bamboo grow thick, leaning in over the road, their trunks slender and tall, glistening in the sweeping headlights.

"Are you here to visit the U Minh National Reserve, ma'am?" I ask, half turning my head toward them.

"Yes." She seems to want to say more but stops herself. "It's a long story."

I keep my eyes on the dark road, a road I know well. But on a rainy night like this, the soaked, windswept landscape loses its familiarity. We are halfway to the inn. Lit by the headlights, yellow flowers of the narrow-crowned river-hemp shrubs seem to float along the roadside.

"Mr. Giang?" Mrs. Rossi calls out.

"Yes, ma'am?" I tilt my head back.

"Is that your last name?"

"My last name is Lê."

"Leh?"

"Yes, ma'am."

"Leh Zhang. I like the way it sounds. May I call you Giang?"

"As you wish, ma'am."

"Giang, do you know this area well?"

"Not really. Any particular place that you want to visit?"

The wind whips. In its rushing sound I can hear her long exhalation.

"I came here," Mrs. Rossi finally says, "to search for the remains of my son."

"Okay," I say with a sudden tightness in my throat.

"My son served in the United States Army. 1966. 1967. He was a lieutenant."

"He died here, ma'am?"

"Yes. Somewhere here. It's been twenty years." Then she drops her voice. "His remains must still be here, I think."

"What makes you say that?"

"This is where he died, and his body was never recovered."

"How do you plan to find him? It's a vast area."

"I have a map. Someone drew it for me. Crudely, but clear enough. A fellow who served in the platoon that my son commanded."

"He saw your son die?"

"No." She pauses. "No, he didn't. But he was in the firefight. When they came upon this fellow, badly wounded, the next day, they said, 'Where is Lieutenant Nicola Rossi?' They counted all the bodies, and all were accounted for except my son."

"But nobody saw him die."

"That fellow saw him, still alive. A mortar blew up and trapped my son beneath a fallen cajeput trunk. The Cong didn't see him or he'd have been killed on the spot. They shot all the fallen men in the head. My son must've known this."

I draw a deep breath. "How would you be able to identify his remains? Unless there're some items with the bones . . ."

"That's what worries me. I pray that I'd find identification."

I say nothing, keeping my eyes on the road, lined with thin-trunked hummingbird trees.

"Are there any local guides I can hire?" Mrs. Rossi asks. "To go out and look for the remains?"

"The owner of the inn can help you." I speak with my face half turned. "She's from here."

"I much appreciate it," Mrs. Rossi says.

I want to tell her not to raise her hopes, but I can't bring myself to say it. I think of the inn owners' son. How many unclaimed remains are there in that wilderness? Dug up, displaced by rodents and wild animals. Long scattered, blown to pieces by bombs. Charred by forest fires. Time and nature are cruel.

That night, the woman inn owner cooks a fat catfish and a pot of white-rice porridge. Outside it is wet and windy. I take our guests upstairs with their suitcases and, coming down the stairs, I can hear the sizzling of onions. The old woman opens the lid, sprinkles black pepper on the plump catfish just burst open, and stirs the porridge until all the black flecks disappear.

We eat with only one fluorescent lamp in the center of the oblong table, rain on the window slats. Before commencing to eat, Mrs. Rossi bows and says a prayer. The girl, too, crosses herself. The old woman pays them no mind as she ladles the steaming porridge from the pot into each bowl, breaks a chunk of the ginger-colored catfish with the ladle, then dusts the bowl with pepper.

As we eat, the old woman slurps the porridge and sniffs the steam. When she finishes, she goes to the sideboard and carries back a plate. She sits it down by the lamp and Mrs. Rossi exclaims, "Look at that! Are they longans?"

The old woman just looks at Mrs. Rossi.

"Yes," I say. "They are in season now."

Mrs. Rossi's daughter plucks one longan fruit and feels its bark-like, yellow-brown thin rind. She looks at me. "How do you say longan in Vietnamese?"

"*Nhan.*" I enunciate the word. "You've eaten it before?"

"I did. In a Vietnamese restaurant where we live."

"Where?"

"Rockville." She smiles. "State of Maryland."

"You liked it then?"

"I didn't eat it fresh. They served it in a sweet dessert."

"That's *chè*. The sweet slushy dessert."

Mrs. Rossi peels the rind and eases the fleshy white fruit into her mouth. She closes her eyes and shakes her head, murmuring. After eating a few longans, she says to me, "Would you mind telling the owner the purpose of our stay?"

Back then, the old woman tells us, shortly after the North and the South were reunited, people from all parts of the country journeyed to the Central Highlands and the Mekong Delta to search for the remains of lost sons, lost husbands. This region, with its vast wetland forest, was known to the North Vietnamese Army as Military Zone 9, the name borrowed from the French colonial days. You would see people at dawn heading into the woodland beyond the inn, across the grassland and rice fields, carrying knapsacks, spades. At dusk they would come back out. Some of them stayed here at the inn. Mostly civilians. Sometimes you would see soldiers, but they didn't stay at the inn. They came in organized groups—called remains-gathering crews—and they would camp in the woodland with their trucks for a week or longer. Many crew members were war veterans who had fought in Military Zone 9 and knew the region well. They remembered where they had once buried their comrades in makeshift graves. Before searching, they would burn incense and pray for the lost souls to guide them to where their remains could be found. During the war, thousands of soldiers were stationed in this region, always deep in the swamp forest. Many died from bombing and shelling and ground assaults. In that forbidden swamp, the flesh and bones of soldiers on both sides lay under the peat soil.

The old woman points toward the unseen grassland and the paddy beyond. "After the war, the people came here to settle in the buffer zone. Many were war veterans. They cleared enough land for raising crops. They burned down cajeput trees and sold the wood."

Mrs. Rossi asks me if the old woman, or any native, knows the region well enough to act as guide.

The old woman says, "I have never been to the swamp forest myself. I have no business going in there. It is haunted." She says that on rainy nights following a humid day when the swamp vapors are thick, some in the buffer zone say they can hear human sounds from deep in the forest. If you listen, they say, you can hear the human screams and sobs, the wind-born wails coming and going sometimes until first light.

Mrs. Rossi asks me, "Do you think anyone would be available for hire?"

"Yes," I say. "They will do whatever you want."

"I have the map. I think that'll help."

"I think it will."

But deep down I know it won't.

During my time with the North Vietnamese Army, we buried corpses under giant trees to shelter the graves from bombing. Flies, wind, sand, and graves. Graves everywhere. Graves we had dug to bury the dead and sometimes to rebury the dead when bombs fell on them again. In time weeds and creepers overgrew the graves. Then you could no longer tell if they were there at all. Sometimes, though, you could spot a grave from the familiarity of the surroundings,

perhaps from a marker you had planted at the grave site,
or from a tree shorn by bombs that still stood in its odd-
looking shape. Then you would unearth the grave only
to find nothing but bones. Always bones because termites
had eaten everything else. Whatever was left was gripped
and twined with tree roots so tight the bones broke. Carefully you would unknot the roots one by one, so the bones
wouldn't snap, the skull wouldn't crack. But it was always
bones. When you held a fragment of bone in your hands, or
a skull marred with spiderweb cracks, you couldn't tell if it
was Vietnamese or American.

1967
Nicola Rossi

Mama, today is my birthday. The Ides of October. I have been here twelve months and twenty days after leaving America on September 25th, 1966. Many of us here are my age or younger. We are young men in body but aged in the soul. I was twenty-two when I came to Nam and now, after turning twenty-three, my bones are buried somewhere in this godforsaken land and I never feel gone in my body except very old like a septuagenarian.

I don't know these people. I don't know their language. I don't know what they think. They smell strange. Talk strange, like chipmunks. They always smile, Mama. They smiled as we left a village and then one of my men lost his foot in the paddy. In this vill I saw these old hags with blackened teeth and bloody mouths. You should see them, Mama. They have snaggleteeth and they keep spitting red spit all over the place. One of my men said to me, "Have you heard of betel nut, Lieutenant?" I said no. He said, "Back home we chew Skoal, Red Man, here they chew betel nuts." I said, "No, thanks." We found bomb shelters in their huts. They hide children in there. This old hag sat in the bunker with two tiny kids, just plain naked. Her lips were swollen red from chewing betel nuts, and she was cracking lice from the kids' hair with her teeth. You can hear the lice pop. There was a rice pot on the dirt floor. Cooked over wood fire. Another pot of greens boiled in water. Coy, our *slackman*, gave her a can of ham. She just looked at him. You often see that same look on their dumb-eyed buffalos. So he left it on the floor by the rice pot. We can't talk to them, Mama. We don't know how. The only words we know are *di di*, that's go away, and *dung lai*, that's halt. If they don't, we shoot. Before we entered this vill, we saw someone slinking away into the woods. Coy called *dung lai*! The figure kept running so Coy opened up. The figure hit the ground. We came up and found a ten-year-old boy.

The first time I saw a Viet kid, perhaps six years old, he was squatting on his heels, with blood caked on his skinny legs. He had an olive-colored can of ham in one hand and a Sterno heat can in the other. With a piece of wood, he wedged open the lid of the Sterno can. A matchbox lay at his grimy foot. He lit a match, touched it to the paste and shrank back when a blue flame spurted. He put four pebbles on the rim of the Sterno can and placed the unopened can of ham on them. I picked up the ham can and opened it with my P-38 on my dog-tag chain. He lifted his face to look at me. His eyes were peppercorn black. His gaze followed my hand.

*H*ave mercy on the younger generation.

Yes, Mama. I remember those words you wrote in a letter. One hot afternoon in the Mekong Delta, I stood watching the Viet Cong prisoners sitting in rows under the sun, none in the shade. Sitting on their haunches, blindfolded with a swathe of cloth over their eyes. Their shirts were torn, their black shorts soiled, their legs skinny. Most of them looked no older than seventeen.

We have boys in our company too. Have you ever had a good look at the faces in a crowd? These young-old faces that I look at every day, I know them but I don't. Some like me from OCS, and others from ROTC, The Citadel. Sons of dirt farmers. Fathers of just-born babies. Many of them will be only remembered under a Christmas tree, gift-wrapped in a photo album.

Today I saw the new boys. They were lining up to get their shots along the corrugated-metal sides of the barracks. They stood shirtless, the sun beating down on them, the khaki-yellow dust blowing like a mist when a chopper landed. Shrouded in the yellow-brown dust, the boys looked like a horde of specters.

Coy was one of them. A week later I made him our *slackman*. He was seventeen. How he got here I don't know. Maybe his Ma and Pa signed the papers so he could come here and die. He left the line with two other boys, walking together like brothers, one much shorter than the other two, past the Alpha Company tents, past the water tower where the local Viet girls would crowd together on the old pallet every morning, washing the troops' clothes in big round pails, walking past the wooden pallet now dry and empty of buckets, going around the cement trucks, the water-purification trucks, crossing the airstrip and stopping at a row of three Conex containers painted in buff color. Dust blew yellow specks on the grass and on a pile of boots.

"What's your size?" Coy asked Eddy, the shorter boy, who was already crouched in the grass.

"Eight."

"Mine is twelve," said Marco.

"Me too," Coy said.

"Fucked-up size," Eddy said, hand on a boot with a name tag. "They gave me size twelve. What the hell." Eddy lined the boot alongside his foot. It was the same length. "Fucked- up," he said, spitting in the grass.

"How do you walk in them?" Coy asked.

"How d'you walk in them?" Eddy repeated, snickering. "Hundred-dollar question, man. You stuff rags in the toe vamp. What choice d'you have? If I don't get me a size-eight boot soon, I'm gonna end up with a fucked-up foot on one side and a crooked foot on the other."

"These are dead men's boots," Marco said, bending to examine the name tags.

"Size eight," Eddy mumbled, his hand hovering over the ownerless boots. "Give me."

"Cause you're short, Eddy," Coy said. "Five five?"

"Exacto," Eddy said.

"He wears boys' size," Marco said. "Down to his boxers."

"Size eight," Coy said, shaking his head. "They don't make them that small, Eddy."

"I don't ever want to wear a dead man's boots," Marco said.

"I do, boy," Eddy said. "How can you walk in the jungle in size twelve with your foot slipping and sliding in it? If I don't get me a size-eight boot soon . . ."

"Dead man's boots," Marco said.

"Maybe they'll have a whole shipload here tomorrow," Coy said.

"You never know."

"More dead man's boots," Marco said.

Eddy was holding up a pair of boots. They looked like boots on display, neatly laced. Eddy weighed them in his hands. "Wonder why they got no tag on them," he said.

"Maybe they're still looking for whatever's left of who-ever," Coy said, looking down at Eddy.

"*Jesus Christ!*" called Marco, who had gone around the Conex containers.

They went behind the containers. There was a mound of body bags in the grass. The grass had yellowed in the heat and the bags were pale green, their nylon zippers white running down the middle. One bag had burst open and the remains, red and pulpy, had spilled onto the grass. Bones, bloodstained green cloths, intestines discolored and twisted.

Marco turned away, slumping. They could hear him retch.

Coy crossed himself.

"It stinks," Eddy said.

Coy held his breath. Marco sniffled, spat, but he wouldn't turn around as he knelt on the ground.

"They musta dumped them way up from the chopper," Eddy said.

"Bastards," Marco said.

Mama, that boy Coy had a full scholarship to Duke University. He had big brown eyes. He still had pimples on his face. The way he smiled and looked at you, you'd know he was a boy. I asked him, "Can you navigate in the jungle?" He said, "Yes, Lieutenant." I said, "Why do you say that?" He said, "I've never got lost anywhere I go in my life, sir." I said, "Well, you'll be our *slackman* when we go out next time. You're Ditch's replacement." He said, "Where's he now?" I said, "Gone." He said nothing, just blinked. Those big brown eyes. I said, "Your other duty is carrying the litter when we're shorthanded. You think you can handle it?" He said, too eagerly, "Yes, sir, it's an honor. I'll never let anyone down."

Mama, that afternoon he was fifteen feet behind our point man, breaking a trail. I heard a round coming over us. That unmistakably long and thin mosquito-whine sound before it shattered. We all threw ourselves onto the dirt. It went off and I saw Coy's back red with blood. He didn't hit the ground. Then I heard a crack of the rifle. It struck Eddy, who was carrying a machine gun to the left of our point man, and Coy screamed as he stumbled toward Eddy, and I don't know, Mama, if he screamed because he was hit or what he saw from Eddy. There was a steady sound of machine guns. We were pinned down, flattened to the ground, the dirt in our noses, our mouths, until we could see the muzzle blasts of the guns hidden under nets of leaves, the white flashes in the over-foliaged jungle. We returned fire, machine-gunning them as we crawled for cover in the whopping sound, round after round, of our grenade launchers.

When it was over, the edge of the jungle, once heavily bushed, was now singed, smoking, and shorn white by our artillery shells. I went up the trail and heard someone say, "He's done, go help our wounded." Then I heard Marco, "He's not done, damn it." I saw Eddy lying on his back. Marco was crouching over him and next to him stood Murphy, our medic.

Mama, these were grown men arguing over a wounded man who was hanging on to his life by a mere thread. Eddy was my machine-gun man. Only five feet five but he carried that twenty-five pounder proudly. The round had torn open his front and he was gurgling, choking on his own blood. Doc and I watched him quake. Doc said, "He's not gonna make it, no, sir." I yelled at him, "You're not gonna let him die," and Doc said, "I wish there was an alternative," and I said, "Give him three cutdowns right now," and we squeezed three blood bags, just squeezing them and all the while watching Eddy's eyes roll into his head, until they suddenly froze like marbles. He no longer shook. Marco was still holding one of his legs, his size-twelve boot pointed away.

"Where's Coy?" I asked Doc.

"Sedated," Doc said. "Over there. Chopper's coming, Lieutenant."

I went to the edge of the trail where the dirt was a darker yellow and dog's tooth grass was a green-gray thick mat on which he lay sprawled, his head tilted to one side. A machine gun's bullet had shattered his cheekbone, knocking out both of his eyes. His nose wasn't there. Just red meat left. Had I never known him, I couldn't have guessed what he looked like before. He still had a pulse. Marco and Doc came and sat beside him and Marco whispered, "Coy, hey buddy," and Coy's head moved just a twitch. I said, "We're gonna bring you through," even though I didn't mean it. Half his face was gone, the pink bubbles rising and breaking from the cavity. I didn't want to turn him over, didn't want to ask Doc about Coy's back, for I knew it was a mess. Marco held the boy's hand and said, "You're going to make it, you hear, you're going back home." And hearing it I thought of his scholarship and his big brown eyes. We gave him more morphine. At first Doc refused—no additional dose in less than two hours—then he gave in. Coy just lay there. If he felt pain, he didn't show it. He was one of the boys I wanted to bring home, but now he just lay there. Just lying there, Mama. Marco held his hand. Doc walked away. When I heard the chopper, the sound of its rotor pitch thumping over the horizon, I looked back down at him and he was gone.

I didn't cry over here. But that time when they took him away on the litter, I cried.

One hot afternoon, Mama, we came to a village on the northern bank of Trem River in Upper U Minh, where a creek meets the waterway. The village was a cluster of thatch huts, with mud walls and roofs covered with palm leaves long faded to a soiled gray. The huts sat on stilts on the high bank, scarred and pockmarked in places where the wet soil was brown. At times you couldn't see the huts because of the screens of nypa palms that rose out of the riverbed, their underwater trunks tinted pale lime. Behind the huts were peatlands, where rice plants grew out of irrigated ditches in long, narrow troughs, the water a mirrored blue.

In this swamp forest, Mama, the soil is mud brown and soft. The rainwater running off the soil is brown. An ancient land. That's what the colonel said. Nature's upheavals over thousands of years had flooded the land with seawater, letting it dry for a couple of thousand years and then overflowing it again. This U Minh forest has grown on a thick bed of marine sediments. In dry seasons, the forest fires repeatedly burned down trees and plants, and then floods from the sea and the monsoon brought back the trees and vegetation. A timeless cycle. And the trees, Mama, the trees. The first time I saw those forest trees flowering white, I wondered what they were. So I asked the colonel. "Cajeput trees," he said. He didn't know how to spell the name, so he said, "In plain English? Paperbark trees." It made sense to me. If you ever see them, you would know. When I first saw them, I said to Sarge, "Don't they look like somebody pasted paper all over the trunks?" And Sarge said, "I reckon you can peel the bark and float them like boats."

Even now as I close my eyes, I can still smell the cajeput flowers and see the silty brown watercourses. The canals are everywhere. The colonel, who speaks some French, said the French had many canals dug when they first occupied southern Vietnam in 1867. *La colonie de Cochinchine*, the colonel said. The colony of Cochinchina. The maze of rivers and canals was evidence of their indestructibility. Along the swamps and cajeput forests were clusters of villages, many laid to waste by bombing and shelling from the nearby military bases. Villagers fled. The burned-down villages became ghost lands. Mama, the only ones left behind were those who could no longer work or walk.

I want to tell you about the Trem River. It runs north-south through the U Minh forest, cutting it in half, so the northern forest is called Upper U Minh and the southern forest Lower U Minh. One day, aboard a riverboat patrolling the river near a creek called Ra Ghe, which flows into the Trem, I saw white flowers afloat along the riverbank. From where it meets the creek, the river runs straight for some ten miles and all you can see are myriad rows of flowers whitewashing the edges of the riverbank. The flowers float on their round-shaped leaves, notched deeply down the center like a heart. The breeze is fragrant, and the fragrance follows us upriver till the river bends and the white flowers and their scents disappear. Someone aboard the river craft said they were water lilies. When I asked the colonel many days later, he said, "The Viets call that stretch the 'River of White Water Lilies.'" At night, when we patrolled the river, we'd often see fishermen out on the water in their sampans, each hung with a lantern on the stern and on the bow, brightly lit, and the river smelled of smoke and glowed with the lanterns' reflections. I was told that they were out to catch prawns—not ordinary prawns but tiger prawns. Mama, these prawns are at least ten inches long and plumb, rusty-brown with black-and-white bands across their humpbacks. But if you ask what I remember most, it would be the floating lily pads and the river that runs long and white with water lilies.

That day we filed along, across the river from the village, moving parallel to the edge of the forest. The grass had turned yellow in the sun. We had a new *slackman*, Marco. When I made him our new *slackman*, he said to me, "Now I'm cursed, sir." I said, "How's that?" He said, "You got Ditch and Coy before me and they're gone, that's how." I said, "Your mind's playing tricks on you. Just do your job and you'll be fine."

We were coming around a bend in the river where the river became narrow-waisted, fifty yards wide, and looking across the water we could see the bank thickly veiled in the sunlit saffron-green of the nypa palms, and behind them glimpses of the gray thatched huts. Suddenly a crackling shot. Marco screamed. He didn't stop screaming until another shot cracked. Two of our men came running up when a barrage of machine guns roared and, just like that, our forward line was gone. We moved back to the forest's edge, keeping behind the trees. The bullets hit the trees and their bark flew like white mulches and their branches snapped noisily. Lying flat behind a double-trunk cajeput with a compass in my hand, I worked my map. A few feet from me the radio was hissing with static, and the radioman lay with his radio cradled in his arms. "You got the grids, Lieutenant?" he shouted. "Getting there," I said, glancing toward the river. The opposite bank was so bright with a saffron-yellow glare of the midafternoon sun you could not see the enemy's muzzle flashes. The voice came across, "Give me what you've got." I heard the whine of his radio. "Lieutenant?" the voice came again in the crackling of the radio. "Shut up," I said. "Here're the coordinates. Send one marking round. Wait for confirmation. Then white phosphorus. Got it?"

Mama, every time I ate my chow, spaghetti and meatballs, I would look at the mushy sauce, the round balls, and see the glob of Marco's brain falling out into his helmet. It had a burned hole on the side where a bullet had gone through. He wasn't dead right away, after the first shot. He should have kept quiet when he was shot. He screamed and their guns found him the second time. When I saw him, after the ambush, he was sort of looking at me like he was half awake, not knowing that his brain was sitting in his helmet like a pulpy thing you see on a skillet. I wanted to turn over his helmet but instead I rose to my feet and walked to the riverbank. Plumes of black smoke were rising over the ruins of the village, ashes swirled, and the air was hot in the lungs. Trees and bushes had become misshapen, singed black and mottled gray with cinders, and wind-born ashes floated across the river and you could feel them on your face. A burned-meat smell hung in the air and anywhere you found yourself in that late afternoon, the smell stayed in your nostrils.

1987
Le Giang

I watch her from the window of my room. The morning heat comes early. In her cutoff jeans with white frays at the thighs, Chi Lan leans against the doorjamb, legs crossed at the knees, gazing at the old man in the back lot with the bone in his hand. She swats at a mosquito, arm cocked, smooth white in her cerise sleeveless blouse.

The old man is tapping down the soil in a fresh hole he's dug under the lemon tree. With the window shutters open I can smell the rusty heat. I draw deeply on my cigarette and cough until my eyes water. When I look up I see her outside the open window looking in.

"Hello, *Chú!*" she says, smiling. Her voice is soft with a lilt in "Chú." Uncle.

I cover my mouth with my hand and nod at her.

"Are you all right?" she asks, leaning in on her folded arms on the windowsill.

"Yeah. How are you?"

She nods. "Fine." The word barely leaves her lips when she drops her gaze to the folding table. Atop it is a stack of paper. A cigarette pack and a Zippo lighter are its paperweights. A black pencil lies across an ashtray. On the top sheet a pencil sketch. She tilts her head, looking at the sketch. "You draw, *Chú*?"

"Yeah." I mash the cigarette in the ashtray.

"May I see them?"

"Do you draw too, Chi Lan?"

"No," she says, laughing lightly. I pass her the stack of papers through the window. She sweeps her hair back over her ear. Her lower lip tucked in, she seems to blend into the sketch. She has a tiny black mole under the corner of her left eye. She blinks when she sees me gazing at her.

"Is this a battlefield?" she asks, pointing to a sketch of a boot.

"What makes you say that?"

"This military boot," she says. "The smoke, and the burned-down trees."

"Okay."

"Okay, what?" She squints at me.

"A battlefield."

"Whose boot is that?"

"An American GI's boot."

Her gaze returns to the sketch. Black, white, gray. The fire-consumed peat ground grays off in its top layer. Tree stumps, fallen limbs in charred black, bare roots like wildly flung arms entwined in black and gray. Wisps of smoke hovering over the ground.

"Are they ghosts?" she asks, tracing her finger on the eddies of smoke.

"Just smoke."

"They have human shapes," she says. "Our eyes trick us sometimes though. And what do you call this, this rooster in Vietnamese? Is it a jungle cock?"

The jungle fowl stands with its combed, wattled head erect between a smoking tree stump and the boot. "*Gà rung*," I say, looking up at her.

She repeats the words, slightly accented. "Where was this battlefield?"

"From my memory."

"From a real place?"

"Does it matter?" I shrug. If she knew this land as well as I do, she would recognize the peat ground that only exists in this U Minh region.

"You were in it, right?"

"I was in many battles. They're all pieces of recollection now."

"My mother said many war veterans don't want to remember their pasts." She turns over one sheet after another. Sketches of people and things. Remembered. Unremembered. And that's how you unburden your memories.

"Oh!" she exclaims. "You have him in here too?"

I look at the sketch I did of the old man, on his haunches in his bone-burying routine. She knows about his routine now because I have told her. She was as much shocked as I was the first time seeing him at it.

"You draw beautifully," she says.

I look away before my gaze makes her uncomfortable. She stops turning the sheets, her gaze fixed on a sketch.

"You drew me?"

"That's not you."

"I'm sorry." She studies the face in the drawing. The only difference between her and the girl in the drawing is the long hair plait. Knotted toward the end with a ribbon, flung over a shoulder.

"I never braid my hair like that," she says. "Maybe I will when I grow my hair that long."

"You've never had it that long?"

She shakes her head. "Who is she?"

"Someone from memory."

"Of course," Chi Lan says. "I mean, who is she to you?"

"Someone I knew when I was your age. Or maybe younger."

"I'm eighteen."

"I was seventeen at that time."

"In the North?"

"How do you know?"

"You told us during the ride when you picked us up. You said you were a North Vietnamese soldier. Born in the North."

"I forgot I said that."

"You're getting old, *Chú*." Her smile makes me smile.

Why a Vietnamese adopted child? Did this somehow allow her mother to hold on to the memory of her lost son? I like Mrs. Rossi. A retired high school principal, a sweet old lady. I admire her determination to find her son's remains. More so, I admire her faith. Still strong after twenty years.

At seventeen, younger than Chi Lan, I was living in the city of Thanh Hóa with an ethnic Chinese family, whose son, Huan, was my good friend. They used to live in my village until Land Reform in the North wiped out the landowner class between 1953 and 1956. As ethnic Chinese, they were safe. Also, his father practiced eastern medicine—herbs, acupuncture—and was not a landowner like my father. By the time the land reform ended, my family was stripped of everything we had owned. Of my family's possessions, my father retained only his moon-shaped lute to remind him of his wealthy past. The lute's two strings were made of woven silk and its back was covered with black-snake skin. Many like us died, old and young, from starvation. When it was over the Party admitted its mistake: It was genocide to exterminate indiscriminately the land-owning class. My father and I lived our banished lives like lepers. He caught snakes as his trade. We, his landowning kin, were shunned by all. He could not find work.

By that time, I had seen many people killed. I had seen deaths during the land reform, when human lives were worth less than a scrap of tobacco paper. My father, a denounced landlord, had crawled on his hands and knees to the platform of the People's Court. He sat in that doglike posture while peasants hurled accusations at him. Before him, a noble Catholic priest, after having his robe removed, looked shrunken. On his hands and knees, the priest sat with a dumb look on his face that made me hate him. Perhaps because I hated the cowardice in myself.

After we had fallen to wearing rags, my father died from a snakebite. That happened in 1960. I was twelve. I left my village for Thanh Hóa and took refuge with my Chinese friend's family. They had been there for four years at that time, after Land Reform ended. My friend, Huan, was my age. He had told me his name meant "happiness," back when his family was still living in my village. He said that many Vietnamese words were borrowed from Chinese, even the pronunciation. I had no quarrel with that. But some boys in our village school loathed him because he was ethnic Chinese. He and his kin were a privileged class in the North, and because their nationality was Han, they were not required to serve in the army. One morning he walked into the classroom with his head hanging. Everyone turned to look. His face was swollen from punches, one cheek bruised to a liver color. The boys had picked on him before. At recess I put my hand on his shoulder. "You want them to call you a sissy? Treat you like one?" At his silence, I continued. "Arm yourself with a knife. Draw it on them, and they'll back off. Do what I tell you from now on, and you won't get hurt again."

In the city of Thanh Hóa, his father continued practicing eastern medicine. His mother still read things the Chinese way, from right to left, so when she delivered an herbal prescription to a Vietnamese family in the city, she couldn't find their house number—it was 23 but 32 to her. They put me in a Catholic school where their son had been boarding.

I spent four years there. The school's headmaster was a middle-aged Frenchman who once managed a rubber plantation in the South. A tall, virile man. Most boys stood only to his shoulders. He had a prominent hooked nose and small ice-cold blue eyes that caused chills when you met his stare. He loved eating raisins, clutching them in his left fist and popping them into his mouth. Then he'd dust his palm with his other hand and run the hands over his cropped hair the color of blond wood. At that time, I wondered about the man's complete change of career. Could a man who used to style himself master of a rough rubber plantation in the South and call the Vietnamese animals recast himself as an educator in a peaceful boarding school in the North?

At a midday recess, the school custodian called for my friend and took him to the headmaster's office. My friend did not return to the classroom. When school ended in midafternoon, I went looking for him in our dormitory. He wasn't there. I asked the custodian about him.

"The infirmary," he said.

"Is he sick?" I said.

"Been sick."

"He wasn't sick this morning."

"Sick now." The custodian shrugged.

In that deserted room I found my friend lying facedown on a cot. A thin olive-colored blanket was flung over his lower body, most of it sagging in folds on the floor. His eyes were closed. His face in the shuttered sunlight was tear-stained.

"You're not sleeping, are you?" I said.

His eyes opened a slit. Long lashes like a western girl's.

"They said you were sick."

"I'm not sick."

"Then why're you here?"

He burst into tears.

"What happened?"

He sobbed into the thin pillow, his arms drawn up to his chest. The blanket fell to the floor. I stared at the seat of his white shorts. There were bloodstains on the seam. "Why all this blood?" I said. "You hurt yourself?"

"Mr. Doig." The words came out of his mouth bubbling with saliva.

"He hit you?"

He shook his head.

"What then?"

"He . . . forced himself on me."

"Raped you?"

He nodded into the pillow.

"How?"

His hand moved down and touched his buttocks. I began to visualize what I never before imagined.

"He did it . . . twice."

"Can you stand up?"

He raised himself on his hands. He rose, wobbling on his feet. He looked like a windblown scarecrow.

"Can you walk?" I asked, seeing him grimace.

"It hurts . . . so much." He wiped his eyes with the hem of his white shirt, the way girls did.

On that rubber plantation, Mr. Doig had done it to boy laborers, I later learned.

In the years after the Indochina War broke out in 1946, the Vietnamese economy was a dying beast. The French control of the Vietnamese countryside was on the wane, slipping to the Viet Minh. The French still had the major cities and the rubber plantations. The plantations had peaked in the glorious years before the war but had dropped sharply in productivity when Vietnamese laborers fled their villages and joined the Viet Minh, leaving behind only the sick and the old. Desperate for laborers, the French army raided

villages and seized people regardless of sex. The captives
were brought to the plantations along with prison labor and
those branded Viet Minh simply because they lacked iden-
tity papers.

They called these plantations "The New World." Most
plantation workers signed a three-year contract, but half
never made it home. Death from exhaustion was common.
Workers were expected to tap a thousand rubber trees daily,
an impossible quota for overworked, underfed laborers,
who called on their children as young as six to help them
meet the mark. Ten-year-olds had their own quotas.

The boys in that rubber forest were Mr. Doig's prey. He
took boys into his bungalow and when he was through, the
boys could be seen crawling out to the veranda. In fits of
bestial passion, he would move through the forest at twilight heading toward the work area, looking for ten-year-old
boys. The last boy he took into his bungalow was carried
out by servants and laid upon the veranda for his parents
to bury. The workers went on strike to protest Mr. Doig's
crime, which took the Michelin Company by surprise. When
it was settled, the company brought in a new manager, and
Mr. Doig was never seen on the plantation again.

At seventeen, I became a member of the Vanguard Youth.
We were to help repair roads and bridges after an air raid.
That year, 1965, the Americans started bombing our city.
They bombed the Hàm Rong Bridge. After two days of
heavy bombing, the Dragon's Jaw still stood. Highways and
bridges came under constant aerial attack.

Schoolchildren were told to move out of the city to the
surrounding villages. My friend Huan and I and another
student roomed together in a peasant's house. We brought
our own rice so the peasant's wife could cook for us. Our
families paid the peasant for our stay. At the end of each

week, we rode our bicycles back into the city, pedaling as fast as we could, fearing the sound of air-raid sirens.

One early morning in August, the Americans bombed the rail yards and a truck depot on the edge of the city. Some errant bombs hit a bordering village, which burned for an entire day. We were ordered to go there to help the victims and clean up. I had traveled through it before, on my way to the peasant's community, and the dirt road was shady under the lacing crowns of ginkgo trees, flame trees, and milkwood trees. I had biked through the village without seeing the sun. When we got there at noon, most trees had burned to stumps. The dirt road glared red. The air singed. Everywhere we went the napalm-burned victims screamed in pain, and the dead shredded of clothes lay bare in the open. A ripe, stomach-sick odor hung in the air. Ashes grayed the hedges, and soot-blackened houses still simmered. Many had no roofs. The straw, now scorched black, lay strewn across the dirt floors. The napalm victims, their flesh burned, begged us not to touch them. We were told to wait for the soldiers to come and carry them away. In the sun glare I stood watching a mangy dog gnawing an old woman's leg bone. I could still make out her face, the black turbaned head, but there was nothing left of her body except shriveled flesh and white bones. Then a little girl came and shooed the dog away. The dog growled and I kicked it in the rump and it trotted off. The girl stood, looking down at the old woman, and cried. Late in the day soldiers and city workers came. They brought no medicine but a few burn sprays. They sprayed the burned victims and then carried away all the bodies, the old woman's body too.

At dusk, the local militia came through the village. I was carrying bamboo trunks on my bicycle to rebuild the ruined houses. I saw militiamen on the dirt road, walking in tandem, flanking a buffalo cart. A large crowd of people followed on both sides of the road, clothed in indigo, black, and brown. I got off my bicycle and edged toward the cart to see better. An American pilot sat slumped against the slatted wooden side of the cart. His cropped hair was sand-colored. Although seated, he filled the cart. You could see his whole upper body above the slats. They had stripped him of his boots and jumpsuit. In his white boxers and white T-shirt, his torso was lean and muscular. They had shot down his plane when his squadron bombed Thanh Hóa City and captured him three kilometers outside the city, still tangled in his own parachute.

The crowd grew bigger going through the village toward Thanh Hóa City. Staccato curses and shouts flew. Some threw dirt clods and rubber thongs. They called him murderer. Animal. Savage. The militia tried to push back the crowd. I saw his face just as a wooden sabot hit his chest. His eyes froze as he looked across at a sea of faces, drawn with hate, the betel-chew red lips, the snaggled blackened teeth. He seemed to shrink. I couldn't help thinking of the Catholic priest, on his knees, disrobed, looking like a half-wit before the People's Court. I hated that dumb look.

I saw a peasant, his head wrapped in a black turban, bull his way through the crowd. He charged in between the two militiamen and came up to the side of the buffalo cart. He raised his scythe, the long, curved blade gleaming in the dying sunlight. The blade scythed the American at the neck and the head fell rolling on the ground. Blood gushed up from his gaping neck, splattering his white T-shirt.

The crowd stood, eerily quiet, gawking at the headless body, tottering in the cart as it creaked along. On the red dirt the head rested facing the twilight sky. As I looked down at it, I saw the eyes blink.

When I come back to the inn, it is still early in the morning. I find Mrs. Rossi in the kitchen boiling water to make tea and Chi Lan standing in the back doorway, looking through her camera at the old man, out in the back lot, digging up dirt to bury a bone. I tell Mrs. Rossi that I found a man whom she could use as a guide.

Her face beams. She grabs my hands. "Bless your heart, Giang. Who is he?"

"His name is Lung. He lives in the buffer zone. A war veteran."

"What side was he on during the *Veetnam* war?"

"Our side—the Republic of Vietnam. He'd also fought in the Indochina War. He was with the *Bawouan*."

"The what?"

"Bataillon de Parachutistes Vietnamiens—the Vietnamese parachute battalion. Or BPVN." I shrug as I catch Mrs. Rossi's confused look. "How the Vietnamese say *BPVN* in their tongue to how the French say it, *Bawouan*, is beyond me."

"I won't try. Believe me, Giang." She pours hot water from the kettle into the teapot. "So he fought the French back then?"

"No, ma'am. He fought alongside the French at Dien Bien Phu in 1954 against the Viet Minh. I was six at that time."

"I'm confused."

"He belonged to the Vietnamese National Army—the French-trained, non-Communist Vietnamese government."

"I understand now." Mrs. Rossi puts the kettle back on the stove. "Say that word again for me, please?"

"*Bawouan*?"

Chi Lan walks back in, camera in hand. "Don't make her say it, *Chú*." She tilts her head toward the back lot. "Yesterday she asked me about the old man's name. She wanted to greet him . . ."

"His name is Qúy." I cut in.

"His last name."

"Nguyen."

"I know," Chi Lan says. "She had trouble pronouncing it. Not *Nu-gen*, I told her. Not *Gwen*."

We sit down at the dining table. Mrs. Rossi pours tea for everyone except me. She knows I drink only black coffee.

"I'm not sure I'm cut out for foreign languages," Mrs. Rossi says. "I only wanted to know the man's name so I could at least say hello to him when we run into each other. Mr. *Nu*—"

"Mr. Qúy," I say. "In Vietnamese your last name comes before your first name. And in greetings, your first name will be addressed. We go by the first name with a title of respect or a kinship term, like Uncle, Aunt." Seeing Mrs. Rossi's grimace, I smile. "Your name will be Rossi Catherine in Vietnamese, and a Vietnamese will address you as Madame Catherine."

Chi Lan puts her cup down and looks at her mother. "I was about to tell you that, Mom. The Vietnamese name is arranged in opposite order of the English name. The family name comes first, then middle name, then given name."

"I believe I already knew that." Mrs. Rossi nods, then turns her face to me. "Your name is *Leh Zhang*. Correct?"

"Right, ma'am."

Chi Lan comes back from the pantry with a papaya on a plate. As she cuts it in half, lengthwise, the tiny peppercorn-black seeds glistening in the pith, a sweet smell wafts up like the smell of an overripe cantaloupe. She scoops out the seeds with a spoon. "Do you want a slice, *Chú*?"

"No, thanks," I say.

Chi Lan places the spoon and one half of the papaya in front of Mrs. Rossi.

"I love this," Mrs. Rossi says. "And the local bananas. They're so sweet and fragrant. What do you call papaya in Vietnamese?"

"*Du-du*," I say.

Mrs. Rossi repeats the word.

I grin. "If you ask for a papaya from a Vietnamese, ma'am, your pronunciation will certainly get you in trouble."

Mrs. Rossi rolls her eyes. "Why?"

"The way you pronounced it could mean . . . sexual intercourse. But it's a vulgar word for it."

Chi Lan laughs. Mrs. Rossi shakes her head. "Well, Giang. I told you I'm not cut out for this language." Suddenly she stops and looks out the slatted window toward the back lot. The old man is dragging his spade toward a fenced-in garden plot. "Giang, he's going to ruin it for you."

I look, half rising from the chair. "That's the mustard greens in the plot I just planted for his wife."

"Poor soul," Mrs. Rossi says as I hurry out through the back door.

To get to Old Lung's dwelling you follow a canal dug by the settlers to bring in water for irrigation. The canal, long and narrow, girds the forest and protects the buffer zone against forest fires during the dry season. The canal runs alongside a dirt path that winds through the communes, edging the rice fields, sometimes through low-lying bogs always glistening with stagnant water, odorous of mud, where aquatic reeds and spiked sedge sprout freely, and passing by you could always hear the *aarf* of the dwarf tree frogs.

The last time I came back from his dwelling, I was drunk. In the dark I walked listening to my feet and the rustle of reeds, the croaking of frogs. There was a mud stench in the breeze. Strange noises rippled the stillness, swooshing and ruffling. I strained my ears, lost my bearing, and fell into the bog. I sat huffing in the mud, rank and warm, smelling liquor on my breath and a tinge of sweetly decayed vegetation. I lit a cigarette. The strange noises stopped. I held up a match and saw two herons standing deep in the bog, their heads cocked toward the little orb of light cupped in my hand. Then heads bobbing, yellow beaks clacking against each other's, they sparred on. The match went out. I remained seated and fell asleep.

Old Lung, the war veteran, is like me. He was a prisoner of war, sent to a reform camp, but only for three years. Unlike me, he had fought for the Republic of Vietnam. Most people who settled in the buffer zone are war veterans and soldiers' widows. Former North Vietnamese Army soldiers, former Viet Cong fighters. Enemies of the former Republic. Old Lung had fought both the Viet Minh in the Indochina War and the Viet Cong and NVA in the Vietnam War. He is like a mongrel among the others. Settlers have cleared several hectares of land to grow rice, vegetables, fruit trees. Old Lung grows nothing on his single acre of land. "The more land you've got, son," he said to me, "the more misery you bring upon yourself."

When somebody dies, the family always calls on Old Lung. He will build the coffin and dress the corpse in a burial garment, a chore nobody wants to do when the body lies in rigor mortis. Old Lung will stand looking down at the corpse, his hand clutching a jar of rice liquor, mumbling a prayer. He will take a mouthful of liquor and blow a spray on the corpse's limbs and start rubbing them down. Soon the limbs will lose their stiffness, and after he straightens them, the corpse, with arms and legs neatly in place, looks like a sleeping person.

He told me he had buried many corpses of his friends during both wars, a time when, for days, it would be impossible to evacuate the dead and the wounded from the battlefield. "Sometimes what you bury," he said, "are hunks of meat and bone. That's what is left after a mortar or an artillery shell hits you. You wash the chunks of meat covered with grime and leg bones with most of the flesh completely gone. Wash them with water from your canteen and then put them together in a hole in the ground. You want to give them a decent burial, though sometimes you can't. Just smell your fingers after you're done burying them. Son, have you ever smelled meat gone bad three days in the heat? Never mind the maggots. They can't smell what they eat. You don't have liquor with you to wash that smell away. Scrape your fingers with sand, with leaves hard as you can. The smell stays."

When they first dug the canal that encircled the forest, a stretch of the canal went through the buffer zone's grave-yard. They had to relocate a number of graves. Old Lung exhumed the corpses and reburied them in new coffins. "You know what, son? Those fresh graves just a year or two gone by are the worst. Those corpses are still rotting. You break a grave open and it smells worse than a basket of stinking fish."

I had seen exhumers patiently wait for the dead man's family to take a first stab of the spade into the grave's soil. They feared to be the first who disturbed the dead from his slumber. But Old Lung feared nothing. He would mumble a prayer, then sink the spade into the yellow dirt. I asked him if he ever left a bone or two behind in the old graves, for stories were told that the dead would come every night in pursuit of those who forgot their bones, until the exhum-ers were at their wits' end. Old Lung grunted, said, "Dead or alive, son. Wouldn't you fret when a body part of yours is missing? But I always take care of them. I tell them so. I say, 'You must forgive me if I make a mistake, but I don't make careless mistakes, so don't bear any grudge against me.'" Old Lung has that unblinking stare that can catch you off guard. He reminds me of myself sometimes. But I know not to stare after I have read a person's thoughts. You can't miss Old Lung's bat ears, which stick out from his inverted-triangle-shaped head. He has a protuberant fore-head creased sharply in wavy lines. On his pointed chin grows a tuft of gray goatee. It sets a contrast to his thin

black hair, still black in his old age, grayish only in the side-
burns. He said, "Know somethin' else, son? One time I was
digging up this grave and it had just bones and a skull,
cause everything else had rotted. Here I saw a gold leaf in
the skull's mouth. Pure gold. Buried with the body as a fare-
well gift to be spent in the other world. I gave it back to the
family, but no, they wanted it reburied with the bones in a
new coffin. I guess as the old saying goes, 'Good as gold.'
The fella's spirit musta never run out of money to spend in
the netherworld."

I thought Old Lung's sincerity must have kept him in
close rapport over the years with the dead. A good heart can
ward off evil, they say. Behind his dwelling is a well, just
a stone's throw away. One night I was too drunk to make
it home, so I slept sitting up against the side of the well.
Sometime past midnight I woke and found Old Lung tapping me on the shoulder. He was holding a kerosene lamp
in his hand and its smoke stung my eyes.

"Why didn't you sleep inside?" he asked.

"I thought I'd just sit here to get my head cleared before
I got on home."

"Done that myself."

"Hey, old man, here to your shack is no more than fifty
meters."

"Son, you mistake me for some octogenarian. I ain't that
old yet. And even when I'm full of liquor, I can always find
my way back to my cot."

"Why out here then?"

"To talk to the ghosts. They keep me company."

"How'd you do that?"

"Son, you see ghosts when there ain't no barrier between
you and them. I took care of them when they were dead.
They owe it to me. When I think of them, they come."

"Just like that?"

"Yeah. But it won't work for you though."

"But how do I see them?"

Old Lung took the lamp with him back to his hut. I sat in the dark, my head heavy, my mouth dry. Fireflies flickered yellow and green and sometimes just glowed steadily in eerie blue dots. The blue-ghost fireflies. The earth and grass smelled warm. Just as my eyes began to close, Old Lung's lamplight again glowed in the dark. He opened his hand. In the hazy yellow sphere the lamp made against the night, I saw a small banana leaf in his palm. A glob of slaked lime sat wet and white in the center of the leaf.

"Dab this on your fingertips and toe tips," Old Lung said.

"Huh?"

"You asked me to show you how to see ghosts."

"With this?"

"Lime paste," Old Lung said.

I examined his wrinkled face, rust-brown and leathery. He kept his hand open until I was done daubing lime on my toes and fingers. He tossed away the banana leaf, blew out the lamp and sat down beside me, his arms wrapping his knees. "Now what?" I asked, my hands open, palms upward. My legs were straightened out, sandaled feet pointed up.

"Just wait," Old Lung said.

"They'll be coming?"

"Quiet."

A whip-poor-will called somewhere in the blackness. When it died out, the night purred with the undulating shrills of toads. My eyelids grew heavy again. As my eyes were closing I saw lights coming toward us. The blue-ghost fireflies came glowing from deep in the night, coming nearer, like myriad stars attracting one another, until a blue light began to shine. In the glow were two human figures standing face to face, for just one brief moment, and then they lunged at each other. The shorter one was an NVA soldier. I recognized his green uniform immediately. The two button-down breast pockets, the pants with thigh pockets. I had for years worn that same uniform. His cordwood sun-helmet was tipped back, no chin strap. The hat fell as he tried to stab the other man with his AK-47, fitted with a spike bayonet. The other man was an American soldier who wore no helmet. His marine fatigues were coated with yellow dirt as though he had wallowed in it. In his hand he held an entrenching tool. He sidestepped the NVA soldier and gashed his arm with the entrenching tool's blade.

I turned to Old Lung. "You see this?"

The scene disappeared. The blue light hung in the night momentarily and it too went black. In the dark I could feel Old Lung shifting on his buttocks. He struck a match and lit the lamp.

"You saw what I saw?" I asked.

"I ain't blind."

"But you've got no lime on your toes and fingers."

"I don't need lime to see them. I told you that, didn't I?"

"You think they heard me and disappeared?"

"I shoulda told you to say nothing, not a word when you catch them ghosts with your eyes."

"They must've died around here to show up in the same place again. Right, old man?"

"If the dead people could stand together on this land for roll call, it would be the size of a division."

"I was here back then. Could've been dead myself and turned into one of those ghosts."

Old Lung said nothing. He lit a cigarette. Twenty years have passed since that war. *Why do ghosts not grow older with time?*

Mrs. Rossi and I go into the forest for the first time, in a sampan. There are four of us. Mrs. Rossi and me, Old Lung and Ông Ba—Mr. Ba. Old Lung found Ông Ba, a settler who owns a fifteen-foot-long sampan fitted with a Kohler outboard motor, the type that has become ubiquitous in the water grid here for many settlers who own a canoe or a sampan; you can never find any sampan in the waterways without a motor.

We follow Bien Nhi Canal, going east. The canal was arrow straight and clear with a paved road edging it on one side, with dwellers' homes on the other side, mirrored in the blue water. Ông Ba said it was an elephant road before he was born—trampled down by traveling herds to become a path—and whenever there was a dirt path there were migrators.

When the sun finally breaks through on the water's surface, we enter Cái Tàu River, the waterway wide and brown. There are fish stakes pounded into the riverbed along the banks. We reach Trem River and turn south, seeing the forest on the far right, green with white flecks of cajeput flowers.

Past a sawmill there are lumber barges moored along the low-lying bank. Ông Ba says, "Yonder it is." He turns right into a canal, the sampan bobbing on the choppy currents where the canal enters the river, the banks high and thick with bear's breeches, glossy- and spiny-leaved, and over the bank you can see the sawmill's brown roof.

When we no longer hear the noises from the sawmill, at least a kilometer behind, Ông Ba brings the sampan alongside the bank where it flares into a shaded cove. Ahead one hundred yards is the forest.

"This is the place," Ông Ba says, cutting off the motor.

I translate for Mrs. Rossi. Old Lung simply watches her. She looks at the hand-drawn map and then across the grassy tract of land, brown in the sun. She gestures toward the open space: "I imagine the American Army base used to be over there?"

"Yes, ma'am," I say.

She tilts back her umbrella, her face full of sun, and gazes into the shadowy space farther downstream where the canal disappears into the forest.

Old Lung opens his knapsack and takes out a cigarette. In the rucksack he carries his lunch packed in a plastic container, a bottle of water, and a large bundle of clear nylon. He lights the cigarette, works the knapsack onto his back, and picks up the machete and the long-handled spade with a small blade.

I borrow the map from Mrs. Rossi. In the hand-sketched map the U Minh forest is kidney-shaped, bisected by a river running north-south. From the confluence, the map says, where Cái Tàu River flows into the Trem, you go north for fifteen kilometers, and there you see the old American Army base sitting westward from the Trem River.

"You've done this before," I speak to Old Lung. "How will you go about it with her?"

"You want to hear the truth?" Old Lung glances at me. "I helped many folks looking for bones. But they're our own people. They're poor and tough, who can put up with hardship and the forest scourge. Still in the end many of them gave up and went back home. They got ill, and there's no infirmary in this buffer zone. You have to go to Ông Doc town for medical treatment." He squints at me. "How long can she last? How much faith does she have? It's a vast area and it's only me and her."

"I know it's a vast area, but I already told you about her son. He was last seen here." I point toward the map of the forest. "If he made it out of the base and into the forest, he wouldn't get very far before the Viet Cong picked him up. There's a creek not far after you enter the forest, and on the other side of that creek are swamps with bogs and many spots of quicksand. If I were you, I'd stay on the one side of that creek that's safe and work your way down."

"I've seen that creek. I believe it goes to the sea several kilometers toward the west."

"Good. It's a lot of land to cover, but not too vast. You do your best, old man, and I trust you."

Old Lung clears his throat and scratches his head. "I should tell you this. There's a woman who works as a medium for folks who came here looking for bones. She lives in our buffer zone and you should see her backyard. It must have more than two dozen graves from the bones she collected by helping those folks search that forest and elsewhere. Unidentified bones that nobody wanted. But that woman has a good heart. She took the bones home, washed them with five-flavor berry leaves, wrapped them in nylon sheets, and buried them, each set of bones in a grave. She put flowers on every grave."

"You mean to tell me that the bones could be anywhere, even in that woman's backyard?"

"Yeah." Old Lung taps his spade. "But I must start some-where, right? You know why I don't carry a spade with a wider blade? This dry season makes the clay soil in there hard as rock and you must use a spade with a small blade. You dig and sparks fly. Eh?"

His machete will help him clear the bushes and branches from giant bamboo and ebony. But he has no help. When the remains-gathering crews go into the forest, they survey the area for half a day and then start digging. At night they hang hammocks and sleep in the forest. It takes weeks; sometimes they find nothing, other times they stumble upon a mass burial ground.

I hand the map back to Mrs. Rossi. "I wish I could go into the forest with you, ma'am. But I'm needed back at the inn. Mr. Lung knows the method. He has a good plan."

"You mean he knows where to look?" Mrs. Rossi asks.

"And how to spot a makeshift grave. Like a hump of earth above the ground. Things like that. I can find more men to help, if he finds that he can't dig by himself anymore."

"I understand, Giang," Mrs. Rossi says. "I understand perfectly."

I ride back in Ông Ba's boat while Mrs. Rossi and Old Lung stay at the forest for the rest of the day.

Ông Ba is a grizzled man with a gray stubbled chin. He wears a brown fishing hat and under the hat is a white towel to keep his neck from sunburn. He knows the region. A war veteran like Old Lung and me. Unlike Old Lung, he was a Viet Cong fighter. Before that he was a Viet Minh fighter during the Indochina War. Now he just ferries farm produce to nearby town markets where he sells them, and then buys household goods and resells them to settlers in the buffer zone.

He asks me where I come from. I tell him. An NVA soldier, then a *hoi chánh*. I offer him a cigarette, cupping the flame in the cross-breeze while he puffs on it. The river is red-brown. It smells of ripe vegetation so strong even the cigarette odor cannot mask it.

"So you're one of those guys from the North," Ông Ba says.

"Yes, sir," I say.

"You northerners are always polite," he says, chortling without any malice in his tone.

I am always on guard against people. I gauge their motives through the fleeting expressions of their eyes, the tones of their voices.

"I was a winter cadre," he says. "I grew up in the delta. Been here all my life."

A shrewd, elusive mole. These "winter cadres" were VC southerners who had fought in the South all their lives.

He says, "I used to know this guy in my three-man cell. He went North in fifty-four. A regroupee. Got all the indoctrination, all the political training. Thinking like the northerners. Damn those autumn cadres!"

I had heard of the animosity the winter cadres felt for the autumn cadres—those who left the South in the autumn of 1954, living in peace in the North, and then came back to lead the winter cadres who remained in the South to fight the Americans.

Averting his gaze, Ông Ba says that when the war broke out in 1945, he had just turned twenty. His father was a tenant farmer in the Mekong Delta. "We were dirt poor," Ông Ba said, squinting. "I didn't know how to read or write. I helped my father who worked for this landlord who owned more than one hundred hectares of land. Other times I joined the crew clearing the canals of built-up silt. Got paid for that. Here the water grid is useful as long as the canals are free of silt deposits. Then I joined the Viet Minh."

He takes a last drag and tosses the cigarette into the water. "I don't know about you, young man," he says. "But joining the Viet Minh was the only way out of stinking poverty. They promised upward mobility to a family whose children joined them. Land redistribution. Lands they confiscated from filthy rich landlords. Promised us literacy. Taught us ignorant farmers to read, write. And that's how I learned how to read the *quoc ngu*."

He meant the Romanized script that was our national language.

Sitting down on the transom, Ông Ba steers the sampan with his bare foot on the motor's tiller. The motor drones in the quiet. Hands in his lap, he begins rolling a tobacco cigarette. He puts the cigarette in his shirt pocket and reaches down into a canvas knapsack at his feet and comes out with a small cloth bundle. A stack of round peanut brittle. Without meeting my eyes, he hands me one. "Try it," he says. "Local delicacy."

In fact I am hungry. We left the inn at seven in the morning and I had time only for a cup of black coffee which I brewed in my room. The peanut brittle is thickly glazed with cognac-colored caramel. I pass it under my nose. The wholesome smell of rice paper. The brown-skinned peanuts burst in a rich aroma as I chew. Ông Ba has already wolfed down his. He lights his tobacco cigarette with a lighter, setting his eyes on the grasslike clumps overrunning the banks and sprouting up above the water. Ghost rice. We used to treasure them during the war whenever our NVA ran short of food. They grow in swampy grasslands, in marshes, along riverbanks.

"I guess no one cares about wild rice nowadays. Right, sir?" I say to Ông Ba.

"I know," Ông Ba says, eyeing the water. "I remember those days when we fought the Americans. Wild rice was heaven sent."

"You were with the National Liberation Front until the war was over?"

"When it was over, they retired me." Ông Ba steers the sampan clear of an enormous patch of ghost rice sprinting up near the bank where sandbars have built up. His eyes clouded by the smoke, he speaks with his cigarette dangling between his lips. "Why'd you quit, young man?"

"I wish I were young again, old man," I say, chuckling. "I gave them eight years. I was seventeen when I joined the army. They paid me back those eight years by putting me in a reform camp for ten more."

"Cause you joined the other side. They put you away for that long?"

"Ten long years."

"I thought once or twice about quitting. When did the thought hit you?"

"A few years after I was already in the South. We were told before leaving the North that the Party and the Front had captured two-thirds of the South, and the majority of the people there were dying to see us, the liberators. I found out it wasn't so. The entire South wasn't dirt poor as we were told. The people weren't desperate for liberation. We were dirt poor, the North. They were rich, the South. We were thieves, robbers on their land. We weren't welcome here. I quickly found out that the jungle was our only haven. I found out the war was far from being over and the Ho Chi Minh Trail was littered every day with Chiêu Hoi propaganda leaflets up to our ankles."

I stick an unlit cigarette in my mouth. After the snack my throat doesn't feel as dry. I have at times wondered why a southerner like Ông Ba could not see what we northerners had come to find out for ourselves. I was a main-force soldier who wore a pith helmet. I was a northerner indoctrinated by the Party. An ox among others herded in an endless line to the abattoirs. He wasn't like us. He grew up in a free land. But he wasn't free from the Party's moles who had stayed behind in the South after 1954 to carry out the Party's plan. He was more concerned with his own poverty and, somehow, fell in love with the Party's rhetoric and promises. Why had it taken him so long to see it?

Ông Ba pinches his tobacco joint between his thumb and finger. "I wouldn't lie to you," he says, "when I say I didn't waste my youth being a Viet Cong fighter. I wasn't miserable. At times I would cry out of happiness. Happy for our battlefield brotherhood, our camaraderie, our common goal. But then things started to reveal themselves slowly. We weren't kin to our brothers in the North. We were being used. The final victory only confirmed that. Those guys from the North couldn't wait to get rid of us southerners."

I watch him stroke his bearded chin, lost in his own recollections. These southerners. Emotional, spendthrift, and fun-loving. They act before they think it through. They don't like northerners, calling us misers, phonies, plodders without any sense of spontaneity. But I have lived in the South nearly half of my life, a double life.

Ông Ba taps his tobacco joint with his little finger to break the ash. "I called it quits," he says, "the day our country was unified and the flag we were told to salute wasn't our NLF flag but the flag of the North. We heard not even a word of compromise."

Ông Ba's face falls into a dark look. Did he still have his NLF flag—half red, half blue inset with a gold star in the center—tucked away in his possessions? Did he hate the sight of the Party's all-red flag with its gold star in the middle, because it brought him memories of loss?

Ông Ba blinks with one eye, peering at me. "Were you at the victory march?"

We all knew the date: May 15, 1975.

I shake my head. "No. Why torment myself?"

"Ah, I forgot, you were a *hoi chánh*. It was a splendid victory march. All units were there, dressed in their attire and carrying their weapons. All-North army. I was there too with my NLF fighters. We were the last unit, like a remnant. No uniform. We never had one. Marching under the North army's banner. We were told beforehand that there was only one banner: the Democratic Republic of North Vietnam."

Ông Ba hawks up phlegm, spits into the water. He and his kin must have hated themselves for their gullibility, to see themselves sacrificed repeatedly in large numbers in frontal assaults while the NVA forces remained in the rear. I was still with the NVA when the Tet Offensive decimated the NLF, its entire regional forces becoming demoralized, and into the vacuum left behind by the NLF, the NVA began filling it with its replacements. Those who rose to power on the graves of his South-born comrades were, "The Men from the North," no others.

I light my cigarette. A quick puff. I look at my nicotine-yellowed fingertips. "You seem to know this region like no one else."

"Young man, you're speaking to one who's been all over Zone Nine. You just tell me the name of a creek or canal, I'll tell you when that waterway was born in this delta. You tell me about a battle, I'll tell you when, what, and where." Ông Ba pauses, blinking with only one eye again. "That Bien Nhi creek where we came in from. I used to go up and down that creek every day, carrying weapons and ammunition in our sampans. Food, medicine, Kohler motors, you name it. We bought those motors from those who got them from the American aid programs to farmers. That Bien Nhi area used to be the South government's stronghold in the U Minh forest. Know what happened to them? They pulled out eventually. They had to. Many of them died there. There used to be a cemetery before the creek enters the forest. Graves of those South soldiers that we killed. Then the whole Bien Nhi area became our stronghold. Home of the 306th Battalion. All the villages there were our families. Six thousand strong."

"Three hundred and sixth battalion," I say, eyeing him. "There were many NVA fillers in that battalion."

"Of course, young man. We were cut down by half more often than I can remember. Had to take in fillers. And we always grew back like a lizard's tail."

"What about the Killing Ground I've heard of?"

"Ah that," Ông Ba says, his voice barely audible above the motor's drone. "You know where it is, don't you?"

"Yes, sir. We've just left it."

"You know about that old American Army base outside the forest?"

"Yes. I heard that it was there after the Killing Ground. Summer of nineteen sixty-six, right, sir?"

"Right. No American base there until then. Just the forest and tracts of land. It all started on that Sunday in June. Our regiment was moving through the forest that day and camped overnight with three thousand men strong. We hung hammocks under trees, so many of them that it looked like a gigantic net hung over the entire forest floor. We packed the floor with our equipment and half the men slept in the tall, wild grass without hammocks. Past midnight they came. You could hear the drone in the sky. Then the sky lit up with flares. It got brighter and brighter and we all woke to see ourselves like pale ghosts in the forest. The jets and gunships came so quick we could barely run for cover before napalm bombs exploded and the forest was on fire and the flames caught us in an inferno and from the sky the howitzers pelted us like red lightning. You could hear the planes' roaring noises, the forest crackling from the heat of napalm, the trees sizzling like meat and falling all around you like thunder. You could hear men's screams above the mayhem. You couldn't breathe. There was no air, and you felt a fire in your lungs and your eyes blurred instantly from the white light of each explosion. When the flares finally went out and the planes left, the only sounds were the cracklings of slow-burning trees, the snapping of limbs finally giving out. In the dark you could hear men crying. Like they came up from underground. The burned men screamed. They had gone out of their minds. Asked you to kill them. Because napalm burns to your bones. Sticks to your skin. Ten times hotter than boiling water. There were gunshots. More gunshots. You smelled something not like air. Something like slow-cooked intestines in a giant cauldron, cooked until all the liquid has vaporized and all the while with its lid on, cooked until the entrails flake because of the heat, and then you open the lid. If you can shrink yourself to the size of a rat and crawl in, then you'll know what the smell is like."

Ông Ba pulls up his trouser leg. "This wound here," he says, "is from that night."

I look at his lower leg. His calf is deformed, a purplish welt running down its length.

"How bad were you hurt?"

"Caught a round in my leg. So I crawled and hid under a cajeput trunk. Many of us got crushed to pulp. Had to doctor the wound myself so I wouldn't bleed to death. But I lost enough blood and the muscle there kinda wasted away."

"You were more fortunate than those hit by napalm."

"Those?" Ông Ba shakes his head. "Even if they survived, it was a living hell for them."

"What happened to your regiment?"

"A few hundred survived. I'm one of those. My battalion, 306th Battalion, went from six hundred men to less than a hundred. All five battalions were nearly wiped out. Took three days to get all the wounded treated. Folks from the buffer zone came and helped. They brought food and water and helped bury the dead. But we couldn't bury them fast enough and the summer heat was so bad the corpses just bloated and cracked open. Then deer flies came laying eggs and pretty soon all the corpses were black with flies and crawling with white maggots. Half of them died in one piece. The rest? Take a guess. They were gone. A hand here, a leg there. You find those on the ground, up on a tree branch, the entrails too, the guts still oozing, stuck to a limb. The whole forest smelled worse than a slaughterhouse. Bag after bag of remains, soggy and bloody, were dumped into a mass grave. You don't know who is who. At least they got a burial and weren't hanging on the trees for vultures and crows."

I remember what the inn owner told us about the forest and recall the spectral scene behind Old Lung's dwelling. The dead remain where they died.

The glare is blinding on the water, the heat suffocating. This humidity and heat, I remember, used to cause our weapons to rust. I wipe sweat off my brow with the back of my hand. Ông Ba lights another cigarette, his face shadowed by the brim of his fishing hat. He doesn't sweat at all. The sampan goes under a monkey bridge. I can see a woman stepping along the log, barely half a foot wide, sitting high on the X supports of cross-leaned poles, and she is looking down at her feet, one hand holding on to a waist-high pole, slimmer than the log, while finding her footing.

"What was your unit?" asks Ông Ba.

"Seventh Battalion, Eighteen B Regiment, First Division."

"Ah. You were here in the U Minh region after all."

I nod.

"So you knew what the American base was there for?"

I nod again and say nothing. I know the base was there to monitor the region for enemy movements and give fire support to the American troops operating in the area. I also know that it was a small firebase, manned by one infantry company.

"You know how that base got overrun?"

"By our men of the NVA First Division."

"So you were in that attack . . ."

The word 'yes' rolls off my lips but Ông Ba does not hear it. I don't care if he did. I don't want to tell him that I know this region well. Nor do I want to tell him how we wiped out the firebase that night.

I am an early riser. For the past two months, in the hour before dawn, I'd sit by the window, my hands resting in my lap, eyes closed. I would work the muscles of my eyes by looking left for several seconds until the eye muscle ached, and then looking right. I kept my head still, moving only my closed eyes like rolling marbles. I continued this routine until I could no longer glance in either direction. By then my eyelids felt warm and my temples throbbed. Then I would massage the eyelids in circular motions. I could hear the sound of ocean waves born on the wind, the time of ebbing tide. I could smell the stale nicotine on my fingertips, rubbing until the pounding in my temples ceased. When I felt the malicious dryness in the throat, I'd stop and sip coffee, which I would brew before my eye exercise routine. I believed you could condition your body to behave in a certain way. It would obey your command if you put your heart into it. I seldom coughed during my regimented eye exercise.

I'd had trouble seeing things in the distance a few months back. I did not want to spend money on prescription glasses. But my eyes tired quickly while driving. Then I remembered a medical doctor I knew while I was with the NVA. The man told me that if you exercise your already weak eye muscles with a daily routine, you could eventually restore the strength in them. How? I asked out of curiosity. He described the routine that would require at least two hours daily. I asked him if he had seen anyone succeed at it. "Yes," he said, "I'm the one." He used to wear thick glasses, he told me. When it rained at night during the treks through forests, his glasses became fogged. Also during surgery, the lenses would fog in confined, unventilated spaces. So he decided he had had enough of the glasses. He began disciplining himself through the eye exercise. Within two months he started noticing the difference. His glasses began interfering with his vision. Like wearing someone else's lenses. After three and a half months, the result stunned him. He had worn prescription glasses since he was a boy, but now could see the world without any lenses.

It has been two months. Two hours each day before daybreak. I have noticed that my eyes, though tired from looking at the road, do not tear. In fact, I have had little eye strain at all.

When she just turned seventeen, Chi Lan won the mathematics championship of her statewide competition. I asked if she was glad to be getting out of high school and she laughed, saying she had been homeschooled all her teen life. She said most colleges were expensive in the States, but in her case, she would go to an in-state college on a full scholarship. While explaining to me about homeschooling, the math competition, in-state and out-of-state college tuition fees, she had to ask me for comparable words in Vietnamese because there were nothing like those in Vietnam. She said she found a small trunk under her bed in the inn. "Not a treasure chest, *Chú*," she said, but an old wooden trunk filled with books and notebooks. Most of them were moth-eaten. In one dusty notebook she saw pencil sketches of flowers and butterflies and several sketches of a graceful-looking girl. "I tried to read the handwritten words in smeared purple ink," Chi Lan said. "But I could barely understand them." She came to a conclusion that it must be a diary, judging from the dates appearing on one sheet to the next. She handed me the notebook, asking, "Whose diary is it?"

"You must wake early," she says. "I smell coffee around four. The owners don't drink coffee. So it must be you."

Her room is above mine. The room windows are open for fresh air day and night.

"Does it wake you?" I ask.

"I like the smell. I usually fall back to sleep. Then my mother gets up and leaves."

"Join me for a cup of coffee then, when you're up."

"You drink it black, *Chú*?"

"Always."

"I can never get used to black coffee."

I tell her to sit on my bed, not on my rickety chair. I have fixed all the wobbly chairs in the inn except mine. She asked when I'd get it fixed, and I said when I went to town the next time to have a haircut and buy some parts for the chair.

She cups her feet with her hands, her toenails painted rose. She draws my gaze to her feet.

"You painted them last night?" I ask.

"You're very observant."

I shift my weight. The chair creaks.

"Your hair is awfully long," she says. "Are you going to town soon, *Chú*?"

"Yeah. And I'll buy the parts for the chair."

"It creaks like a mouse. Doesn't it annoy you?"

"No. It's an old chair."

"Everything is old in this place." She motions to the notebook on my table. "That notebook must be very old, right?"

"Do you know why most old books are eaten by moths?"

"Why?"

"Old paper is porous." I thumb through the notebook, its yellowed sheets brittle and smelling like dust. "You know how old this notebook is?"

"Moth-eaten sheets, smeary ink," she says, tapping her lips with her finger. "Older than you!"

"Be more exact."

"Sixty-nine years old. And how old are you, *Chú*?"

"Thirty-nine," I say. "So you remember the dates in the diary . . ."

She breaks into a smile. "It is a diary, isn't it?"

"A diary from 1918."

"Whose is it?"

"The inn owner's father."

"The old woman's father?"

"Right."

"Who's the girl in the sketches?"

"Her mother. Before she married him."

"Is that what's said in the diary?"

"Yeah. He was in love with her when she was living with her parents and her grandma. Well, that grandma is the inn owner's great-grandma. She didn't love him, but he kept coming to her house . . ."

"Then what happened?"

"She said to him one day, 'Grandma is half blind from cataracts. She can't read anymore. She loved reading Chinese classics in Vietnamese translation. I read for her whenever I can. Would you like to help me?' He said, 'I don't know how to read.' She said, 'How old are you?' He said,

'Nineteen.' She said, 'Why didn't you go to school?' He said, 'I help my father till the land and there are no schools here.'"

Chi Lan lifts her chin. "What school did the girl go to?"

Her astuteness gives me pause. "I don't know," I say. "Rich families back then usually had private tutors in the home."

"How old was she?"

"Seventeen. She was fluent in French too. She said to him, 'Go learn and come back and read for my grandma. Then you can be my friend.'"

Chi Lan wraps her arms around her knees.

"So he left," I say. "He went home and begged his father to let him go to school because he wanted nothing else but the girl in his life. That angered his father, who didn't need an educated son to help him with the land, but at the son's persistence he relented. So every morning before sunrise the boy would walk to the country road and catch a ride to the city. The city-bound black Renault minibus, packed with villagers, would come clanking up the road and the boy would cling to the side, standing on the running board, holding on to the side-mounted spare tire. In the city he asked the school principal to take him in. A French-run elementary school. He joined a class with six-year-old Vietnamese and French children and learned how to read and write from a teacher three years older than himself. At sunset he'd come back, standing on the running board of the little bus. It became a familiar sight. Everyone—the passengers, the driver, the schoolchildren—knew about his determination. Some jokingly called him 'bird of a different feather.' He thinks he can feed his family with fancy words, they said. The boy ignored their taunts. But he remembered their ignorance, the smells of fowl and vegetables. One morning the bus hit a pothole and he fell off the running board. His head bloodied, his arm broken. They treated him in a city hospital, putting his arm in a cast. He caught the Renault for the ride back at sunset. That was the only day he missed school. A year later he visited the girl and said to her, 'I can read now.' She said, 'Can you write?' He said, 'Yes,' and he showed her a notebook."

I lift the notebook from the table and thumb through the brittle sheets.

"So," Chi Lan says, peering up, "he wrote his thoughts each day?"

"Yeah. Sincere expressions, simple words. But he wrote with clarity. A good writer."

"Did he read to her grandma?"

"Yeah. Chinese classics in Vietnamese translation. Then the French original works by French authors. *Les Miserables, Le Comte de Monte-Cristo.*"

"So he learned French too? He had beautiful handwriting."

"He became the village schoolteacher. The only one in the village."

"But you said there was no school in the village."

"He opened one. Poverty isn't a sin but ignorance is, he convinced the villagers."

"I understand."

"You do?"

"Yes, I do." Her eyes never trail away as she speaks the words.

The sound of her voice, not the words, remains foremost in my mind.

1967
Nicola Rossi

Brown earth, brown water. Mama, I step out of the Jeep and walk to the riverbank. I look at the aquatic plants that float on the water, the lush green of vegetation that grows wild on the banks. Riverboats and barges. The natives, tiny and lithe. You have never seen so many streams and canals and rivers, so much water it drowns you in your dreams and in a dream you flow like driftwood, bobbing and swirling mindlessly, smelling the salty air and the water tastes briny and you know then you have returned to the sea. Brown water, rustic, muddy, tranquil as it flows and nurtures the Mekong Delta.

Mama, you can see those waterways ablaze from the helicopter. White serpentine ribbons entwined and gleaming among the greens. You can see the seaside mangrove forest below. A glimpse of sunlit canals and the sparkling water of a waterfowl breeding colony. There's a flower I have seen in this coastal mangrove forest. It looks like jasmine, has that same fragrance. But it's false jasmine. The Viets call it *lá ngón*. We call it *heartbreak grass*. On the edge of the forest it flowers yellow in straggling shrubs, twining the tree trunks seeking sun. We might never have spotted it. If you chew its spearhead-shaped leaves or its yellow flowers or eat its egg-shaped brown fruit, you'd find yourself frothing at the mouth, jaw locked, teeth clenched, and then death would follow in no time. That day we were sent to rescue Echo Company trapped in this mangrove forest by the Viet Cong 306th Battalion. Before we even had a firefight, we had a death in our company. The fellow chewed a handful of false jasmine's leaves. He had a violent fit of stomach pain. He was foaming at the mouth moments before he died, eyes dilated like he saw something terrifying. Later on, an investigation led us to believe that he ate the leaves on purpose—a suicide.

His death took something away from me, Mama. Combat deaths often make me hollow inside and saddened. Like Marco, Eddy, Coy. But suicide disheartens me. It has stayed with me since Papa. I was in high school when he came back from Nam, this God-forsaken land. He never talked about it though. I only knew from what you told me—that he was with the CIA, heavily involved with the Green Berets even before they came under the United States Military Assistance Command, Vietnam. I knew nothing about Vietnam from him until I went to Officer Candidate School. Then I knew what MACV was about. They were here to help train the Army of the Republic of Vietnam to defend South Vietnam against the Viet Cong and the North Vietnamese communists. Later on, MACV carried out a covert operation that became officially known as Operation Phoenix. Then I knew he must have been involved in the program's main objectives—neutralizing Viet Cong suspects outside judicial controls, killing every identified active Viet Cong cadre and every South Vietnamese suspected collaborator. He wasn't the same man, you said to me, after he came back from

Vietnam. Mama, I can't recall what he was like before he left for Nam. He was a reticent man. Even with you, Mama. Then he became even more distant, the time he came back. Then how quickly things fell apart for you and him. You were forty-one then, I remember.

Mama, I died once as a stillbirth but was reborn as your son. By dying, as Saint Francis of Assisi said, we are born to eternal life.

The nurse said she would wash the baby as the doctor removed his latex gloves. The doctor patted Papa on the shoulder and said, "I'm sorry." After he left, the nurse brought the baby to the bed and placed him in your arms. The baby was wrapped in a small blanket. In a hushed voice, the nurse said she would be back for him.

The baby looked as though he were asleep in the cradle of your arms. You were sitting up on the bed, your back cushioned by a pillow against the head railing. You bent your head to look at his face and parted a corner of his blanket to look at his limbs. You touched his nose, his closed eyes, his tiny mouth, trailing your fingers along his jawline. Gently, you pulled the blanket over his chest as if to keep him warm. With one arm cradling the baby, you freed the other and peeled back his pom-pom cap. The baby had dark hair in thin curly wisps. You caressed his pate, then combed his hair with your nails, brushing it back and forth, like someone strumming guitar strings. You held your gaze like that without moving your head and you kept gazing at him, waiting for a miracle to breathe life into this stillbirth. After some time, you broke your gaze and dipped your head to kiss him on the brow. You pressed your lips against him, not moving, in that eternity. Quietly, you cried. Papa leaned over the bed to hug you.

"Do you want to hold him?" you asked.

Yes, Papa wanted to. This tiny thing. Brownish. Dry chafed skin. Smelling of antiseptic. Still warm. His small mouth was red without the fine curves of the lips. His tiny hands clenched. He had fingernails too, and his hands felt soft. Papa said, "So this is you who kicked and turned and moved around playing hide-and-seek in Mama's tummy. Did you hear Mama and Papa talking to you? Did you hear Mama sing?"

He kissed the baby on the forehead. His skin no longer felt warm. Watery discharge was seeping from his nose and the corners of his mouth. The nurse came back. She asked to take the baby away. "I'm sorry, sir," she said. She wrapped the baby in his blanket and you said you would like to hold him for the last time. Holding him in the crook of your arms, you rocked him and you kept on rocking him as tenderly as a mother would rock her baby to sleep until the nurse held out her hands. You shook your head. Your lips parted but no words came out and the nurse touched you on the elbow.

"I must take him," the nurse said. She stroked your hands until they yielded their grip and the baby was back in the nurse's arms, tucked neatly in his blanket, the knitted cap pulled down to cover his brow, and the nurse said good-bye and left the room with him and the door clicked shut.

In the night came the sound of a baby crying. Perhaps just born.

You had insomnia, Mama, during your pregnancy. You could sleep only after a glass of wine. The insomnia got worse after the stillbirth. You couldn't sleep at night. The piano you played downstairs would wake Papa in bed. *Go to sleep, baby child, Hush-a-bye, don't you cry. When you wake, you will have, All the pretty little horses.*

Papa worried about biochemical imbalances in the brain. The doctors suggested a lamp with a bluish luminosity. Rainy days and wintry weather made Papa fret. Did she have enough light? Would she stay balanced? He grew accustomed to seeing the lamp glowing blue, and still there was too much darkness.

Papa stayed up late in bed one night, reading a CIA briefing. The program waiting for him in South Vietnam nagged at him. He wasn't a man for myths and abstracts, so he realized the scope of the proposition the agency asked of him. He was to develop a pacification program targeted at the Viet Cong in South Vietnam. The agency gave him time to bring himself up to speed with the fledgling program. Also, he was to learn the language. "If you speak their language," the director said to Papa, "the Vietnamese will treat you like a family member."

Papa read until his eyes grew weary. Lying beside him, you needlepointed a stocking. Occasionally you glanced up at the black-and-white TV. Papa finally put the papers back in his attaché and got in between the sheets.

"Can you turn off the light?" he asked.

You clicked the lamp off. Papa turned on his side away from the glare of the TV. You held the stocking in your lap, needles in your hands. Could you finish it by Christmas? This stocking showed a little boy sitting under a white pine with sugarplums hovering in his thoughts. You wanted to leave a memory under the Christmas tree. For the lost child.

Soon Papa began his snoring. Your eyes followed the scenes on the screen, your thoughts returning to what Papa had said about his duty in Nam. How long this time? You cried when he was sent to Nam the first time. But you had managed on your own.

The man kissed the woman on the screen. Back then you would long for him on nights you couldn't sleep. A woman's longings opened a new realm of sensuousness. You discovered pleasures you only heard whispered about in girlhood. In those moments you imagined his body.

On the TV screen the woman broke away from the man, lit a cigar for him. The man puffed on his cigar as the match flickered. He gripped both her wrists, steadying her hands, and the match burned down to her fingers. She tried to look calm.

You turned off the TV but still saw the man gripping the woman's wrists. In the dark the images pricked your imagination. You turned on your back, felt dry in your mouth. Your body wasn't ready for bed. It felt warm, though you hadn't touched a drink this night. You turned to Papa, placed your hand on his hip. His breathing was shallow; his snoring stopped. You ran your hand along the curve of his hip, his thigh. You stopped as Papa woke. He turned toward you. He smelled of fresh linen, eyes confused from half dreams. You touched his chest, unbuttoned his top. He followed your hands with his. You bent over him, your hair covering your face, his hands on your hips. He was still half in his dream, half in you when his desire peeked. You clutched his shoulders, your hair falling over his face. He said, 'I'm sorry,' stroking your shoulders. It had ended so soon, so abruptly. Your skin cooled. In Papa's arms you thought of the man in the movie and finally slept.

1987
Le Giang

She leans on the windowsill, watching me place the slow-drip coffee filter on a cup. The stainless-steel filter looks like a square-topped hat, a morning-light luster in its metal.

"I've never seen how it was brewed before," she says. "The brewing with this filter . . . the waiter said *phin*. *Phin* coffee?"

"Café *phin*." I add two spoonfuls of ground coffee to the filter and screw the strainer back on. I pour hot water from the thermos, enough to wet the packed-down coffee. She leaves the window, comes to the table. The coffee aroma begins rising.

"Let me guess," she says, breathing it in. "You get the strongest flavor just now in the cup. Right?"

"Yeah." I pour more hot water until it nearly tops the filter, the steam curling and some black specks of coffee now floating up from under the strainer. I lid the filter.

"How long do you wait?"

"About ten minutes." I glance up at her, pausing at the sight of her thigh-length cutoffs pressed against the table's edge. Her blue cutoffs, the hems frayed, have a sewn-on green-stemmed rose on the left thigh.

"Slow-drip coffee surely takes time," she says.

"You could wait, or meditate . . ."

"I saw you meditating when I passed by yesterday. I couldn't sleep, so I thought I'd go for a walk."

"At five in the morning?"

"I love the fresh air." Her lips curl into a teasing smile. "You were sitting on the chair, looking out the window with your eyes closed. I could smell the brewed coffee."

"I could sleep sitting up."

"You don't like sleeping on the bed?"

"I do. But I'm up at five every day. And I brew coffee because I know you love the smell." I keep my voice nonchalant, watching her reaction.

"At least you were successful," she says. "I was coming down after all."

"I was working on my eyes." I tell her of my self-healing routine. She listens, leaning into the morning light.

"Two hours every morning?" she says.

"I have nothing else to do."

"I mean, the patience. Like the patience waiting on the drip coffee."

"We live a slow life here. I'm sure you'll forget everything by the time you go back home."

"I keep the things I learn—things I select to remember."

"Like what?"

She shrugs. "Like the drip coffee," she says. "I'll remember that. And I'm fascinated with those rivers and canals around here. And the lives that depend on them."

She took many photographs during her first trip to the forest with her mother, Old Lung, and me. Her young mind sponged up things, and I felt lively in her presence. Yet I could never think of her as a Vietnamese.

"Do you feel like a foreigner to your own birthplace?"

"I don't feel foreign to Vietnam. I remember the place where I came from. It looks just like the places around here."

"Where? You've never told me."

"You never asked."

"Where then?"

"Plain of Reeds. In the delta too."

"I know where it is. What do you remember?"

"The floods that came every year after summer. The canals that took you to the big rivers. The mangrove trees in the plain. The stilt houses along the rivers."

"And you left Vietnam when you were five?"

"Yes, *Chú*." She recrosses her legs, her finger tracing the sewn-on rose. "Do you remember those empty stilts along the riverbank? Just stilts on the mud bank with no houses on them?"

"What about them?"

"The other day, I photographed them. I thought, what happened to the houses? Stilts but no houses. I wanted to ask you but you were busy talking with my mother . . ."

"They were destroyed during the war. Just ruins now. Like people. Died, or moved away."

"I used to see them when I went to the riverbank with the nuns. I grew up in an orphanage run by the nuns."

She pauses, glances down at the filter-covered coffee cup. "Is it ready now?"

I lift the lid. The slow-drip coffee has pooled black, glossy, filling half the cup. She inhales the rich aroma. I pour a dash of black coffee into a fresh cup and add some hot water. She palms the cup with both hands, head lowered, the cup raised to her lips. She takes the first sip gingerly, her brow furrowed.

"Bitter," she says.

"Medicine taste?" My gaze fell on the tiny black mole under the corner of her left eye.

"Better than medicine," she says. "Do you know why?"

"Because it's coffee?"

"Because your mind tells you so. And more so, the aroma."

I sip. "Do you want to visit that orphanage?"

"It's no longer there. Some foreign company bought the surrounding land a few years back for business development."

"How do you know?"

"I keep in touch with the head nun. But recently I lost her. She said she'd write me when she knew where they would relocate the orphanage. She sent a photograph of the old orphanage with a church fronting it. I'll never forget the white steeple of that church."

"Why?"

"I got lost in the marketplace one day, separated from the head nun. I was scared but I didn't cry. I found my way out of the market and took the road we came in on, remembering the scenery, and kept walking until I saw the tower, and then I knew I wasn't lost anymore."

"How old were you at that time?"

"Barely five."

She has serene eyes, elongated and pretty. She is getting used to the bitter taste of the *phin* coffee. This orphan child, having been displaced to grow up into a beautiful girl, who exudes liveliness and consideration.

She tells me about the place she came from: the one-story, L-shaped, tin-roofed, mango-wood walled house that sheltered nine orphans, four to ten years old. Behind the orphanage and the white-steepled church was a fish pond, and behind that a plot overgrown with banana trees whose fronds the nuns would cut and wash and later use to wrap food. In that banana grove, caught by a sudden late-afternoon thunderstorm, the head nun held her tight against her bosom, both crouching from the lashing rain. The nun broke the fronds at the stems to screen themselves and took off her scarf and wrapped it around the little girl's head. A streak of lightning struck at ground level, like a sudden flash out of a mirror. Then followed an ear-splitting thunderclap. The girl plugged her ears as another crash shook the ground. She heard the wind ripping through the banana trees, and out in the open the hummingbird trees bent and snapped back and leaves flew fluttering like birds. The pebble-sized raindrops pelted her face and the banana fronds and pockmarked the pond's water. A white flash hit the ground across the pond, searing a hummingbird tree in midsection. The tree snapped. The girl could smell the burned smoke. She said, sobbing, into the nun's chest, "I don't want to be here," and the nun cradled her in her arms. "We'd better stay for a little while. I promise nothing shall hurt you, my dear." The girl inhaled the nun's warm, sweaty smell. Suddenly the nun squirmed, saying, "I've got something under my blouse." The nun eased herself out and her hands came up unbuttoning her blouse. The little girl stared, seeing a black thing against the nun's chest. A caterpillar. Across the air suddenly flashed a jagged line. Then an explosion so loud her ears rang. She mashed her face in the nun's bosom, the nun shielding her now with the open fronts of her blouse. Eyes shut, she heard the nun cooing. She felt the flesh warm and abundantly soft, smelling like wet leaves, and she felt raindrops trickling down to her lips. The thunder came less and less now and soon rolled into the distance and then just the rain clattered on the leaves, the smoky smell now gone from the air, and it felt dank in the wind. The nun gently pulled her away from her chest. "It's safe now, child," she said. The girl wiped rain from her cheeks, following the nun's fingers trying to match a button against its buttonhole. She kept gazing at the ample flesh of the nun's bosom, then at a pink ridge of a scar across her breasts. She didn't ask. But the sight of the scar stayed with her.

At dawn she would rise to help the nun in the rear kitchen, sitting on her heels on the packed-earth floor, stacking coconut leaves, brown and dry, then stripping the leaves from the stiff midribs. The nun would light the leaves and feed them into the hearth, and when the flames spurted she poured a bowlful of rice husks into the fire. The hearth crackled, the husks exhaled acrid fumes, and the flames rose in blue tongues. She would save the midribs and the stems for the nun. The children would tie the stems together into a multilayered fan-shaped bundle into which they would fit a handle. That was how they made brooms. The nun would let her pour rice flour evenly onto a white gauze that screened a wide-bottomed pot, the square cloth stretched and held down drum-tight by four bricks, the pot steaming with boiling water. The rice flour—a creamy white mixture of sugar and coconut extract and sesame seeds—was spread out in a round layer and the nun lidded it with a cane cover. The girl would stare at the rice crepe after the lid was removed, the crepe so thin now, opaque-white. The nun would slide a wide wooden blade under the crepe, lifting it gently so it hung flapping, round-shaped and wet and paper-thin, and then drop it on a palm-woven sieve. As the nun bent to scoop up rice husks with a bowl to add to the fire, the girl could see the nun's breasts through her collarless blouse, the long scar, braidlike, across her chest. They had to use up the flour just before the sun had burned off the morning mist, so they could put out the sieves for the crepes to dry in the sun. By noon the crepes would be dry and the children took the sieves back in and stacked them by tens, tied them down, and wrapped them in brown papers. Later

a nun would carry them to the local market and sell them
on consignment.

Then the flood season came. One morning after a three-day
rain she woke and saw floodwaters rising to the doorsteps.
By noon the water was coming into the house. She could
no longer see the long table where they ate, but only the
tops of the straight-backed chairs. The nuns put the children in three canoes, the long, slender canoes always tied
to the trunks of the hummingbird trees behind the house,
and now with the children safely together, all bunched up
in their clear-plastic raincoats, the nuns began paddling
away. The plain behind the house was a steely white sheet
of water brimming to the horizon. Yellow-flowering river
hemp bushes marked the boundaries between landowners'
paddy fields in the gray water. She could tell where they
were by the familiar sights—clumps of half-submerged flat
sedge fringing a pond, the pond now rising with cloudy
water. The head nun handed her the short paddle and
reached out for a blue water lily. She gave the girl the flower
and took the paddle back. The girl asked if the nun's arms
were tired from rowing, for the nun had taught her how to
row with the *cây dầm*, much shorter than an oar, made of
thingan wood, polished and always light. The nun shook
her head and rowed on. They would stop when they spotted small crabs taking shelter on a floating quilt of water
hyacinths, so the children could pick them up and play
with the mottled-brown crabs that always camouflaged
themselves with the color patterns of their surroundings.
Sometimes late in the afternoon when the water stopped
rising, the nuns rested with the canoes leaning against the
crown of a young bushwillow with its trunk, at least two
meters tall, submerged in water. Neighbored by nothing but
gray sky and white water, the nuns began setting the fishing

poles, fitting their butts into a bored hole in the upper side of the canoe. The poles arched over the water and the lines plumbed the water's depth. The children ate rice balls out of their banana leaves. The girl, too, chewed a rice ball, long-grained and sticky with ground, salted sesame seeds. She could taste its roasted aroma. Her mind grew dreamy. They caught several perches. One hand holding the line, the head nun held up a perch, its dusky-green body quaking in her hand, as the children gawked. The nun told them this fish could walk. The children giggled and asked how. "It uses its tail and fins," the nun said, "to move over land." The girl remembered that. The walking perch. They rowed on, the nuns stopping at times to untangle feathery roots of water lettuce from their paddles. Passing an earthen dike with only its top above the water, the head nun pointed toward a paling of cajeput stakes, closely joined, and asked if anyone knew what the barrier was for. The girl said it was to catch fish. The nun said, "You're very smart, child, but this isn't a fish weir." As the canoes came alongside the wet, battered-looking paling, the nun told them to look down into the water. "A fish weir," she said, "has stakes with a fair distance between them, and with horizontal wattling between stakes to trap fish. Do you see any wattling down there?" The children said no. The nun said, "This paling is to protect the dike from further water damage. You as my children live your protected lives in the orphanage, but out here people's lives depend on the waterways and some-times water encroaches their habitats and so their work never ends, the year-round mending of things in the delta." Beyond the dike, they came around a hummock rising above the water like an elephant back. The nuns shipped the paddles, docked the canoes, and led the children up the knoll. Twilight was falling, spreading a fan-shaped glow across the water, luminous water swelling to the sagging sky. They walked under cajeput trees, between their thin pale trunks into the gloom harbored by their damp leaves, now black and dripping rainwater. In a clearing, a stilt hut sat three feet above the ground. Flanking the steps were clay vats, lidded and waist-high. Beneath the stairs was parked a skiff covered in a moss-green plastic sheet. An old man sat outside the hut on the bottom step. The girl recognized him. Leathery, sun-spotted face. Gap-toothed grin. He was the janitor who helped fix things around the orphanage. He built all the furniture—tables, chairs—and one time made a pen nib for her. She remembered one morning seeing him on the doorsteps pounding a leaf of gray metal cut out from a milk can. She sat by him. "Making you a new pen nib as she told me to," he said, referring to the head nun, as he cut the metal into a sliver. "So you can write again," he said. "You write, eh? How old are you?" She said, "Four." He looked her up and down. "I don't even know my age," he said, "but I can count with my fingers." With the tip of his tongue protruding between his lips, he began hammering the metal sliver.

Now he raised his hand to greet the nuns. So this is where he lives, she thought. In the ash-blue twilight beyond the clearing where bushes grew wild, she saw humps of graves plagued by needle grass and false daisy. The white, small flowers glimmered. She'd seen these same flowers around the orphanage. When they followed the old man up the steps and into the hut, she could hear from behind the hut the hens clucking and the throaty gargles the ducks made in their pens. The old man lit the kerosene lamp, hanging from a hook on a maroon post. The hut glowed eerily in the trembling light, the corners full of shadows. The floor, lined with shorn boles of cajeput, glowed with a bone shine. A lute hung next to the lamp, odd-shaped, its body as round as a coconut. The hearth crackled with a fire going strong, the old man feeding the fire with cajeput wood, then dropping dry cajeput leaves on the flames, giving off a foul smell. "Keeps out the mosquitos," he told the children sitting around the hearth. She followed a nun outside to get away from the smelly smoke. The nun knelt on a flagstone by a vat and began gutting a perch with a knife. Watching the nun prepare the fish, the girl heard heavy wings up in the dark tangles of cajeput trees. She looked up and saw white storks and white egrets coming home to roost for the night. The twilight stillness was broken by the incessant, raw beating of their wings.

The head nun came out of the hut. "Are you hungry, child?" The girl nodded. The nun said, "We're staying here until the water goes down, then we go back home and start cleaning up. I'll be back soon." The girl asked, "Where are you going?" The nun pointed toward the gloom beyond the clearing. The girl saw the humps of graves, now just blurred swells. "What's there?" she asked. The nun looked down at the ground. "My daughter's grave," she said. The girl said nothing but felt a deep separation. "Can I go with you?" The nun patted her head. "Yes, child." And they walked in the rustle of wings to the graveyard.

The small grave sat on the rim of the knoll, which sloped into an overflowing canal. The ground felt soft around the grave, matted with toothache plant. "Aren't they pretty?" the nun said, bending to pluck a handful of the flowers. The girl asked, "What's this plant?" The nun gathered the long-stemmed flowers, each shaped like a yellow-colored eyeball with a red dot in its center. "*Co the*," the nun said. "Like its name says. It tastes like mint, strong enough to numb your gums." The nun placed the small bouquet of toothache plant on the grave. The girl gazed down at the restless water rushing headlong, as though the earth were tipped on its side, a dank smell rising from the canal. Then came a sudden wing rush. A pond heron shot up, coming over them so low she could see its brown-streaked plumage as it sailed into the dark vault of trees. She looked at the nun, who stood with head bowed, forming words of prayer. She crossed herself. The girl imagined a presence in the grave. Forever out here in the heat and rain. "Why did she die?" she asked. The nun took a sharp breath and slowly exhaled. "She drowned in the flood." The girl remembered stories about drowned people who would float back up, bloated and blue-cold, after three days in the deep. The nun said softly, "Since then I've been always prepared for the flood, so you children will always be safe with me." She patted the girl's head. "She was only your age." The girl noticed the small grave, small enough to be overlooked had it not sat alone on the tip of the knoll. "It's so small," she said. The nun said, "It is small, my child. Just a grave. Nothing in it. I could not recover her body. But I want to remember her, that's my wish." The nun squeezed the child's hand. The vegetation-damp smell coming up from the water below reminded her that she would always be safe on high, dry ground like this. Walking back toward the hut, the nun said, "She had eyes like you. You have the Virgin Mary's eyes, my child."

From inside the hut came a thick smell of smoked fish. The fire in the hearth made shadows in the doorway. Leaning against a broken vat the girl stood watching the head nun cleaning her neck. Then unbuttoning her blouse, the nun began washing her chest. In the yellow glimmer the girl gazed at the abundant flesh. When the hand went away, the flesh was bare and milky, and across the ample flesh was the long ridgelike scar.

She puts her cup down on the windowsill, raises herself up on her arms and sits comfortably on the sill with her legs dangling. It is bright outside and the breeze is warm coming into the room and you could smell the wild grass and the old peat soil.

I try to picture her as a child. I imagine hearing her gentle voice, speaking in Vietnamese. "Maybe someday you'll find the nun," I say.

"I hope so," Chi Lan says. "I will come back here."

"You will?" I cough, reaching for the cigarette pack on the table.

"You cough a lot, *Chú*. Maybe you should see a doctor."

"Maybe I should."

"How long have you smoked?"

"As long as I've drunk black coffee."

"Well, how long then?"

"All the vices I picked up when I was fifteen."

"You were fifteen going on fifty."

I chuckle. My throat feels raspy. This morning she wears a scarlet, collarless blouse which has no white fringe around the neckline like the one she wore on the rainy evening at the pier. A lock of raven-black hair curls over her clavicle. The neckline, held by a button, opens out in a small V.

"The nun," I say, "how did she have such a scar?"

"From a rape."

I draw back. The chair creaks. "During the war?"

"Yes. She fought him and he cut her with a bowie knife."

"Who did?"

"An American marine—when they raided her village."

"What village?"

"One in the Plain of Reeds, where she ran her orphanage."

"Her daughter was the result of the rape?"

Chi Lan nods.

I raise my cup to my lips. "When was the last time you saw her?"

"After she agreed to have my American mother adopt me. I cried when she told me. She held me a long time and when I stopped crying she told me it was the right thing to do. For me. That I would have a future that would allow me to grow as a free spirit. That night she woke me before midnight and told me to come with her. She said, 'I want you to see something that you will never see again once you leave Vietnam.' I asked, 'What is it you want me to see?' She said, 'A marketplace.' I said, 'But it's night now.' She said, 'Yes, child, it's the hour that matters.' I asked, 'But why a marketplace?' She said, 'You'll see, child, it's called The Yin-Yang Market.'"

I interrupt her. "Do you mean *Cho Âm Duong*?"

"Yes." She flicks a smile. "I had the words translated in my head before I told you, because I didn't want to say it incorrectly."

"I know what it is."

"Do you? What is it then?"

"We had it in the North. It's hard to explain to outsiders what it is."

"I want to know if we're talking about the same thing."

"In the North, in this particular village in Bac Ninh Province in the Red River Delta, there was this marketplace called 'Cho Âm Duong.' It opened only once a year on the fifth day of the Lunar New Year."

"*Chú* . . ." She cuts in.

I pause, peering at her, and take another sip of coffee.

"The nun," she says, perking up, "was born in the North and came to the South in 1954 when Vietnam was separated into North and South. She said the people who started this *yin-yang* market in the South were northerners, the anti-communist Catholics." She stops, smiles at me. "Now you can go on."

"It makes sense," I say, drawn by her gaze. "And so they said the location of this marketplace used to be a battlefield centuries ago in the feudal time. So many had died their tragic deaths there the *yin* force just shrouds the place. On that day, just past midnight, the market opened. Nobody carried a lamp. In the dark, people came to buy things. Then the market closed before first light."

"Yes, *Chú*." She palms her cup in her lap. "The head nun took me to the market outside our district, near a river. An empty tract of land with stilts standing but no houses atop them. The nun said, 'There used to be a village here ten years ago. In just one day it was gone.' She said the Viet Cong took cover in the village to ambush the Allies and the Allies counterattacked and shelled it to ash. They all died. The Viet Cong and the innocents."

She sets the cup down. "It was past midnight when we got there. A new hour that began a new day on the fifth of the Lunar New Year. There were no lights. I asked the nun, 'Why is it so dark?' She said, 'Just follow me, child.' So she held my hand and we found our way in the dark, walking on bare ground, stepping between people who sat with baskets and bins in front of them. I could hear my footfalls in the stillness. And wisps of murmurous voices. I could smell the steam of rice porridge, the rich odor of beef broth they used to brew porridge with. White steamed buns, rice balls, *bánh lá*—the leaf-wrapped dumplings—were laid out on the sieves. The familiar odor of steamed noodles. Finally the nun found someone. A turbaned woman who sat with a tray at her feet. The nun made me sit between her and the old woman. I bent to see what the old woman had on the tray. 'What are those?' I whispered to the nun. She said into my ear, 'Betel leaves and areca nuts.' She picked up a betel leaf, tore it halfway, and held it to my nose. I winced at the dark, spicy smell. That old janitor always chewed this sort of leaf with a sliver of areca nut. We children were fascinated how he prepared his chew—he would drop the slice of areca nut in the center of the betel leaf and brush the leaf with wet white lime. Then he would roll the leaf into a tight quid and ease it into his mouth. He spat a lot after he chewed. The first time I saw him spit, I thought he spat blood. When he grinned—he had no front teeth—you could see his tongue, and his gums looked as though they were bleeding badly. Now I thought this was some strange market. It was chilly. The nun held me to her side and I rested my head on her shoulder. People were sitting all over the ground in an eerie stillness. I could smell the river in the breeze, its old muddy smell. The sky was low and moonless. I fell asleep on the nun's shoulder, I don't know for how long. Then someone spoke, someone answered, and I woke. A woman wearing a conical hat was standing before me. She folded a betel leaf into a quid and then worked it into her mouth. The oyster-gray skin of her palm-leaf hat glimmered, covering most of her face; her *bà ba* blouse was so white she seemed to glow. She handed the turbaned woman a coin, then turned and walked away. The whiteness of her blouse sank into the blackness. Like stepping into a dark doorway. There were more people now, shuffling about, indistinct, shapeless, wearing the *bà ba* blouses, the wide-legged pantaloons. They sat down, eating from the vendors' bowls. I could hear the slurping noise they made. The air felt cold and damp on the skin, a shivering dampness not there before. I snuggled against the nun and she put her arms around me. *Who are these people? Where'd they come from?* Nobody spoke. It was like seeing things in a dream, black-and-white, soundless. Someone came for a betel chew, then another. Older women. When they came the air would feel colder, like when you open the door and the rain-damp air comes in after it has rained all night. I fell asleep on the nun's shoulder and when I woke the market vendors were packing up. Some vendors had lit their kerosene lamps, the glows painting amber lights and shadows on their faces. The turbaned woman had sold out her betel-chew condiments. The nun said something to her and she began emptying her blouse pockets onto her tray. Wrinkled arrowroot leaves, dried-up banana leaves, holed seashells, pebbles round and square. Like a child's things. 'Why do you carry them in your pockets?' I asked the woman. She looked down into my eyes, about to say something, when the nun said, 'These aren't hers, child. They came from the people who came here to buy things from her.' I said, 'Are they worth anything?' The nun shook her head and said, 'No, child. Themselves they aren't worth anything. But they were money when those who came here paid her and other vendors.' I said, 'But they're not money.' The nun said, 'They were money when those people were here.' Picking up a round pebble, the nun put it in my hand and said, 'This was a coin when they paid her.' She picked up a dried arrowroot leaf and said, 'This was paper money when they gave it to her. You see, child, those people aren't living people, like us. They have been dead for many years now. They came back from their *yin* world into our *yang* world, this market-place, so they could enjoy again our worldly pleasures for one brief moment. There was no bargaining, no haggling about the prices in this market. They came, bought things, paid for them. It was real money when they paid. The coin money, the paper money. Only after they have left to go back to their *yin* world, the money turned back to its true origins.' The nun patted my head. 'Now, do you understand why I said that you shall never see anything like this again after you leave Vietnam?' I stood looking at the pebble in my hand. A child's thing, like when children play *buy-and-sell*. We'd use seashells, pebbles, cutout papers for money."

When we leave the café in Ông Doc town to come back to the car, Chi Lan notices a red-inked, handwritten sign hung on the door. She reads it, puckering her mouth. "What exactly does it mean?" she asks. "Something about café *phin* for serious men?"

I thought the figure of speech would be hard for her to understand, but she caught on. I point at the particular words for which I can't find a comparable expression in English, and she says, "It means 'for the birds.'"

I put the cigarette back in my shirt pocket and translate, "Sweet dreams are for the birds. On sleepless nights real men drink only café *phin*."

She smiles. "Like you, *Chú*. Now, go buy your stuff, have your hair cut, and I'll meet you soon."

A boy walks past the café, carrying on his head a wicker sieve covered with a white cloth. "Sugarcane!" he calls out. "Sugarcane!"

I stop him. The boy sets down the sieve and peels back the cloth cover. Round chunks of pale yellow sugarcane fill the sieve. I buy half the sieve and the boy wraps the chunks in a moist cloth. Chi Lan and I suck on the cane cubes, and flies come whirring around. I tell her it is sugarcane season, and she, wiping the juice from the corner of her mouth, leans toward me, and asks. "What's that noise I keep hearing in the air?"

"The chirping?"

"Yes, the chirping."

I take the cigarette pack from my shirt pocket; the last cigarette I have put back wrinkled and bent. "This town is a bird town," I say. "They raise swiftlets everywhere and profit from selling their nests. The birds build the nests with threads of their saliva." Restaurants serve bird's nest soup, I tell her. Expensive. Rich people buy it as a delicacy and eat it for health benefits. At least that's what the merchants had them believe. Credulous people and greedy opportunists. Perfect combination. And the chirpings? They come from those birds, and if the birds stop chirping then what you hear is mechanical chirping. The town's breeders dedicate a whole story of their homes as a bird colony. They lure the birds with the birdlike mechanical sounds. They build tubes for the birds to make nests in. Neat, cup-shaped nests. After a nest is built, the breeder will take it away and the bird has to build another one to lay its eggs in. But day and night this town is kept awake by the birds' chirping.

I offer her another chunk of cane. She shakes her head, wiping the corners of her mouth again with her thumb and finger. "Such a bizarre business," she says, "as bizarre as the *yin-yang* market."

We come back to where the Peugeot is parked. Before we split, I give her the extra car key.

"This Ông Doc town," I say, "has one main street and backstreets are the rib bones. Find the main street and you won't get lost here."

She drops the car key into her purse. "*Chú*, you make a good teacher."

I gaze at her before she goes off on a shopping spree. "Never pay the price they ask for. Haggle—down to every knickknack, for they can tell you're a *Viet Kieu.*"

"Overseas Vietnamese? From my accent?"

I shrug. "Sure. And because you look different."

She leans her head to one side, her lips parted with an unasked question.

"You just look wholesome," I say. "So beware. This dog-eat-dog town is full of drifters."

"Like you?" she asks with a giggle.

"Like me." Most of them, I tell her, rent a squalid room somewhere, a pay-per-day room, for hired hands, who go to sea at dawn, sometimes for several days, and the wives work odd jobs, sleeping alone at night. Between fair weather and big catches, the wives hoard money and in time use their husbands' cash to open knickknack shops and stash away the profit little by little in gold leaves until one day they cash them in to buy a fishing boat. This town abounds with opportunists. Some of them may someday own a fleet of fishing boats. One used to own a seafood plant that employed a third of the town's population, another a boat-repair factory, and another an ice-making plant. Now one drives a taxi for a living, another works as a coolie on the dock, and the other died alone in an alley.

Sauntering off she throws me a sidelong glance. "Don't worry about me."

From behind the rain-streaked windshield, I watch the street. It's raining hard now, like the evening I picked them up at the pier. Since then Mrs. Rossi has bought two rain-coats. In fact, I bought the raincoats in this seaport town on one of the crowded backstreets where you have to duck your head going under suspended wickerwork and colorful apparel, where the broken pavement is ribbed with green moss in dark crevices, damp year-round in a sunless gloom.

I light a cigarette and roll down the window a crack. The window fogs quickly and I wipe it with my forearm. Across the street, a woman peddler is walking under the awnings with a large sieve atop her head filled with white dumplings. Rainwater drips in quick-glinting beads onto the sieve and the woman walks unhurriedly, like a somnambulist, the sieve her umbrella. Chi Lan might be sheltering under a shop's awning on some backstreet, watching rivulets of rain running off the street where its blacktop is so far gone the surface is patched with shorn boles of black mangrove.

A knock on the car window. I peer up and see a hooded face. A girl wearing a pink, clear-plastic raincoat bends her head toward me. I roll down the window. She wipes her face and smiles. I notice her eyetooth.

"Remember me?" she asks.

"I remember you."

"What're you doing in town?"

"Some business to tend to."

"Why don't you stop by anymore?"

"I might, sometime." Leaning back, I look at her until she starts giggling.

"Why're you looking at me like that?" she asks.

"You have lipstick on, so I didn't recognize you at first."

"You like it?"

"You didn't have it on then."

"You mean, the first time you met me?"

"Yeah."

"So you like me better plain?"

"You look fine either way."

"You're always polite. You're not like any of them who went in there." She looks the car over. "This your car?"

"I don't own a car. It's the inn owner's car."

"You told me about the inn." A wind gust nearly blows her hood back. She grabs the top of it and holds it down.

"Are you on your way up there?" I ask, glancing toward the café, the second story of which has three curtained windows overlooking the main street, the pint shutters wreathed with red bulbs.

"I don't have to be there for another half hour," she says.

She rests her hand on the edge of the rolled-down window glass, her fingernails painted a gaudy red. I motion with my head to the passenger seat. "Come sit inside. It'll be clearing up soon."

As she comes around the front of the car, I push open the car door.

"I'll mess up the seat," she says.

"Just get in."

She flops down, shuts the door with a *clunk*. Wet strands of hair mat on her brow. Her hair is longer now, touching her shoulders. She wears a rooster-red plastic hairband, as bright as her lipstick, which smears toward a corner of her mouth. She dries her face with the back of her hand, then pulls down the visor to look at her face in its inset mirror.

"Where're you from?" I ask.

"Not here," she says. "What'd I tell you last time?"

"I wasn't there long. Didn't get to know much of you."

"I remember. You paid. And did nothing." She studies herself in the little mirror. "You didn't tell me why. Just left."

I say nothing, watching her fix her face. When she turns toward me, she breaks into a nervous laugh. "Why d'you keep looking at me like that?"

"You were too young. That's why."

"I didn't tell you my age."

"You can't hide your age with makeup."

"Nobody told me that before. They don't know. Or care."

"Obviously."

"How old d'you think I am?" She touches her lips and clears her throat. "You have a cigarette?"

I fish out the fresh pack, tap it, and watch her pinch a cigarette between her red-nailed fingers. I click open my Zippo. She coughs immediately, waving the smoke away from her face.

"This isn't mint cigarette," she says, picking some tobacco shreds off the tip of her tongue.

"Not mint, not filtered."

She hands back the cigarette. "Not for me."

I look at the red-lipstick stain on the unfiltered tip, then with my thumb and finger snuff out the burning end. She pulls back a little. "Hurt?" she asks.

"No." I slide the cigarette back into the pack. "When did you pick up smoking?"

"Not long ago. All the girls in there smoke. We've got nothing else to do."

"You're the youngest."

"Guess how old I am then."

"Sixteen?"

She brings her hand to her lips, chewing the tip of her fingernail. "I'll be seventeen soon. The three other girls are older, one eighteen, the others twenty and twenty-one." She gnaws at her pinkie's nail. "You've done it with them, haven't you?"

"I have. Before you came there."

I crank down the window halfway to let out the cigarette smoke. Rain drums loudly on the car roof and window glass. I feel droplets of rain on my face. When I turn back she is gazing at me, her eyes plain, her eyebrows full. Perhaps it won't take but another year before those eyelashes will be thickened with mascara, those eyebrows plucked, sharply aslant toward the ears.

"Is there something wrong with me?" she asks.

"You're just too young."

My calm voice seems to convince her, for she drops her gaze and plays with her raincoat's front zipper. "Some guys say I'm too skinny. Am I too skinny to you?"

"Yeah."

"So it's better with those other girls than with me?"

"No. It's just didn't feel right."

"Why not?"

"There are certain things one doesn't do. Some personal rules you cannot break."

"Mmm." She brings her hand to her mouth again, stops as she sees me staring at her gesture. "Your wife knows what you did, I mean, visiting that place?"

I chuckle.

"What's funny?"

"What would you do if your husband did that?"

"I don't know. Ask me when I'm married." She scratches her head with a tip of her long nail. "What about you? So you're not married?"

I shake my head. Someone is hurrying across the street, stopping to find footing in the running water, bundled up in a yellow plastic raincoat. She stops at the passenger door and knocks on the window glass. The young girl cranks down the window and a hooded face peers in.

"Can I get in?" She speaks in English with her lips hardly moving as rainwater drips freely down her face.

"Open the door," I tell the young girl.

"Who is she?"

"She's our guest at the inn."

"She's Viet Kieu?"

"Yeah. Vietnamese from America. Open it."

The girl pushes open the door and struggles to get out. I watch her exit the car, work her hood back over her head. The girl waves, just one quick hand motion, and turns and walks up the sidewalk.

Chi Lan flops down on the seat, swinging shut the car door. Rain slants in on the dashboard, staining it quickly. I reach over and roll up the window. The wet creaky sound of her raincoat, yellow as banana, makes me pause.

"Where'd you get that?" I ask.

"I bought it from a street vendor." She pulls back the hood and gives her head a shake. "I had to buy it. I didn't know when it'd stop raining."

"Did you have any trouble with the vendors?"

"Yes . . . no." She hangs her head to one side. "I walked away and he called me back. Because I remembered what you paid for our raincoats not too long ago. This one . . ." She looks down at the front of her raincoat glistening with moisture, "is just like the one you bought, but he asked for twice the price."

"If I hadn't gotten you that raincoat, would you have paid what he asked?"

"Well . . ." She rolls her eyes. "I took your advice, *Chú*. I bargained. That's why I had some money left and bought you something."

She runs her fingertips through her hair, tangled and damp, gathering it over and behind her ears, and unzips her raincoat. She has a purse slung over her shoulder, a brown bag clutched in her hand. "I bought these near where I bought the raincoat," she says and offers a lidded Styrofoam cup with a white plastic spoon.

"What is it?"

"*Chè*."

I pop open the lid. Longan *chè*. Inside each succulent pearly longan is a paste of yellow mung bean. I can't help laughing. "Is it your favorite?" I ask, remembering what she'd said about eating longan *chè* in America.

"Favorite?" Her brow creases. "I only tried one flavor of *chè* back home."

"I'll get you some other flavors."

I spoon a longan fruit, cool, pulpy, into my mouth, let-ting the faintly sweet taste of mung bean melt on the tongue, and sip the ginger-flavored, sweetened juice. I lid the cup.

"Don't you like this flavor?"

"I'll save it for later." I want a puff of cigarette very badly.

"This flavor's the only flavor I know. They've got thirty some flavors and they all look yummy. What's your favorite?"

"I don't know. I'm not too crazy about sweet things."

"You don't have a sweet tooth, huh?"

"What's that?"

"A sweet tooth? A craving for sweet things."

"Mmm," I say, putting the new words away in my mind.

"You didn't get your hair cut, *Chú*," she says.

"I was stuck here with that girl."

"Who was she?"

"That girl?" I tap the spoon on the lidded cup. "She's a local prostitute."

"A hooker?"

"Yeah."

Chi Lan tilts her head back and looks at me. "She was here soliciting?"

"You mean her asking me . . ."

"Yes."

"No. I asked her to sit out the rain. I saw her once three months ago and she remembered me."

"Saw her where?"

"Above that café." I motion with my head toward the café up across the street.

Chi Lan ducks her head trying to peer through the rain-smeared windshield. She sits back, nodding. "I saw the red bulbs on the second-story windows when we left the café. Kinda odd looking, I thought." She raises the cup to her lips. "So that kind of business is legal here?"

"Of course not."

"So that café is also a brothel?"

"A what?"

"A whorehouse."

"Yeah. The café's owner pays off local police. Always been like that."

"She looks very young."

"Younger than you."

"So you visit that place every time you go to the café?"

"Only three times since I came to the inn. Will be two years this month."

"So it's roughly every eight months that you visit the brothel."

"Give or take." I smile.

"If you can quit going there, you can quit smoking." Her eyes drop to my shirt pocket, which shows a one-humped camel.

"What else did you buy?" I ask.

"Nothing else. I took many pictures though. Some of the town in the downpour."

She always carries her camera in her handbag. "You must be very good with the camera," I say as she spoons the last longan into her mouth.

"On the spur of the moment." She drops the empty cup and spoon into the brown bag. "Anything that captures my imagination in such a moment becomes my subject. Just like you, *Chú*. You draw, I photograph."

I nod. I could have drawn the young prostitute and someday I might. The subject must first capture your imagination, like Chi Lan said.

"Are you going to draw her or have you already?" she asks.

"That girl?" I ask. "I don't do it without that special feeling. It's different with a photographer though. See, you must capture the subject with a camera on the spur of the moment. Or lose it. An artist waits until a subject matures in him. He has time because the subject has already entered his memory."

"But they say memory is the ability to forget. Have you heard that?"

"No. If something's gone from the memory, it's not worth remembering."

"Will they be gone after you've drawn them?"

"No. The artist is giving them a decent burial. The ghosts are never gone. They just rest in peace."

"Because they were painful memories?"

"Not really. If I draw you someday, it won't be from a painful memory."

"There must be many stories in your drawings, *Chú.* Like a diary in pictures."

"Because I'm not good with words."

"I want to know every story behind a photograph, every story behind a drawing. I love to hear stories like those in the diary you read for me. And the stories untold in your drawings." She shrugs, her lips curling with a smile. "So the drawing of the battlefield, the one with the jungle cock, is one of your painful memories?"

"Yeah."

"But the girl with the plait is not, is she?"

"She is not."

"Where is she now?"

"I don't know."

"You know her name?"

"No, I don't."

"Did she know your name?"

"No. I never told her."

"But you remember her till this day."

"Yeah."

"You draw her beautifully."

"She was beautiful."

"How old were you then?"

"Seventeen. Almost the same age as you are now." I take her in with my gaze. Turning away I start the car. I'm sure when I finally draw this girl, I won't forget to dot the corner of her left eye with a tiny mole.

When I was seventeen I first saw the wild banana's red flowers. Early one Sunday afternoon I was returning with my Chinese friend Huan from a peasant's house, where we students took up residence during the week. With our school, we had moved out of the city after the Americans began bombing North Vietnam. On this morning we heard the air-raid sirens and we tried to cross the bridge into the city before the planes showed up. But we made it only halfway when the American jets came roaring over. I had barely jumped off my bicycle when the explosions blasted the air with a furnace heat. The river gushed up as a bomb hit the water, then the bridge shook and clanged. Dirt stung my eyes. The air singed, hot on the skin. Suffocating with a burned-match odor.

I was lying on my back. Pain shot up to my head. I found myself away from the wreckage of the bridge. Metal scraps, bent and twisted, smoked. An iron top brace from the bridge, completely torn off, had trapped both of my legs. With my arm flung over my face, I saw a blue sky. Dust fell into my eyes. I turned my head sideways and saw the railroad track gleaming down the center of the bridge and metal debris strewn everywhere. The pain throbbed in my temples.

"Giang!" My friend Huan began pulling at me.

I heard shouts, footfalls. I shook my head at Huan. His face, smeared with dust, looked like a stranger's face. People were looming up from the other end of the bridge that led into the city. They wore dark-colored pantaloons, black trousers. Like a horde of giants about to trample me. They all wore pith helmets. They stared down at me and someone touched the heavy iron bracing that trapped my legs. "How're your legs?" he asked, bending over me. "Can you feel anything in your legs?" Another man peered into the dark crevice under the iron beam. "How do we get him out of this?" the first man said. I looked up at Huan, his face drawn up painfully. Suddenly I heard more planes. "Comrades!" a man shouted. "Take cover!" They all dove to the floor of the bridge and Huan collapsed on top of me, his hands covering his head. The planes swooped down low, so close that I could see the pilots' heads in the cockpits. The planes fired at the bridge and the flashes of the gun muzzles were sudden flares in the sun, the throaty bursts of guns steady, the shrieking noises of metal against metal when volleys hit the bridge. I wrapped my head with my arms and forgot the pain in my legs. The floor shook. Bursts of gunfire came up from the ground from the other end of the bridge. The machine guns, the antiaircraft battery. Windborn smoke thick and pungent, drifted onto the bridge. Soon the guns died down; the planes droned away, and the air was tinged with an acrid-charcoal, hot-metal smell. My friend rose, dusted his hair with his hands. "Will you lose your legs, Giang?" he asked. "Will you?" I shook my head, licking away gritty dirt on my lips. "How bad?" he asked, clasping my hand. "It hurts," I said. His soft hands pressed hard against my hand. People were yelling from the bridge's

end, where the gun emplacements were dug in, well camouflaged with green-leafed branches. They came running onto
the bridge, joining those who had showed up earlier. Two
men, wearing goggles, appeared to be the gunners, and a
girl in a white short-sleeved shirt and black trousers carried
a first-aid bag over her shoulder.

The goggled man, the tallest, pushed up his goggles to
the crown of his head and looked me over. "Gotta send for
help," he said. "We can't do a thing here for the boy."

The man in the pith helmet, who had wondered how to
remove me from the wreckage, raised his voice: "We can't
cut through the iron with bare hands."

The tall man singled out a man who had high sharp
cheekbones. "Go to the city. Get those who can do the job
out here. Hurry!"

"Yes, comrade," said the chosen man. "The city got
bombed too. Don't know if they will send anyone our way."

"Tell 'em we've got no equipment here. They'll understand."

"Yes, comrade."

The tall man looked at the girl, then back down at me.
"She'll take care of you. We have to use runners now for
things like this. Our telephone lines are down."

I nodded. He had a solemn face like one of my schoolteacher's. A face I could trust. His olive-green khaki shirt
had sweat stains on the armpits. After he ordered his men
to their tasks, he knelt down beside me, across from Huan.
"You must be brave," he said to me.

"Yes, sir." I felt drained from fighting the pain.

He looked at Huan. "Are you with him?"

"Yes," Huan said meekly. "He's my friend."

"Stay with him or go tell his parents."

"Yes, sir."

The man studied my face. I fought back the pain, trying
to look calm. I felt sweat break out on my forehead. The

man, pushing on his knee to rise, said to me, "I have to leave you here. Is there anything else you want to ask me?"

I hadn't asked him anything yet, but I shook my head. "Can I have a cigarette?"

He sat back down, his shoulders drawn up. "You need a cigarette? Ah. The pain must be very bad then." He went into his shirt front pocket and placed a cigarette pack in my hand. "Keep it, son. It'll be a while."

He dug into his trousers pocket, fished out a matchbox, and placed it in my hand. I said, "Thank you, sir," as he left. I grabbed Huan's arm. "Go home. It's not safe here."

"What about you? You're not safe here either."

I raised myself up on my elbow. "If I could walk like you—" I stopped. Pain seized me.

The girl swung her bag down. It had a red cross painted inside a white circle on its front. "Let me wash your face," she said gently, flinging back her long hair plait over her shoulder. She poured water from a bottle onto a white kerchief. My throat felt sand dry.

"Can you spare me a sip of water?" I asked.

She handed me the bottle and waited as I tipped the bottle. Her eyes watched me calmly. When I handed her the bottle back, my hand touched hers. Something tender permeated my soul. I kept myself propped up on my elbow. I didn't want to lie down while she cleaned my face. I held still. A sudden stab of pain in my legs jerked my body uncontrollably.

"You must be hurting badly," she said.

"Do you have aspirin for him?" Huan asked.

"Yes," she said. She searched through the bag. "I was about to give him some."

She let me hold the bottle and fed two pills into my mouth. They tasted sour. I swallowed them with a swig from the bottle. My throat felt thick.

"That should keep the pain at bay for a while," she said, folding the kerchief.

"How soon can they be here?" Huan pulled at her elbow.

"It'll be a while," I said. "Go home. There's nothing you can do here."

"But I can't leave you here," he said, almost pleading with me.

"I'll keep an eye on him," she said. "Because I don't know when help will arrive."

"Go!" I raised my voice. "Your parents might try to find you."

He rose to his feet and stood looking around. "What about your bicycle?"

"Leave it there," I said.

"Do you want to read in the meantime? I'll leave you a novel. You want it or not?"

The pain flared. "Read a novel?" I snapped at him. "With this pain—"

"Do you want me to read it to you?" she asked.

I nodded, then shook my head. The pain clouded my thinking. But I would not let her treat me like a person on his deathbed. My friend waved at me as he walked to his bicycle. I watched him tottering to find his balance on the wheels until he rode off. I should have kept my temper with him. I dropped my gaze. Her sandaled feet were next to my elbow. Plain toenails, neatly clipped.

"Where do you live?" she asked.

Her voice startled me. I caught my breath and told her where I stayed in the city.

"Your parents might worry themselves sick," she said.

"I live with my friend's family."

"Are you from the city? Born here?"

Again I nodded. Her large eyes held a gentle look.

"You don't speak with the city accent," she said.

"No, actually I'm not from here. Where I'm from . . . it's in the countryside, an hour from here by train."

"So your parents have no way of knowing . . ."

I shifted my body to ease the numbness on my arm and lit a cigarette.

"Do you want to rest your head?" she asked.

"Rest my head?"

"Yes. Here," she said, placing the first-aid bag behind me. "Lie back and rest."

I did what she told me, the cigarette in my mouth, my face upturned looking at her long plait hanging down her front, black against her white shirt.

"How old are you?" she asked.

"Seventeen." I took another drag. The nicotine helped relieve the pain. "What about you?"

"Eighteen." She glanced at my cigarette as I tapped it with my finger to break the ash. "You smoke often?"

I nodded.

"Since when?"

"Fifteen."

"Fifteen?" She arched her brows. "Why?"

"It kept me warm. Those cold mornings when I had on just a shirt. I sat in a market and wrote letters for those who couldn't read or write."

"You were a scribe?"

"Something like that. If they wanted to make out an application or petition, or needed to write a letter to someone, they would tell me their stories. I put them down in words. It was so cold some mornings my hand shook. I couldn't hold the pen. A man let me have a puff of his handrolled cigarette and said, 'Keep ye warm, eh?' It surely did. I smoked their cigarettes till I had enough money to buy our northern cigarettes."

"Your parents didn't reprimand you for smoking?"

I inhaled the smoke deeply, held it until the pain dimmed. The sun was behind her, bronzing the railings of the bridge, and the contour of her head glowed golden. I pinched a shred of tobacco from my lip. "My father just let me take care of myself. I was old enough."

"At fifteen?"

"He wasn't around anymore when I was fifteen."

"What about your mother?"

"She died when I was five. Then when I was twelve my father died. So I left my village and went to the city and stayed with my friend's family. We used to go to our village school together before the Land Reform in the North." I took one last drag, drawing hard, until the cigarette burned to my thumb and finger and I flicked it away. The men in pith helmets were directing traffic on the bridge—cyclists, pushcarts, light trucks—routing them to the other side of the track, leaving it empty on my side. They were tossing the metal bits onto wheelbarrows and the metal clanged noisily, and soon they carted off the rubble in wheelbarrows one after another, rolling on their squeaky rubber wheels into the slanting saffron-yellow beams of sunlight. "I used to be my father's helper after school when I was eight. Learned how to haggle for every xu we earned from selling stuff."

She rested her chin in her hands. "What stuff?"

I did not look at her but at the rusty red on the collapsed brace that weighed on my lower legs. I tapped out another cigarette and saw her eyes fall to the cigarette. I waved the match out, holding the smoke in my mouth as long as I could, and drove the smoke out of my nostrils. "My father," I said, meeting her gaze, "caught snakes for a living. Eventually he died from a snakebite. Before that he was one of the wealthy landowners in the southern region of the Red River Delta."

She nodded. "Land Reform changed many people's fortunes. But I've never met anyone in real life—victims of the purge. At least until now."

"Those people died from execution. If they survived that, they'd later die from hunger. They weren't allowed to work a decent job unless they left their native place." I cupped the cigarette against my lips so she couldn't see me swallowing the smoke. It numbed my head, took my mind off my lower limbs. I spoke through my clenched fist. "In the beginning, my father broke rocks. He owned a hammer and anvil, nothing else—except for his moon lute. He broke rocks and sold the chips to those who needed them for road and housing construction. Sold them or traded them for food—manioc, rice vermicelli, salted duck eggs. Broke rocks from dawn to dusk. I helped. I was eight years old then. He got me a smaller hammer, taught me how to pound rocks without hurting my wrist, how to whack them without blinding my eyes with flying chips. Broke rocks, both of us. Till one day his back gave out. Then he started catching snakes. Breaking rocks you sit in one place all day long. But catching snakes you must go from place to place. By evening your legs are dead. He got a large jar of *tam xà* liquor, his only treasure besides his moon lute, and he rubbed his legs at night with the snake liquor."

"What's the *tam xà* liquor?" she asked.

"You catch three kinds of snakes and then preserve them whole in a jar of liquor. The *tam xà* make up that special liquor. Through that clear jar you could see them coil up in it, one on top of another in their beautiful colored spots."

"Heavens!" she blurted. "Three kinds of snakes? Dead?"

"Dead for sure. The spectacled cobra, the banded krait, and the rat snake." I drew deeply on my cigarette. "After he killed them, he would hold each of them up by the head and squeeze its body down the length to the tail until a green slime oozed from its anus. He said if you don't do that, the snake liquor will stink."

She shook her head.

"He smoked hand-rolled cigarettes," I said, "and drank snake liquor every night till he passed out. Played his moon lute in our early days after we'd lost everything. The lute was the only thing left with him, kept him company at night when he played. Then he started getting drunk every night and I had to wrap the lute and put it away. He didn't want to look at it anymore because it reminded him of his wealthy past. He kept going because of me. Without me he was better off dead. I knew that."

"I thought they killed all the landlords during the Land Reform."

"The People's Court did that to most of them, those condemned by the peasants, the wretched poor, the labors-for-hire. If you were rich and cruel to the poor, you were doomed even before the People's Court handed down the verdict. Most of them got buried alive because the firing squad couldn't shoot them dead—they never fired a gun before. But if you were rich and your cruelty wasn't notorious, you'd get sent to prison. And if you were rich and not cruel to the poor, you'd only lose all your wealth and get the first taste of how to be dirt poor. That was my father's fate."

"Where were you when all this was happening to your father?"

"I was in the crowd watching him suffer humiliation."

"By whom?"

"Those who worked for our family. Now they turned against him. They accused him of all things imagined. Many of these folks couldn't read and write, so the Viet Minh cadres would put them through rehearsals before the denunciation sessions. The cadres taught them the hand gestures, made them memorize words and phrases so it would look real and spontaneous. I watched my father crawl on his hands and knees to the dirt platform before the tribune. Fourteen of them, all illiterate peasants, sat on the lowest tier and seven more on the middle tier, and there were huge pictures of Mao Tse-Tung and Ho Chi Minh on the top tier. His former employees took turns to denounce him with insults and accusations. The committee chief, a woman on the middle tier, would shout down at him, commanding him to rise and fall on his knees again and again. My father lasted the early part of the day before he was dragged to the tribune to sign his confession. He confessed to everything he was accused of. Many of the accusations were make-believe. The most wicked landowners would suffer the trial for two or three days before they were executed."

She cupped her face and peered down at me through the gaps between her fingers. "They took everything away from him after that?"

"Yeah."

"So where was home after that?"

"In a graveyard. He fixed up a shelter and we stayed there and soon I found all kinds of snakes also living there. The graveyard soil was peat soil and during the rainy season the top layer would drift and what grew on it were sedges and peat moss and reed grass, which attracted the cuckoos to build their nests there. Soon I found out that cuckoos fed on snakes. They would pound the snakes to death with their strong bills and swallow them headfirst. We got used to living with birds and snakes. We knew about snakes like we knew about the weather. So when my father quit breaking rocks, he knew what to do next."

"But how do you make a living catching snakes?"

"You sell snake meat to the eateries and the gallbladders to the Chinese herbal stores."

"I could imagine eating birds in any imaginable way." She shook her head. "But not snakes."

"Snake meat is tasty. You can't tell if it's chicken or fish—if you don't know what you're eating. My father used to roll small chunks of snake meat in a flour-and-egg mixture and fry them. He used the eggs of the birds he caught because we couldn't even afford chicken eggs. I told him the meat tasted like chicken and he said, 'Right, son. I soaked the meat in saltwater for two days so it wouldn't taste of blood and gaminess.' But the snake's gallbladder is what medicine men like those Chinese herbalists wanted most."

"Gallbladder? Why would they want that?"

"He said different parts of a snake have different medicinal values. Said if you sun-dry a snake body and then cut it up and grind the pieces into powder, then you can cure stomach and intestinal problems because it's high in protein and enzymes. But the *tam xà* gallbladders brought him more money from the Chinese men than anything he could make off a snake without its gallbladder."

"Why those three kinds?"

"They're poisonous snakes. My father hunted just those three kinds. After he got a basket full of them, he'd bring them to the herbal stores. He laid down the basket on the floor and began chewing a wad of wild tobacco he used to roll cigarettes with. Then he rubbed his hand and forearm with the chewed tobacco and opened the basket's lid and snatched up a spectacled cobra. He got the cobra by the neck with one hand and squeezed it so hard its mouth flew open wide and you could see its long ugly fangs. Behind the counter the Chinese owner folded his arms and watched as my father drove a small pointed knife into the midsection of the cobra and slit it open. In no time he gouged out a blue-black thing like an egg. He plopped it down on a saucer and tossed the dead snake back into the basket. The dead snakes would later end up in the eateries. Brought him much less than gallbladders. Then he grabbed a banded krait. Beautiful snake with black and yellow bands. This type has a blue-green gallbladder. Then he got the rat snake, the smallest of the three."

"But what kind of medicinal value do these snake gallbladders have?"

"For treatment of bronchitis and cough." I waved off the cigarette smoke that made her squint. "They heat-dry the gallbladders and grind them with dried tangerine peels to powder. It's one of the best cough medicines."

She laced her hands in her laps, watching me draw my last drag. "Someday you'll need that cough medicine yourself. My uncle is a heavy smoker. Whenever I hear the sound of coughing, I know it's him."

Her tone soothed me. I cupped the cigarette with my other hand and spat out shreds of tobacco on my tongue. "My friend Huan said the same thing. His father is a Chinese herbalist, lives a healthy life, so I respect that. At night when I need a puff of cigarette, I go outside on the street."

"Has his father ever bought snake gallbladders from snake catchers?"

I couldn't help grinning. She smiled.

"He has," I said. "Sometimes they bring him one of those three kinds because they know what he wants. These weren't snake catchers by trade, though. So none of them knew how to remove a snake's gallbladder. I would slit the snake open and take out its gallbladder for him."

The noises of the wheelbarrows grew fainter beyond the bridge. A breeze came up, fanning my face. In a brief lull I heard my stomach grumbling. She asked me to sit up and reached for her bag. She went through it and her hand came out holding a small bundle of brown paper. She slid the bag back under me.

"You're hungry, right?" Inside the paper was a smaller bundle wrapped in a banana leaf.

I was starving. I had not eaten since we left the peasant's house in the morning. She peeled away the banana-leaf wrapping. I could smell the fragrant leaf as she gave me a rice dumpling.

She brought the other dumpling to her lips and took a small bite. Inside the white glutinous dumpling was a paste of red bean. It tasted faintly sweet.

"Where'd you get them?" I asked.

"I made them. They're my lunch."

I stopped eating. "Now you'll go half hungry."

She smiled. "I wish we had mushroom and pork cubes to make the fillings. Tastier. We can only buy fish once a month. Rarely meat."

"Do you have a big family?"

"Five of us and my parents."

"What's your father do?"

"He works at a factory. My mother and I wake up at five in the morning, so she can cook breakfast and lunch for Father to take with him to work. The same for breakfast and lunch every day: cooked vegetables and rice. Sometimes she packs a steam-cooked manioc and sprinkles brown sugar on it. That's dessert for him. We have government food ration. For all city people. We might get chicken once every three months. And since we can only afford fish once a month, it's a treat. I don't remember what pork or chicken tastes like anymore."

I suppressed a deep sigh. The last bite of dumpling seemed stuck in my throat. She saw me try to sit up and quickly got out the bottle of water.

"Take a big gulp," she said.

I washed it down and handed her back the bottle. She still had half the dumpling between her fingers. I had drunk her water and eaten her food. She'd hardly sipped her water. I knew how it felt living on food ration. Your life was continually preoccupied with food. Looking at her holding half the dumpling in one hand, the bottle of water in the other, I felt very tender toward her. I told her in the city quarter where I stayed, there was a public water tap on each street. I always drank from the tap, never bottled water like her. She said she never drank tap water but would carry it home in a five-gallon pail. She had to make several trips, standing in a long line each time, to fetch enough water for the whole family to cook, bathe, drink. For drinking water, she boiled tap water and bottled it so her father could make tea when he got home from work. By the time he came home, her mother had already gone to the city stores to buy food and household items. Rice, firewood for cooking and heating were the most expensive.

"What're you doing out here on a Sunday?" I asked as she eased the last bit of dumpling into her mouth.

"I'm a volunteer in the City Vanguard Youth," she said, covering her mouth with her hand.

"Some of the boys I know volunteer too. They said if you volunteer, the government will exempt you from the military service. Said if you're classified as sons or daughters from a bourgeois or landlord class, the government will erase it from the record."

"Why didn't you volunteer then?" she asked as she folded the banana leaf.

"They can erase my bad classification all they want, but that won't make it right for me and my father."

"But you can join the Vanguard Youth to help clean up the city, help the wounded after we're bombed by the Americans." She said she belonged to a platoon that was stationed at this bridge. Her platoon was part of a company which made up a battalion that employed the city youths like her to repair roads and build pontoon bridges where main bridges got bombed.

I dropped my gaze to her hands. She was wrapping the folded banana leaf inside the brown paper and folding them up together. She saw me watching and said, "I reuse them. Sometimes we can't even buy banana leaves."

The sun was low now on the horizon where the river glinted red. Shades grew across the bridge spreading to the riverbank, which was thick and green with banana groves. In the deep green of banana fronds were splashes of red.

"Aren't they beautiful?" she asked, following my gaze.

I nodded, enthralled by the banana flowers' breathtaking, cardinal red. There was a racket on the bridge and we both turned to look. A railroad trolley was coming toward us. One man was pushing it and three others were running alongside the track.

"Here they come," she said. "They'll have the equipment to cut the metal for you."

Suddenly I felt hollow. I didn't feel relieved as the men arrived. She stood up, looked down at me, her plait falling across her chest. Her face looked shadowy in the twilight, and on the riverbank the last glimmer of sun glowed golden on the pointed tips of wild banana flowers.

The painted stork steps gingerly along the water's edge. The shallow water is a clear blue, so the stork can see the small fish roused up by its pumpkin-yellow bill sweeping from side to side.

With the motor turned off, our boat bobs on the canal. A breeze is coming through the tall grass on the bank, and the water shudders when fish nib at the water lettuce's trailing roots. In pale-green rosettes they float. Chi Lan raises her camera, rotating the lens toward the stork as it cocks its head, flashing a yellow glint on the down-curved tip of its bill. In the water, you can see the motionless stork on its reedlike, coral-pink legs.

I cough. It comes suddenly. The stork startles, twitching its rump, then shoots up in a whoosh. It glides over the water, neck outstretched, legs trailing long and pink, the great underwings soot-black, like a Japanese fan.

I cough until my eyes water. I spit into the water. "I'm sorry."

"I ought to be quicker." She still fingers the camera's shutter button.

"Like a photojournalist?"

"Yes, *Chú*." She gazes after the stork downstream. "I've taken tons of still-life photos. But live things move quicker."

I sip from my bottle of water. "You ever seen the napalm-girl photo?"

"The little Vietnamese girl running naked down the highway?"

"Yeah."

"If you fail to capture that special moment, it's gone forever."

"Maybe so." I cap the bottle. "But I can bring back that stork. And its mirrored self in the water in a drawing."

"That's the difference between the camera's eye and one's memory."

"Yeah."

She caresses her neck strap. "You know something, *Chú*?"

"What?" Her morning-fresh face in the mild sunlight holds my gaze until she blushes.

"If I had one wish, I'd rather be a painter than a photographer."

"One wish," I say, nodding. In the brief silence a fish rises to the surface and snaps at a water bubble.

"*Chú*," she calls to me.

I glance up. Aiming her camera, she adjusts the lens with her fingers.

"Smile for me," she says.

My lips form a smile. *Click*.

"I've got your smile now," she says, teasing. "You rarely smile, *Chú*." Her voice is soothing. I should have smiled more naturally for her.

"Have you ever had a moment when you wish for that one wish?" she asks.

I shake my head. Perhaps too quickly. I do have a wish. That she would never leave. I lift the cigarette pack from my shirt pocket and her eyes follow my gesture. I hold the cigarette's end close to my lips, inhaling the dark tobacco smell.

"I'm not going to light it," I say. "I never had that one wish. Except perhaps one time . . ."

She blinks. It must be my humorless tone. Saying nothing, she taps her finger on the film advance lever.

"I helped carry out someone's wish," I say.

"To make it come true?"

"Long time ago."

"When?"

"When I was about your age."

"The one wish in someone's life?"

"Yeah."

We were ordered to consolidate with another unit in the Mekong Delta. Both of our forces had been decimated. At first light our undersized battalion came out in an open field. We were moving toward the woodland, only a kilometer from it, when the enemy shelling began. Suddenly the ear-prickling whines of incoming rounds, big as a house, shattered the air. The earth gushed up, the bone-crushing blasts threw us up and slammed us down. We reared, ran, our guts hanging out, we ran into the agonized squeals, the scalding screams that imprinted themselves forever in ourselves, and everything around us peeled off in a flash— flesh, innards, blood, bones.

In the elephant grass we hid, crawled, and overhead came two Skyraiders. They swooped down so low over the scrub trees I could see bombs hanging under their wings. Our soldiers dreaded them more than the jet fighters, for these Spads could fire dead-on. They could hang around for several hours until we turned white with fear. That day we all turned white. I lay in the grass, my rucksack on my back, watching the sky. I had my arms covering Huan's head. He lay on his back, his abdomen split just below his diaphragm. His hands, pressed down on the wound, were wet with blood. Our doctor was nowhere to be found, so I cut off a sleeve from a dead man's khaki shirt and wound it around Huan's torso. Men were crawling through the tall grass toward the woodland. I thought, dead or alive, I will carry him on my back, walking. Our uniforms were quickly stained with sweat, with blood, smelly and sticky. I dragged my rucksack and our rifles, walking slumped, with the cawing of crows, some circling the sky, some already on the ground picking at the flesh of the dead, my throat searing with thirst, his moans soon in rhythm with my panting, my eyes blurred from dirt, from sweat dripping down from my brow, stumbling in stunned exhaustion, in the shame of defeat.

For two days we subsisted on water and rice rations during our trek until we arrived at the rendezvous zone. We hooked up with our other unit and, much undersized now, the combined forces made their way to the hideout in the bowels of U Minh forest. Huan's wound had turned green. He babbled in his fevers. The doctor examined then sedated him, said it was only a matter of time. I trusted this doctor, who no longer needed eyeglasses. I had also seen him experimenting some healing method on a dog. He had snipped off two inches of the dog's intestines and then pieced the severed ends together. I didn't think the dog would live with the patched-up entrails, but a few weeks after I saw the dog again. I pled with the doctor to save Huan. He pondered. He said there might be a chance, in theory. For a deteriorated spleen, what might help boost up the immune system was spleen extracts. From not one but at least a dozen human spleens to produce just a small amount of extracts. A dozen human spleens?

It was sultry that night. The ground still breathed warm vapor, the air reeked of wild vegetation. In the wavering lights of gas lamps we hacked away waist-high bushes of toothed fern and fox grape, the air soon foul with fresh sap and gas-lamp smokes. We hung our hammocks between trees, double-decking the hammocks and stringing them from one tree trunk fanning out to others in that neighboring fashion so we could hear each other, see each other, and sleep safer. My hammock was above Huan's. He couldn't move around much. We slept with the lamplights burning in the night, hearing the hooting of owls, *whooo-whooo*, waking and falling back to sleep in the restless sawing and whirring of insects coming from the peat-covered earth, from the dark crevices of underbrush, filling the forest like an ocean of sound and here and there the viscous *krek-ek*, the throaty *gwonk* of tree frogs.

At two in the morning the first bombs fell. No one heard the coming B-52 bombers. Then the forest heaved in one cataclysmic bang and then another and trees snapped, toppling in a hair-raising whoosh, cracking loud, and the smells of burnt fumes seeped through the air like air blasted out of a furnace. We were thrown off our hammocks. Lights flickered, dirt clods rained down, the lamps spurted and quivered. We crawled, we groped for one another, we flattened ourselves on the ground, our ears hurt, our heads rang, our eyes teared from dirt and smoke. I found a hand clawing mine. I heard Huan's voice. He was alive. A tree, broken in half, splintered in a shotgun burst and men screamed like they were machine-gunned down. Huan was sobbing: "I can't see!" I shouted, "We don't need lights!" He screamed louder, "Something busted my eyes . . ." I squeezed his hand. "Keep still. If we move, we'll die." Voices erupted. "Comrades! Help me! Please, comrades, help!" Explosion after explosion ripped through the forest, the earth ruptured, the human cries drowned out in the successive blasts; we went deaf, we tasted blood salty on our tongues. Overhead came the screeching sounds of the escorting jets. The air grew hotter, the sap smells grew stronger, the white glares lit up a corner of the forest after each thunderous bang, the forest floor spewed, raining down clods and shreds of vegetation. Then the sounds of hell died out. So did the cries for help.

It was pitch black. Half past three in the morning. The burned smells of fumes and vegetation filled our lungs. Shouts and moans. The eerie moans drifted through the blackness. Men weeping. Find them before it got light. Find them before the reconnaissance planes would show up at dawn and, if they spotted us, hell would repeat itself.

"Giang."

"Your eyes, Huan?"

"I'm cold."

"It'll pass."

He had chills and fevers, despite antibiotics the doctor had given him. His hand felt clammy in mine.

"I'm bleeding," he said.

I struck a match, held it toward him. Smudges of dirt covered his face. He looked black, you couldn't see his girl-like fair skin. I peeled off a leaf stuck on his forehead and saw blood glistening on his lips. I wiped my wet nose, the back of my hand stained red. I was about to tell him we all bled from the bomb concussions when the match went out. He groaned about his stomach and I lit another match. His wound was bleeding. The dressing was soaked with blood.

"Lie down," I told him. The match died. In the dark I took off my shirt and, using both sleeves, began wrapping them around his wound. People were clearing branches, pushing and rolling broken tree limbs out of the way. The air hung thick, the evil fumes refused to vaporize. My hands felt the shaking of his body. He was sobbing.

"I'd rather die . . ." His voice sounded muffled because of blood in his mouth.

"Stop that!"

"Bombs should've killed me . . ."

I was about to snap at him but his shaking gave me pause. Would I wish to suffer a slow, agonizing death if I became an invalid like him? I cared for him. I always did. More than that, his family wanted me to look after him when we were sent South.

I heard the relayed order: Go retrieve the bodies. Rescue the wounded. Use flashlights. No lamplights. Without seeing his face, I said to him, "I'll be back."

I stood in the blackness, saw circles of flashlight bouncing and colliding around me. Moans and cries came up from underground, from the monstrous tangles of collapsed trees. Shielding my eyes, I crawled through a net of tree branches. I couldn't see my own hands in the dark. Deep in the branches I heard moans. They came up from beneath a severed tree trunk. I shook my head, crawled on. The raking flashlights gave me pause. Pit after pit opened up in the ground. Those cavernous holes could swallow a tank. There were bodies down there. My foot kicked at something. A rucksack. As I picked it up, my hand touched a body. I sat down, shook it. Then I drew my knife. I felt with my hand for his heart and, certain that he was dead, tore his shirt open. My left hand's fingers probing around his abdomen, I brought the tip of my knife to where my fingers stopped. Firmly I sank the knife's tip and slashed across the left side of his abdomen. The knife's blade cut him open just enough and I reached in with my hand. The cavity was still warm. I felt around with my fingers. They touched the spleen. Slimy and pulpy. I yanked it.

I dragged the rucksack with the spleen in it. Men called to each other, crying, the whimpers that soon became part of the night. I kept moving. My shirtless torso became drenched with sweat, my hands slick with blood. One corpse came alive when my knife tore through its flesh. I thought I heard him scream, a choked scream. I said a silent prayer. To whom I did not know, but I wanted him to bear me no ill will.

When it started getting light, my rucksack was full. The moaning from underground had stopped. Death had taken all of them.

For several days it was hot and muggy. Then one night the rain came and it rained with no respite until it leached the white out of the sky. It rained into the eighth day, the ninth day and sometime on the tenth day the rain let up long enough for a glow to spread across the sky, and the forest shivered just once so we could hear the damp wind sough through the drenched foliage, and, in the lull, rain-drops trickled like the sound of pebbles. That evening rain fell again, crescendoing madly, tinkling and spattering like musical notes made of steel beads, a wet symphonic murmur that soon settled into a steady mindless cadence. We rushed out to snatch all of our uniforms and linens, still drip-dry-ing, that we had hung on the strung-out twines between the trees near the cooking fires, which had barely dried.

In the hut I could smell the wood smoke. It smelled odorous whenever a fire was suddenly put out, and now the rain that had doused it brought a stink that seeped through the clammy air. Under the cot a red centipede came crawl-ing out. I watched it measuring the soggy ground with its whisker-thin legs. They would come out at night, the red centipedes, the brown centipedes. The earthworms too. All except the yellow and black deerflies. They swarmed around my Chinese friend Huan, when I carried him on my back for two days after the carnage by the American artil-lery until we reached the forest. It had been thirteen days. Now he lay on the cot, his stomach wrapped with a soiled cloth strip. At least, for now, the rain kept the flies at bay.

You could see them feed on the open wounds until their striped abdomens bloated. If you don't clean the wounds soon, the next day the gaping wounds seem to move with tiny, dough-white maggots.

A hand touched me on my elbow. Huan's face went dark when the lantern on the ammunition crate suddenly wavered. The forest groaned in the wind. I moved the crate closer to the cot. A rusty metal crate stamped with a single star on its grooved top. I bent to his face.

"Water," he muttered.

His breath smelled. I raised his head until his lips touched the rim of the tin cup. His cracked lips opened to receive the rainwater. It was our drinking water now. The rain had become our savior. We also had a shortage of cooking utensils after the last B-52 bombing had shattered most of our porcelain wares. Now most of us used the tin cups from our mess kit as rice bowls and drinking cups.

"You hungry?"

He did not answer. His eyes were closed. Their long lashes brought a softness to his repose. He hadn't opened his eyes much these days. His pretty-girl eyes. Gently I lay his head down. He didn't weigh much and every time I changed his dressing I could feel his bones. Life was ebbing from him. Shadows pooled on his sunken cheeks. I dabbed some water on his lips and said, "You must eat something." I pulled a hunk of cooked manioc from my trousers pocket. I broke off a piece and pressed it against my palm until it softened. His lips felt like hard rubber. "Eat," I said, "you hear me?" But his jaw was set. "Huan?" I pried open his lips with my fingers. His teeth were clenched. His skin felt hot. He was burning up.

"Giang . . . save it," he slurred. "You're hungry too."

That hunk of manioc was my whole day's meal. We had run out of food because of the siege. Trapped deep in the forest by the surrounding Americans and ARVN soldiers, we had eaten wild banana flowers and scorpions and snakes. We went looking for the snakes. Before that, we all dreaded seeing them. We ate wild taros, even those that caused itch, and afterward many of us retched and clawed at our throats, finger-forcing ourselves to vomit, and our doctors had to calm our throats with saline water so that after gargling a mouthful, it eased the killing itch. We ate cocoyam, the giant ones. They rose abnormally tall. Over two meters. Their trunks, thicker than wild bananas' trunks, exuded a glossy look of unhealthy green, and their underground stems in the somber year-round shade twined deep in the earth where, in earlier days, corpses of our comrades had lain unburied. After vultures had picked away the flesh, the crows came, then centipedes and ants. Then worms and maggots. Then forest rains. Rains washed the human remains into the depth of soil, which nourished the flesh-loving cocoyam, which then nourished us, day to day now.

I put my hand on his forehead. The heat shocked me. I looked at the manioc hunk in my hand and put it back in my trousers pocket. My fingers touched the butt of a half-smoked cigarette. With the cigarette ration, we were running out of them. I plugged it in my mouth and dragged on the unlit cigarette. In the dry tobacco smell hung a malevolent odor of rot. It came from his stomach wound. One that had damaged his spleen. The soiled dressing looked wet.

"Giang."

"Yeah?"

A silence. "They . . . told me."

"Told you what?"

He was breathing through his mouth. His long black hair on the back hung over his shirt collar. None of us had had a haircut for many weeks now. His hand rested on his thigh. I looked at his long fingernails, so long they had begun curving down and a thought hit me. He might not ever have a chance again to cut them. Me? I just chewed on them every day so they stayed snub.

"Doctor told me," he said, without opening his eyes.

"Your condition?"

"How you got the human spleens . . . for me."

I said nothing. I felt empty. All I did for him was in vain. My stomach gnawed.

"They told me . . . they could do nothing more . . ." His voice trailed.

I already knew that. He choked on his breath. I bent down. "Hey." His face simmered with heat. The doctor had made him swallow the little black pellets to ease his pain. But now they had to conserve the black opium's supply for those who needed it most. He was dying nevertheless.

"If they can spare you some of that painkiller," I spoke without looking at him. I meant the black pellets.

"It . . . hurts."

He wasn't sleeping. He could hear me.

"I know," I said. I thought of the time on the bridge back home when I was hurt by the American bombing and how he worried for me. A dark feeling enveloped me. The lantern light made shadows on his cheeks. I looked closer at his abdomen. His blue sweatshirt had a dark, wet stain under his diaphragm. It smelled like rotten eggs. I had washed his green uniform, blood-soaked and foul, and put on his spare uniform. A sweatshirt and cotton black trousers. The only spare we each had.

"Giang."

"Yeah."

"Seven hundred and fifty-three days . . ."

"What?" Suddenly it dawned on me. He had counted the days we had spent in the South. "You remember?"

"Wrote each day down . . . in my diary."

He would never write again. Tears were seeping from his eyes. Those pretty eyes. The day his family received news that he was drafted, they panicked. Ethnic Chinese like him hadn't been called up until then, when the North began drafting every male between eighteen and thirty-five. I was already drafted. I had seen what the boys tried to do to shun the draft. They hid away when summoned by the recruiting center only to see their family's rice ration cut off. They chewed tobacco leaves and their blood pressure shot up just before the physical. None of them, though, could fool the examining doctors and the recruiting officials. Yet I had seen other boys disqualified from the draft—those from wealthy families who bribed the examining doctors. Or those from influential families—the government officials, the Party leaders, the politburo members. Those boys were sent overseas to study. The northern army was taken mainly from the countryside—the poor, the illiterate, the naive. The morning Huan was to take the army physical, he put iodine in his eyes. When I saw Huan's eyes, I thought he was bleeding. His bloodshot eyes couldn't see well for two days and I thought his eyes were ruined for good. He went in for the physical with his vision foggy. It remained foggy for several days after when the news came. His classification was "A"—to be drafted. That afternoon I didn't see him at his home. His younger sister said, "I saw him out crossing the railroad track." "When?" I asked. "Short while ago," she said. "To the market?" I asked. "I guess," she said.

I headed out toward the track. He must be going to the marketplace to buy some eyewash, I thought. The track cut through a heavily foliaged area with tin roofs peeking between the sun-bronzed leaves, and above them were inked the electric wires between poles, evenly spaced, watching over the track. I walked on the graveled shoulder until I saw ahead of me someone sitting on the bottom of the shingled slope where it met the grass. A train was coming around the bend. The ties rattled. The horn wailed. The train went *shussh-shussh*, thunking and rumbling, the couplings clanked in the high-pitched *clickety-clack* of the wheels. It came up blasting its horn, roaring toward me like the blackest demon. Just then I heard someone scream. It died out in the rumble, but I could hear it. Huan's voice. Like a horror that had no face but all sound and can't be mouthed in words. He was slumping on the grass, blood oozing from his wrist, his palm laid open on his thigh. I stood rooted to the ground, staring at the blood. Quickly I took off my shirt, twisted it, wrapped it around his wrist. I tied it. Hard. My hands turned red. I picked up the knife he'd dropped. I wiped the bloodstained blade against the grass, jammed the knife down behind the waist of my pants, and hoisted him up to his feet. His face was full of sun when he looked at me, his eyes red. The iodine trick didn't save him from what he feared most.

I will never forget the pain that contorted his face. I said nothing. There was nothing to say. I hoisted him onto my bare back and started home.

"Giang."

"Huh?"

"Tell my Ma and Pa . . ." Huan's jaw clenched. "Write them a letter . . ."

"I will."

But the letters would never get to them. Before I left the North, I knew those who had gone South to fight the Americans. Some of them were my friends. Going South. One by one. Nobody had heard anything from them since. I asked people why none of them ever came back and they shushed me. Most of them my age tattooed their arms with four words, *"Born North Die South."* Like it would boost their morale. Most of them died—true to their tattoos—and no news was sent home. You can't win the war with damaged morale infecting the people at home. The messengers of death came not from telegram but from the returning wounded who eventually reached the unfortunate families.

To hide the most demoralizing picture of the war, the government quarantined the wounded—they were not to see their families. But that only came after they had been seen in public. And the sight of them, maimed for life, had painted a Biblical hell about the war.

Now I put my hands between my knees. I didn't want to touch his inflamed body. Two years in the South for both of us. I had once or twice thought of the day we would return home together. The thought was like a thief hiding in my head. The day I killed that thief, I stopped daydreaming. That day on the way South on the Ho Chi Minh Trail I saw camouflaged trucks heading North. It was raining. Rain fell on our nylon raincoats, fell on the open beds of the trucks. We stopped, exchanged greeting words. I saw human bodies, alive and packed under the cover in mottled shades of green and brown. The wounded. Some had no legs. Some were burned by napalm so severely they looked leprous. Rain dripped on their limbless bodies as they slept. After the trucks came the stretchers. Sticks and bamboo slapped together. Lying on them were the blind. Some had no faces. We couldn't greet them. They couldn't see us. Some struggled on their crutches, finding their footing in the mud-spattered tracks the trucks left behind. The armless ones had had their raincoats tied around their waists so the wind wouldn't blow their coats away. They moved past us, huffing and puffing. Rain-smeared sallow faces. Malaria-wrecked skin. They were all bones. So they headed home. Up North. I looked at them. I wasn't afraid. Just queasy. We stood off the muddy trail, letting them pass. One day someone going South on this trail would look at me heading North. I might not then have a face. Or limbs.

Huan began to wheeze. Like he needed air badly. His hand on his thigh twitched. I got up to soak my handkerchief in the pouring rain. I wrung my kerchief and placed it on his forehead. I sat hunched on the edge of the cot, hands between my knees. Rain clattered on the foliage. Rain fell sluicing from the leaves. Rain. The white noise played on our nerves. Rain. The hunger that growled in our stomachs. Rain. There was no rice or grain left. Now we ate centipedes. Then earthworms after.

Now I saw his lips move. "Why . . . Giang?"

"What?"

"Why . . . you did that? With those spleens?"

"I thought they'd help save you." I looked at the half cigarette between my fingers. "Our doctor gave me the notion . . ."

"You know what . . ." Huan's voice came like from a ventriloquist.

"Yeah?"

"The dead men's spleens . . . you took . . . will add to my karma . . ."

I heard every word. I thought about what I had done for him, the absurdity of it when, in the end, nothing worked. I had felt bitter. I had loathed the miserable life we had lived. The venom had slowly built up in me but, then, hearing what he said I couldn't help pitying him for the little worries, among other trifles, that had hounded him all his life. I turned away from him and looked out to the darkness. Where had all the fireflies gone to? The wind howled. A mournful wail sighing through the forest.

"How many . . . you took?" came his voice again.

"A dozen." I didn't turn around. His hand grabbed mine.

"Help me . . ."

His knees banged each other. I lifted my bottle of water and brought it to his lips. "Drink some."

He gripped my hand tighter. "Hurts . . . so much . . . I can't take it . . . anymore . . ."

I turned over the handkerchief. The side pressed against his brow was warm from his burning fever.

"I'm here," I said, looking down at his parched lips. "I'm not going anywhere."

His head shook side to side. "Hurts," he said, the kerchief slipping off. I put it back on his forehead.

"I know," I said. "Damn all this."

"Giang . . ."

"Yeah?"

"I have one wish . . ."

"I hear you."

"Can you . . . help?"

"Tell me."

"Will you . . . help?"

"I'll help you."

"You promise?"

"I promise."

"Swear . . . you must . . . swear!"

I took a sharp breath. "I swear."

"Let me die . . . now."

I clenched my jaw, staring at his emaciated face.

His eyes shut, his lips moved speaking soundless words. His odor grew. It got into my breathing, seeped to the root of my brain. I didn't wince, didn't reject it. The stench made my heart weep. I had done everything I could, even inhumanly, to save his life. I had sat by him for hours in the sultry heat, the morning after the bombing, fanning away deerflies and horseflies that came to feast on his festering wound. The only time I was called away came in midmorning. We had to bury the dead. They began attracting flies. Striped abdomen, green-eyed flies. Metallic-blue blowflies. Wherever we were that morning, the flies followed us, humming. The blood-darkened soil, plowed by bombs, looked like a confetti ground speckled with yellow and black flies coming in myriads for the sugar in the blood and for the shredded flesh buried like fibers in the soil.

I took the kerchief from his forehead and went to the door of the hut to rinse it with rainwater. The cot creaked loud. I turned and saw him shaking from side to side, knees clapping, hands clawing at his stomach dressing. His mouth fell open and out of it came a garbled sound. "Huan!" I held him by the shoulders. He kept quaking. His hand grabbed my forearm. I pressed the wet kerchief hard against his nose and kept pressing it and I did not lift my hand during the whole time until he stopped shaking and kicked out one foot.

I stood looking at him for some time, like watching someone sleep. Then I walked out of the hut. Rain smelled of wet ashes and coals and the charred smell was in the air and followed me through the forest, and I kept walking in the pitch dark until I came to the bomb craters where we had buried our comrades.

I stood over the rim of a crater, looking down into the black pit, until my drenched body and my head went numb.

We have new guests who arrived at the inn three days ago. A couple from Ireland. They drove down from Ho Chi Minh City. The husband is a journalist. Since their arrival he has gone around the U Minh region, always with a camera, backpack, and palm-sized voice recorder. The wife, in her late thirties, made friends easily with us. When she first heard of the purpose of Mrs. Rossi's visit, she said to her, "Jasus, ye break my heart."

Bundled up in my raincoat, I quickly step onto the veranda and set down the two bags of groceries and household supplies next to the entrance door. I get out of my raincoat and hang it on a wall hook, one of several I have put up on the veranda walls, front and back.

The door open with the familiar scratching noise the bottom-edge wire mesh makes against the cement floor. Since I came, I have sealed each door's bottom edge with a wire mesh to keep out bugs and rodents and even snakes, especially during floods. Chi Lan stands in the doorway, holding a mug in her hand.

"*Chú*," she says, "give me a grocery bag."

I put the bag in the crook of her arm. "Where's everyone?"

"My mom's in the back with Maggie," she says. "Washing clothes. Alan went off somewhere in their car."

I notice steam rising from her mug. "What're you drinking?"

"Café *phin*. I made it myself."

"Black?"

"No. With condensed milk. I can't drink it black like you."

"I've got you into drinking café *phin* now, huh?"

"We'll be even when I get you to quit smoking," Chi Lan says. She steps back for me to come in. Barefooted, her toenails look rosy, freshly polished.

I smile at her gentle tone. I have indeed thought of cutting back on smoking. It is cool inside the house. She wears a black T-shirt and white shorts. My sandals squeak, leaving a wet trail behind me on the gray cement floor. Clean, as the old woman of the inn demands it. At the end of the big room is a pantry that has a refrigerator. Chi Lan sets her mug on a shelf and puts the groceries into the refrigerator. She stops and holds up a paper-wrapped baguette.

"*Bánh mì!*" she says, sounding as if she's just found gold.

"I bought plenty of them for lunch. Hope you and everyone like it."

"I love it. What do we have in them?" She takes off the rubber band, opens the wrapper and peeks inside the baguette. The fillings—pork bellies and liver pâté garnished with cilantro, chili peppers, cucumber slices, and pickled carrots—seem to please her. "I've tried to make these at home," she says, wrapping up the baguette and tying it with the rubber band, "and they never came out like this— the smell, the taste."

"Because most of the fillings are homemade. The pork bellies in particular. They made the bread themselves too."

"And because I'm an amateur cook." She picks up her mug and sips. "Are you a good cook, *Chú*?"

"I can manage on my own. Alan asked me about a snake dish the other day. I told him before he and his wife leave, I'd cook a snake dish for everyone."

"Oh my." Chi Lan closes the refrigerator. "Did you tell him you used to catch snakes with your father? And about the snake gallbladder?"

"No. I've never told anyone that. Except you." I set down the supplies bag, squatting on my heels, and inspect the four legs of the cupboard, each leg shod with a tin cup half-filled with vinegar. In one cup floats a mass of dead black ants.

The air stirs faintly as she kneels beside me. "Must be the sugar jar in the cupboard that attracted them. Look at them." She bends closer, sweeping back her hair over her ear. "That looks like a moat around a fortress—the water and the cups. Is this your idea, *Chú*?"

"Yeah."

"You're a good custodian."

"It's not water in those tin cups. It's vinegar."

She looks again. "What's the difference?"

"Ants might survive in water and they'll crawl up into the cupboard."

"I didn't know vinegar kills them." She turns to face me, her eyes gently holding my gaze. "My mom appreci-ated having that clothing trunk in our room to store our clothes. I didn't know why it's lined with tin till you told us. Otherwise our old suitcases would've crawled with moths and cockroaches."

"I'm going to replace the vinegar in those cups." I take out a bottle of vinegar in the bag. "When I lift a leg up, can you remove the cup under the leg for me?"

"Go ahead, *Chú*."

She remains on her knees, head bent, as I plant my feet and slowly raise a corner of the cupboard. I glance down as she slides the cup out, and through the open top of her T-shirt I can see that she's braless. I hold my breath, set the cupboard back down. She tilts her face up at me.

"What now? Should I empty the cup—and the ants?"

"Yeah."

Each time I heave the cupboard, despite my knowing what I will see when I drop my gaze at her, I still look down through the crescent opening below her clavicles, admiring the milky white of her skin, the fullness of her bosom. What comes to mind is the long scar on the head nun's chest.

On the rear veranda, Mrs. Rossi and Maggie, the Irish woman, are scrubbing clothes in a round rubber tub. The inn owner normally does this chore. Though old, she can still scrub and wring garments with her small hands. At times she would tread on them the old-fashioned way, while hoisting the legs of her pantaloons.

"Giang," Mrs. Rossi calls to me, "you're back already."

Maggie, her face wet, raises her voice with a toss of her head. "Made it back in one piece in this bloody weather, didn't ye?"

"Roads are flooded now," I say to them. "Where's your husband, Maggie?"

"Went to meet his local guide and then off to the jungle." She means the U Minh forest. "I said go aisy on a day like this. He's beyant control. Wouldn't you say, Catherine?"

Mrs. Rossi shrugs. I step closer and look at her lower legs. Above her ankles are crowds of deep purple marks like she has been hit with a buckshot.

"Leech bites?" I ask her, pointing at them.

"How d'you know by just looking?" asks Mrs. Rossi.

"I've got scars on my legs from them." I pull up my trousers legs. The women and Chi Lan stare at the pea-sized scars on my shins and calves.

Her face scrunched up, Chi Lan shakes her head. "You got them during the war, *Chú?*"

"From years in the jungle."

Mrs. Rossi drops a wrung-out sock into an empty basket next to the tub. "Every night when I take off my socks, they're bloodstained from those suckers. The first few days in the forest I was near tears from putting up with them. Mr. Lung, he seemed unperturbed by leeches and bugs. You know how he got rid of those leeches for me?"

"With his cigarettes?" I ask. "Make them drop away?"

"That or I just pulled them off my legs."

"That's why you've got scars like these." I sit down on my heels and put my fingertip on her calf. "Do like this. Slide your fingernail under the sucker's mouth. It'll break off. Won't leave any scar mark on you, I guarantee."

"Is there any way to keep them from latching on to you?"

"I'll get you some chopped tobacco. Soak your socks in the tobacco water and then dry the socks before putting them on. Leeches won't bother you again."

"Does it really work?"

I nod. "Or you can cut the leech in half."

Looking at me, Mrs. Rossi leans back slowly and smiles. "But it'll regenerate itself, won't it?"

"No, ma'am. Mother Nature is fair to us that way."

Mrs. Rossi pats my hand. "You're a kind soul, Giang. I know yesterday was your day off, and you volunteered to go with me into the forest to help Mr. Lung. Bless your heart. I'm thankful for this torrential rain that keeps us from going out."

Maggie laughs. "*Zhang*, people like you will do us all the good in the world, won't you?"

She rises with the tub in her arms and empties it over the edge of the veranda, then refills the tub with rainwater sluicing like waterfall from the edge of the roof. I have seen her and Chi Lan washing with rainwater, cleaning and scrubbing themselves until their faces glowed. Precious rainwater. When it rains I would fill jugs of it for the old woman to wash and bathe the old man, and for cooking and drinking too. Once, while filling the jugs, I told Chi Lan that in the jungles we soldiers used to wait for rain so we could shower, and sometimes it was just a passing shower which stopped before we could get all the suds off our bodies. She laughed.

"Is she sleeping?" Chi Lan looks back into the house for the old lady.

"She's feeding him," I say.

"You want me to fill the water jugs for her?"

"No." My hand touches my shirt pocket where the cigarette pack is. "We have all we need for now."

I catch her gaze at my gesture for a smoke. I leave my hand on my chest and in my mind I see the creamy white skin of her bosom. She squats down and begins scrubbing a mud stain off her mother's jeans in the tub.

Mrs. Rossi arches her back, drawing a deep breath. "I must say I admire the old lady for washing clothes like this. My back is killing me already."

Maggie is wringing her denim shirt until veins bulge on the backs of her hands. "That's why that oul' lady walks bowlegged." She shakes out the shirt loudly. "Mother o' God give us a washer and a dryer. That's one thing we need here."

I have told them to air-dry their clothes in the sun once a week, so the sun would kill any eggs that might have been deposited in their garments. The books they brought with them too. Shake them out once in a while. On the first day of their arrival I heard her scream upstairs. I saw a trail of black ants that led into their room and heard her say to Alan, her husband, "I wouldn't even give them the steam of my piss." So I went in and there I saw a dead scorpion under the dresser. I picked it up and told them I would get rid of the ants for them. "Oh, you're a treasure," she said. "Please make them bloody eejits go 'way."

Now Maggie hangs up her shirt on the cord strung across the veranda and clips it with a wooden clothes-peg. In her late thirties, she is lean, small-bosomed, her sandy-blonde hair tied into a ponytail. Bony in the face that's freckled heavily under the eyes, clear blue eyes, she smiles a lot, the ear-to-ear smile that brings a smile to your face too. She comes back to the tub for her cotton slacks. "You ever got caught with this sorta rain in the jungle while ye go about yeer business?" she asks Mrs. Rossi.

"Oh, I've been in those downpours and the misting after the monsoon rains. It's miserable, Maggie."

"Tell me, love, how on earth can ye find anything in such a place? In that wilderness God doesn't plant a sign that says, 'Dig here!' Ye know what I mean."

Mrs. Rossi skims the suds off Chi Lan's forearm with her finger. "Mr. Lung has a method," she said. "We kinda divided up the area and went from one section to the next. When we spot a mound of earth here and there, he'd dig and dig, bless his old heart. He never stops going until I beg him to take a breather. Then he'll take a sip of water, have a smoke, and then be back at it. Most of the time we find nothing. A few times we found bones, human bones, and God Almighty I'd feel myself shaking. And you know something? You can't tell one skull from another. They all look like they were cast from the same mold. Those unclaimed skulls belong to unknown soldiers and that's why somebody like me is still searching for them."

Listening to Mrs. Rossi, I couldn't help thinking the same thought. You can't tell those skulls apart. You can't tell a Vietnamese skull from an American skull.

Mrs. Rossi shakes her head, as if trying to chase away something unpleasant. "One time we found a penicillin bottle among the bones. It was closed tight with a rubber cap. Mr. Lung opened it and there's nothing but a piece of paper inside. Well, he doesn't speak English like you, Giang, but after a lot of gesticulating and with much pidgin English, he got me to understand that it had to do with a soldier's identification. Things like name, combat unit, rank, birthplace, and hometown. He said that back when the remains-gathering crews would arrive, searching for the remains of their comrades, the bones they found without penicillin bottles would be brought back and buried in the National Military Cemetery in Ho Chi Minh City. The unidentified bones would be interred in the section for the remains of unknown Vietnamese soldiers."

Maggie frowns. "The Americans must've bombed the bejesus outa the jungle. So what's left in there to find?"

I cut in. "Sometimes all you rebury are a few bones. The rest got blown away."

"And if ye find them," Maggie asks, "how d'ye take them oul' bones back?"

I plug a cigarette in my mouth without lighting it. "They pack them in nylon bags and hang them on tree limbs. Keep them away from termites because the remains-gathering crews would stay in the forest for weeks. They bring all the bags back to the cemetery when their stay is over."

Maggie screws her eyes at me. "Say ye stumble on a skull of an orangutan. Can ye tell? Or ye bag it up and bury it in your National Military Cemetery among the oul' souls of yeer soldiers?"

Mrs. Rossi eyes Maggie with a bemused expression. I take the cigarette from my lips. "The men of the remains-gathering crews know about bones. They know how to tell a monkey skull from a human skull. A woman's skull from a man's skull . . ."

"Seriously?" Maggie chirps up.

"Yeah," I say. "They can tell. A woman's chin bone is smaller than a man's chin bone. The eye sockets are deeper. That sort of thing."

"Ah, now," Maggie says, nodding. "Nurses, weren't they?"

"Soldiers. Women fighters."

Mrs. Rossi wipes foam off Chi Lan's cheek. "We did find a couple of skulls and Mr. Lung said they were women's skulls. I had not the faintest idea why he said that. But women soldiers?"

I told them the women's skulls must have belonged to a vanguard unit of women fighters who took risks to spearhead into enemy territory. That was their mission. All of them were women.

Maggie whistles. "All women, eh? Aw for Jaysus sake . . ."

Mrs. Rossi sighs. "Mr. Lung was respectful with the bones we found. You must see how careful he was with them when he came upon them . . ."

"He's a gravedigger and undertaker around here," I say.

"I admire him for his professionalism," Mrs. Rossi says, "but more so for the personal feeling in the way he treated the bones. Before he dug, he'd light a stick of incense. Then you just watch him stab and stab the ground with his shovel and sometimes it'd hit rocks and sparks'd fly and then he suddenly stopped and looked down and there lay a small bundle in the hole, just a nylon bunch tattered and gray and when he ran his hand over it, the nylon fell apart. Like ashes. A skull cracked and chipped. Like broken china."

"What'd he do with them?" Maggie asks. "In the name of Jaysus, Mary and Holy Saint Joseph!"

Mrs. Rossi's voice drops. "He rewraps the bones in a clean piece of nylon he brought with him and shovels dirt over the pit and says a prayer."

I feel as if she's living her wish through Old Lung's acts, to see her son's remains ever cared for by a stranger in an unknown place.

Mrs. Rossi continues, "After he reburies the bones, sometimes with a skull, Mr. Lung flattens the dirt and removes the incense stick. I asked him why he did that and he explained, while miming, that'd wipe out any sign of a grave. 'Why,' I asked. 'So the bad people wouldn't come upon it,' he said. That's as far as I could get to the truth."

Her wrinkled face holds a dogged patience. "Mr. Lung did the right thing," I say. "There are bone crooks who go around digging up bones and selling them."

"Selling bones?" Mrs. Rossi's mouth falls agape.

"Swindlers. Bone profiteers."

"Selling bones to whom?" Mrs. Rossi asks.

"To contractors who build the National Military Cemetery."

"I might be obtuse," Mrs. Rossi says. "Would you please explain *that*?"

"These bone crooks go into the forests. The worst of them follow the poor folks after they've recovered the bones of their relatives and outright rob them. Then they sell the bones to the contractors in the city. You see, ma'am, for each tomb the contractors build, they charge the government. The more tombs the more profit. The contractors divide up the bones they buy from the bone crooks, and instead of building one tomb for a dead soldier's bones they build two, three tombs and charge the government. For the unknown remains, they'll end up having several unknown markers for one dead soldier. But the worst, ma'am, are those who rob the relatives. Instead of being properly buried back home with a tomb and a headstone, a dead soldier will be buried in the National Military Cemetery as an unknown soldier with his bones in multiple tombs."

Maggie taps her forehead. "Aw, Gawd, I sure never heard of this meself."

"Me neither," Mrs. Rossi says. "Who could think of such an inhuman thing?"

The next day the heat comes early, and by sunrise I have to open the window shutters in my room. Ông Ba arrives shortly after sunrise and drives Mrs. Rossi to Old Lung's where they will go to the forest in Ông Ba's motorboat.

Before the sun is high and the heat becomes unbearable, I pick up a machete and begin clearing the bushes along the front base of the veranda. In the bushes I find some old moss-covered logs, still damp from yesterday's rain and ax them to small chunks so rattlesnakes will have no place to nest. With the bushes uncovered, I can see the rocks worn slick by the coming and going of snakes. Under one bush I find a small carton of seeds. It dawns on me that they are watercress seeds the old woman has asked me to sow. Summer heat is so thick now the seeds would sprout in a week. She told me to plant them in the back, next to the lemon tree where the old man buries and reburies his ox bone. The last time he did that, unearthing all the freshly planted seeds of mustard greens, I had to erect a wire-mesh fence around the plot. I try to keep an eye on him.

I pick up the carton and empty the four tin cups half filled with vinegar. We have many cartons of vegetable seeds we plant year-round, and I fit each carton's bottom with four wooden pegs. Each peg rests on a vinegar-filled cup. Without protection, ants would devour the seeds. Before I came up with this solution, the old woman told me about the disappearing seeds. She said once she saw a patch of watercress sprouting up in the rear land, as though someone had sown the seeds there. I told her the ants did that. They eat the seed caps, which have nutrition for them, and leave the seeds behind. The seeds later sprout where the ants have left them.

I've left the carton behind the bush when the Irish couple arrived. I remind myself to plant the seeds today before the old woman asks again. She said most of our guests like watercress among the greens. After leaving the carton on the rear veranda, I go around the inn and empty all the receptacles of standing rainwater. I've forgotten to turn those planters and flower pots upside down, and now several of them are filled with rainwater, becoming a breeding ground for mosquitoes. After dark those whiners will come out. They can't fly far, but they breed and multiply where they find water.

Everyone else except Mrs. Rossi is still in bed. It's quiet in the rear of the inn. The air stands still as I go about sowing the watercress seeds. With this heat, I believe, we could be eating watercress in the next couple of days. When I stop to wipe my face, I see a lone stork flying across the hazy sky. I can see its trailing pink legs and the black stripes underneath its wings. On the skunk tree a yellow weaver is coming back with blades of grass in its beaks. The agave at the base of the tree is flowering for the first time. Strong, broad, and fleshy leaves are spiny along their edges. It must have flowered overnight. The flowers are bursting forth in busy bottle brushes, and their sunset red strikes the eye against the cactus-green of their leaves. When Chi Lan first saw the agave by the skunk tree, she thought it was cactus. I told her the old woman had wanted it uprooted so she could use the area for a vegetable plot, but to do it you'd need an ox to pull it up. Chi Lan smiled and said she liked its lone, fierce look. I said to her, "Looks unusual but pretty when it flowers." And she said, "I'll photograph it when it does."

I go into town to shop during a downpour. Around noon the rain begins slacking off. The sky is clearing and the breeze carries the heat south, leaving a breath of moistness in the air. The Irish couple must have gone out, for their car isn't there. After putting the groceries away, I check on the old man and see that his wife is bathing him in the bathhouse, adjoined to the side of the inn. Upstairs the Irish couple has locked their room. The door of Mrs. Rossi's room is open, but I do not see Chi Lan. I go back down and out to the rear. The field blazes in the sun. Hazy wisps of vapor are curling over the ground. I see a sudden glint of beaded water on the agave bush.

I run down the veranda to the rain-soaked field and find her lying on her back behind the agave. She is drenched. Her leaf-green T-shirt clings to her skin and her hair is matted in strands on her face. Slung across her shoulder is the camera strap, the camera itself in the crook of her arm. I grab her arm and check for a pulse. Her eyes are shut, lips parted slightly. I can feel her pulse. There are mud stains on the sides of her white shorts, and her legs fold into each other at the knees as though she's sleeping. No bite marks on her legs, which would have told of snakebite. None on her neck. Then I see a small red bump on her upper arm near the elbow. The red looks fresh on her light skin. I see the stinger. A wasp sting. The old woman got stung once by a wasp and fainted after she made it into the house. I pinch the end of the stinger with my long fingernails. The hard stinger comes out like a fishbone.

I gather the girl in my arms and carry her up the veranda and into my room. She must be allergic to the wasp sting. I lay her gently on my narrow bed and work the camera strap off her neck. Water is dripping from her clothes. The purplish color of her lips makes me wonder how long she has lain in the rain. When I look again at her soaked-through clothes, especially her T-shirt, I know I must do something. I snatch a bath towel from the wall hook, and after some hesitation, begin drying her. Her skin is cold and her T-shirt is soggy. I manage to peel it off her body. It drips onto the floor as I drape it over the back of the chair. I pull out a clean shirt in the old mango-wood dresser and, sitting down on the edge of the bed, look at her. Her face is pale against her strikingly black hair. I look at her nakedness and hold my breath. My worry for her becomes muted, for I am drowned in the moment. She is so beautiful. I dry her hair, her face, her chest. A bright red mole beckons me to her bosom. A crimson mole on the creamy white of her skin. Unspeakable beauty. I struggle to get my shirt on her. As if changing a shirt for a child that needs care. My short-sleeved shirt sags at her shoulders. I want her to wake. Yet I want the moment not to end. Her breathing comes heavier now.

I boil water on the hot plate and while waiting for the water to heat up, I cut some ginger slices and drop them into my coffee mug together with a tea bag. She begins to stir. When I glance over, she is trying to sit up.

"*Chú,*" she says with some difficulty.

"Lie back," I say, moving to the bed.

She looks down at herself and touches her face, then her arm, her eyes unfocused. "What happened?"

"You were stung by a wasp." I take out a cigarette. "Were you out there photographing something?"

"Yes, *Chú*. The agave flowers." She looks at my cigarette. "Your cigarette is wet."

"From carrying you in."

"It won't light."

"Maybe it won't." I tear the cigarette paper, set it on the bed and point at the brown tobacco. "I'm going to put this on the sting."

I hold her arm by the elbow, feeling her faint breathing against my forehead, and squint at the reddened bump.

"Is the stinger venomous?" she asks, drawing a sharp breath.

"No. But it can knock you out." I daub a pinch of tobacco with my saliva and paste it on the lump. "Does it hurt?"

"It's stinging now." She bites her lower lip, rubbing the swelling. "You said a wasp did this?"

"Could be a digger wasp or a great black wasp. I've seen those around the inn."

After I bandage her arm, she pulls up her soiled legs and rests the bandaged arm on her knee. She massages the swelling. "I don't remember anything." She leans to one side, her eyelids fluttering. "Well, maybe I do. I felt something very painful on my arm. I took a few more pictures then suddenly felt dizzy."

"It'll take a day or so before the pain goes away."

The water boils. I pour hot water into the mug. Blowing on it, I bring it to her. "This will ease the sting."

She looks down, not taking the mug from me. "I'm wearing your shirt, *Chú*."

"Yeah." I keep my voice even. "You were soaked through. I was worried. Have a sip of tea."

She says nothing, keeping her head down. The mug breathes curling vapor. She lifts the mug with both hands but avoids meeting my eyes. Her face reddens. She hides her expression behind the mug with only her eyes visible. She glances at her T-shirt still dripping over the back of the chair. The tiny black mole dots the corner of her left eye. I think of the red mole. My gaze makes her drop her head. She shifts. The bed creaks. Its white sheet is wet and stained black.

"Your bed is messed up," she says.

I nod just as she winces and touches the bandaged bite. Her mussed-up hair, still wet, gives her an untamed look, so pale, so raw that I feel a man's desire for her.

"I'm surprised," she says with the mug still covering her face, "you could carry me in from out there."

"I had to. You're as light as air."

She watches me wipe her camera dry with the towel. "Thank you, *Chú*," she says, peering across at me. "Did you buy the tobacco today? My mom said she'd do what you've told her."

"She must soak her socks in the tobacco water. Make sure they have enough time to dry before she wears them in the morning."

Chi Lan caresses her bandaged forearm. "Are you sure it'll take the sting out of me, this tobacco treatment?"

"I've done that myself. For a wasp sting."

"You got stung by a wasp?"

"It knocked me out, like it did to you. We're both allergic to their sting." Picking up the torn cigarette off the bed, my hand brushes her foot. "I was an NVA soldier then. We were behind the lines, deep in the jungle."

At that time, I tell her, I was deserting my unit. For the whole night I kept moving, not resting for a moment. By morning I came upon a trail. Just as I took to the trail, I got stung by a wasp. It left its stinger in my forearm. I pulled it out and kept walking but soon felt miserable with that numbing pain, like someone had punched a hot needle into my arm. The trail took me to a graveyard in a clearing. Then everything suddenly went black before me. When I woke, I was lying facedown and around me the earth was red.

Red dirt, red humps of graves, red-stem taros with their giant elephant-ear leaves flopping. This vision of red made me believe I was dying. I heard a shoveling noise. I sat up. Nearby a man in a visor cap looked over at me. He was an old man. When I told him I'd passed out after a wasp sting, he began doctoring me with cigarette tobacco. He told me he took care of the graveyard. He said he'd thought I was a corpse and he was ready to bury me. He said he buried corpses every other day when trucks brought in bodies from the front line. Or he buried the remains of those mauled and eaten by tigers that ran out of the regions destroyed by the American bombing. Sometimes he buried the deserters' corpses.

Chi Lan lowers the mug and her face looks calm again. "I wonder what would have happened if you had slept longer."

I smile at her remark. "He would have buried me. And I wouldn't be sitting here telling you this."

She gives a small laugh. "I'd be dead now if it were a poisonous snake."

"So be careful when you're out there."

"I remember that you told me about your father." She offers me her mug of tea. "Would you like some?"

"Just one sip." I receive the mug from her, cupping my hands over hers.

"Didn't your father know how to doctor himself against snakebite?" She sets the mug back on her knee.

"He could have. With an antidote. Did you know that they make the antidote for snake venom out of the venom itself? My father used to sell the venom he extracted from snakes to the professional snake catchers. I used to watch him squeeze a snake at the throat so hard the snake's mouth opened wide enough to jam in a cup. You should have seen how the snake's fangs hooked inside, and when he raked them, the venom started oozing into the cup."

"Ew." She shivers. "What color?"

"Yellow." I look down at her mug. "Like that."

"Stop that." Giggling, she draws up her shoulders. "I wouldn't drink it now that I know."

"You can drink snake venom. It's harmless."

"No way, *Chú*."

"My father used to mix it with rice liquor and drink it in one gulp. Said it's good for digestion."

"I thought it's deadly."

"If the snake bites you, yeah. Because its venom goes into your blood stream. But not when you take it by the mouth."

"Why the difference?"

"By the mouth? The venom goes down to your stomach. The acid there will neutralize it." I pause, with a grin. "And it's good for digestion."

"Yes. But not for me."

She brushes strands of wet hair over her ears with her fingertips. In that moment I feel as if I were looking at the girl on the bridge when I was seventeen. The inky-black eyebrows that arch gracefully, the melodious voice. Her foot shifts and touches my hand. In the silence I can feel her tense.

"Why didn't your father protect himself with an antidote?" she asks casually.

"He was careless."

"And you were too young to tell him otherwise?"

"It made no difference. He used to tell me, 'Son, if a snake bites you on a finger and you've got no antidote around, chop off the finger. If it's a toe, chop off the toe. Then you'll live.' Easy to say. I'd seen men do that in the jungle during the war. Men with missing fingers and toes."

She sips, listening. "One night," I say, "my father saw a girl sleeping outside our shack under the weeping fig. The base of that huge tree was a snake colony. With snakes crawling in the bushes around the tree, my father thought she must have been dead. But she had passed out from hunger. This beggar girl was in her early twenties. So my father fed her a bowl of snake meat and some rice and let her sleep on the floor in our shack. She would come back to the graveyard whenever she was hungry and father would take her in. When he asked her where she came from, he found out that she was the daughter of one of his former servants, a man who had denounced him during the People's Court. She cringed when he told her who he was: a former wealthy landowner with ten servants in his household. He told her not to be afraid. 'We're equal now,' he said. 'Think of the one million people already dead from starvation. You and I are blessed.' He would drink himself into a stupor every night and one night he took the girl outside our shack and they slept there. From then on, he never slept inside when the girl came. He had a jar of antidote we kept in the shack. But my father never carried it with him. Like he had a death wish. Or just careless. Then one morning I woke to her cries. I ran out and saw her weeping over his body. I found snake-bite marks on his leg. Even the girl did not know what happened to him, and so I believed that he died in his stupor."

Rubbing her arm, Chi Lan says, "That's very sad, *Chú*."

"I was worried when I saw you lying out there."

"What if someone here is bitten by a poisonous snake?"

"The old woman has antidote. There's a jar in the refrigerator. It has a label in both Vietnamese and English."

She laughs. "*Chú*, I won't mistake it for the cooking broth."

A bead of water rolls down the side of her face. She hunches up one shoulder and dries her cheek with her shirt—my shirt. Breathing in sharply she says, "Now I smell of tobacco, just like you."

1967
Nicola Rossi

G ood old Ian Vaughn.

He was a fine young man, Mama.

One day we were out at first light on patrol outside a Viet village. A hazy morning. We were wading single file across a canal that hugged the side of the village. Hedged by water hyacinth, the bank was thick with a barrier of bamboo, to prevent against water erosion of the soil. Where the hedge ended you could see the soil so fretted away by water that the roots of bamboo stuck out dangling. Brown thatch huts, at times only their roofs, peeked through the green foliage. A figure slunk out behind a clump of reed. A kid. He was lugging a rifle. Ian, our point man, hollered, "Who goes there?" The kid turned, looked back. Then he bolted. A gunshot rang out. The kid fell. Sergeant Sunuk-kuhkau lowered his M-16 and climbed the bank and walked into the tall reed. The kid lay prone. His wound still leaked blood like thick nail varnish.

Sarge picked up the kid's gun. An old battered Thompson submachine gun. Its walnut-brown buttstock, badly nicked and chipped, had a faded look, like it had been buried in the paddy since World War II.

Sarge turned his snake-eyes on Ian.

"Did you really say that?" he asked. "'Who goes there'?"

Ian looked down at the kid's lifeless body and back at Sarge. "He was just a kid, Sarge," he said, as if apologizing to the dead kid.

"And this?" Sarge thrust the old Thompson against Ian's chest. "A toy?"

"Maybe they made him do it. Told him to shoot at us."

"May I ask?" Sarge tapped the twenty-round box magazine. "What would've happened if he'd emptied this on us?"

Ian said nothing. He stood hunched like a lonely heron. A tall boy, his hair, flame-red in its root, was straight like the Viets', with only a patch on the top and the rest was shaved all around down to the back of his neck. His freckled face looked boyish, as if someone had pulled him out of bed one morning, slapped the fatigues on him, and said, "We'll make a man out of you."

He once said to me, "Lieutenant, I don't want to kill anyone."

"Then you'll get killed," I said, "if that's your choice."

Talk about fear of the damned, Mama. He was full of it. The kid was a good Christian. When a man kills another man, he told me, he will be damned to hell forever. Although I believed in none of it, I could still hear the words they drilled into us through basic training: "What's the spirit of the bayonet?" And the lot of innocent boys shouted, "Kill, kill, kill, no mercy!" And the drill sergeant bawled, "What makes the green grass grow?" And the boys shouted back, "Blood, blood, bright red blood!" Ian despised all this; he loathed himself for yelling out those words. He spoke Sherman's words into my ears with absolute conviction. "Lieutenant, you know this general in the Union Army during the Civil War, William Tecumseh Sherman? He said, 'There is many a boy who looks on war as all glory, but boys, it is all hell.'"

Once we were moving into enemy territory and everyone went to lock and load. The man next to Ian doubled
back and whispered to Sergeant Sunu—few remember his
full name, none can spell it. Before long, Sarge came up the
line and pointed his finger at Ian's M-16.

"Remove the magazine," Sarge said.

"Why?" Ian said.

"I want to see it," Sarge said.

Ian pressed the magazine release. The magazine fell out
and before he caught it in his hand, Sarge seized it. One
peek into the magazine and he grabbed Ian by the collar
of his shirt. "This," he said, shaking the empty magazine
in Ian's face, "is unthinkable. This is close to treason, boy.
Someone from our side could pay a dear price for this. You
don't want that on your conscience, do you, boy? You kill
the slopes or they kill us. It's as simple as that."

Beyond the base was a little Viet town. A red dirt road ran
through it, and along the dirt path in groups of threes and
fours were the odd-sized shanties, the Viets' crude abodes,
and among them, right in the middle of the dusty road
under the shade of a chinaberry stood a tin-roofed house
with a white red-lettered sign that said, "Refreshments."
Mixed in were a few stores that had no signs—their owners
were migrants who would leave the day our American
base was abandoned—or older stores that everybody knew
about, signs or no signs. Late afternoons a Lambretta minibus would come chugging down the dirt road, sputtering
and spitting smoke, and stop in front of the tin-roofed house
long enough for the town dwellers, mostly women, young
and old, to run out of their shanties, each hugging a big plastic bag full of onions, raw and freshly diced, and the driver,
a lanky black kid, got out and, saying not a word with a
smoldering cigarette stuck in his mouth, began tossing each

bag into the passenger cab and shoving crumbled bills into the women's hands. Soon the Lambretta turned around and headed back the way it came on the same dirt road rutted and ridged, hollowed with mud pools left behind by the olive-colored trucks, with a white star painted on the cab doors, that carried water to the base. We called this little town "Blind Colony," Mama. It was the same age as the base, built a few years ago. Like parasitic climbers on old tree trunks. And the sight of our star-painted trucks was as familiar as the sight of the old Lambretta that came chugging in every day at daybreak, unloading bags of fresh onions in front of the refreshment store, and returning before sunset to collect the onions now neatly diced. They must have good soil somewhere to grow those onions, for each bulb was big and smooth and shiny, and those bulbs could stay fresh for a few months. You know why, Mama? After they were harvested and dried, those who grew them preserved them in DDT and gypsum powder to keep off fungi and onion flies and eelworms. Otherwise the onions would rot in a week. Now the Viet women would receive bags of them at first light and all day long they slaved dicing up the onions. At day's end, eyes teary and red when their bags were filled with diced onions, they must have wiped their eyes a hundred times. Before long their eyesight was affected by the DDT and eventually they went blind.

There was a Viet kid always standing outside the refreshment shack. He was out at dawn every day when the Lambretta came and the black driver, a Vietnamese by birth, Mama, perhaps between a Viet woman and a black Senegalese from the Indochina War, would toss him a couple of onions and the kid would work them into his shorts' side pockets until they bulged like two grenades.

One morning when Ian stopped outside the refreshment shack, the kid came up to him.

"Hey, GI," he said looking up at Ian. "Me you same same, hah?"

Ian nodded. "Right, right." Ian was redheaded and his eyes were hazel. The kid was redheaded and his eyes were blue. He did not look Vietnamese.

"GI, wan oh-ni-on?" The kid pulled out the two onions in his shorts pockets and held them up for Ian to see.

Ian looked at the sleek bulbs, bright red like two pomegranates. He took one, weighed it in his hand. "Nice," he said, sniffing it.

"Gud to eat, hah?"

"Big onion. How much?"

"Gib me one dollah."

"I'll give you a pack of gum for that."

The kid took it. Then he gave Ian both onions.

"I only want one," said Ian, thinking to give the cook on the base this beautiful onion to make omelets.

The kid pointed at himself, then at Ian. "Me souvenir you."

"All right, thanks." Ian rubbed the boy's head. He knew he could rub every Viet kid's head but never a grown Viet's head unless he wanted to invite his wrath. The head was the holiest place in a man's body. That was their custom, he'd learned. "What's your name?" he asked the kid in Vietnamese.

"Mao."

"Mao? Like Mao Tse-Tung?"

"Hah?"

"Okay. Little Mouse. My name is Ian."

He looked into the refreshment shack through the white, green, yellow plastic strips that hung from the doorway. In the back of the shack was a room where you could buy pleasure from a Viet girl. He'd only heard about the back room; he himself was still a virgin. "Your Mom, she works in there?"

Little Mouse had a blank look on his face. Ian asked again, slower in Vietnamese. This time Little Mouse pointed toward the base. "Got ya," Ian said. Guys on the base paid a couple of Viet women to wash and iron their clothes, make their beds, and shine their boots. They earned 118 piasters to a dollar, better than selling your body. Ian imagined the room in the back of the shack his friends had told him about. A thought struck him. Who might be the father of Little Mouse?

The next morning when Ian met Little Mouse outside the refreshment shack, Little Mouse held a Zippo lighter. He was toying with it, flicking open the lid and clapping it shut, listening to the sound it made. Ian stood looking down at him. Little Mouse struck the flint wheel, and his nose wrinkled at the whiff of gasoline smell.

Ian noticed imprinted lines on the side of Little Mouse's cheek, probably from a rush mat or bamboo cot.

"Zippo," Little Mouse said, waving the lighter with the little blue flame still burning.

"Where'd you get it from?"

Little Mouse slapped shut the lid. He lifted his face. Sleepy blue eyes gazing into Ian's eyes. "Ma gave me this." He spoke Vietnamese in that quick, lilting southern accent.

"Let me see." Ian put out his hand. The plain brass lighter had many tiny scratches. One side was etched with something that caught his eyes. A carefully carved NVA pith helmet. It had a chin strap, a star inside the round badge on the crown. Beneath the hat the Vietnamese handwritten words said, "*U Minh, 1967. Yêu em.*" Ian mouthed the words silently. "Can you read them?" he asked Little Mouse.

Little Mouse looked at him.

"You can't read?" Ian asked.

Little Mouse shook his head.

"You know how old you are?" Ian asked.

Little Mouse scratched his head.

"Seven? Eight?"

"Không biet."

No bic. Don't know. Ian had heard those words from fellow GIs when they interrogated the villagers. Ian read slowly to Little Mouse the words on the Zippo, running his fingertip along the words *Yêu em*. Love you. An NVA soldier must have carved this message for someone he loved back home. How did the fellow get this Zippo? From a dead American GI?

"You wan?" Little Mouse said in English, shaking the lighter in Ian's face.

"Sure." Ian leaned his head back. "How much?"

"Gib me fife dollah."

"Five dollars? I give you three for it. What d'you say, Little Mouse?"

Little Mouse looked at the three bills. He blinked, then clutched the singles tight in his fist. He looked at the Zippo one last time and gave it to Ian. "Numbah one," he said.

Ian wasn't sure what he meant, the Zippo or the consummated deal. For a kid who couldn't read, he surely knew how to count. Ian wondered who might have given Little Mouse's mother the Zippo. He thought of how to ask it in Vietnamese. Instead he said, "Your Mom will be mad because you sold her souvenir."

Little Mouse shook his head. "She don't know."

Although he didn't smoke, Ian would take the Zippo out of his shirt pocket now and then to admire it. Each time he read the Vietnamese words, *Yêu em*, he thought of her. *Love you.* She was pretty but she had a face that would leave nothing in your mind. How could a pretty face leave nothing in one's memory? He could never figure that out. He never had a chance to photograph her, because he thought he was so happy around her in that tiny Viet village in those days, so all he had left was a memory of her—and the words, *Yêu em,* the words he spoke to her that first time, which made her laugh and blush and say to him, *You silly silly silly oh silly you,* but the way she said it warmed his heart.

Five days after he bought the Zippo from Little Mouse, he sat in a stud game with four others. Sergeant Sunu was one of them. High stakes. He was low on money when the last card was dealt. He got a pair of aces. As he peeked at the corner of the last card, he saw an emerging big A. *Lawd.* Sarge raised the bet. Fifty dollars. That was half his monthly paycheck. Two guys slapped down fifties. One quit. Ian peeked at his cards again. *Damn.* He had thirty left. He took out his Zippo. "Check it out," he said. Two fellows looked at it. One said, "What's this worth? Five bucks in a PX. Guaranteed."

"Look at the other side," Ian said.

The fellow looked at the engravings of the pith helmet and the Vietnamese words. "So?" he said, glancing at Ian.

"It's worth twenty bucks minimum," Ian said, "and I'll buy it back for that next month, if I lose."

"Lemme see," Sarge said, scratching his biceps, where a grinning red-devil tattoo bulged.

Sarge turned the Zippo back and forth in his big hand, his face blurred from smoke of the cigarette dangling between his lips. He looked at the inscription on the bottom of the lighter. Four vertical bars on each side of the flourished Zippo logo. His lips moved as he read the Vietnamese words. He shoved the lighter toward Ian, pointing at the words *U Minh, 1967.* "I know this," he said. "What's this? *Ewe am?*"

"Love you," Ian said.

"You sure?"

"That's what it means, Sarge."

"You got this from one of them gooks?"

"Yeah. But if I lose it, I want to buy it back next month from whoever. Deal?"

"I want it," Sarge said, the cigarette jerking, dropping ash in his lap.

"I said I'll buy it back," Ian said, his eyes narrowed at Sarge.

"Either you fold. Or lose this, if I win."

Ian felt hot in the head. Sarge liked collecting so-called war memorabilia, especially gook knickknacks. In one game, he won a pith helmet a guy pawned for ten bucks but never bought back. A special pith helmet made of heavy compressed board, not the thick hardboard helmet equipped with a leather strap. The last game, Sarge added to his collection a Viet Cong metal cup, a surefire collectible item. It had a lid with a cute little knob in the center. On one side of the cup, you had a gook wearing rubber-type sandals trampling on an American soldier's helmet. The gook, holding an AK-47 fitted with a bayonet, was charging under a Viet Cong red-and-blue flag emblazoned with a gold star in the center. The enameled cup, scuffed here and there, had a Vietnamese line on the bottom edge: *Dánh Tan Giac My Xâm Lang*. Nobody knew what it meant, though Sarge said it probably meant this cup was used for eating rice and drinking green tea, which he could have been right about. But Ian thought it must mean "beat the crap out of the Americans," based on the picture. But he didn't tell Sarge that.

Now Ian glanced down at his last card again. *Sumbitch.* "I'm in," he said, hearing his voice shaking. One guy had two tens, two kings, and the second guy three queens. When Ian laid down his cards someone said, "Hot damn." They all looked at Sarge. He took one last drag and mashed the cigarette in the ashtray. Then he laid down his cards. Four jacks.

For three days Ian didn't feel like going to the Viet town, for Little Mouse standing outside the refreshment shack would remind him of his lost Zippo. But it wasn't the Zippo. It was those words, *Yêu em*. He could have been the one who carved them for her, and memory without a souvenir was a bitch. So was love.

That morning on the third day was sultry. Midmorning heat made guys sweat like they were being boiled in a sealed tank. Ian sat on the edge of his cot, scratching sores on his arms and legs. Raw, red-looking sores. The hooch smelled of sour sweat from unwashed bodies, lying in the two dozen cots. He could feel sweat tickling the sides of his face as it ran down. Sweat beads stung his eyes. Sweat tasted like salt on the tip of his tongue. *Holy Jesus.* He worked his legs into his fatigue pants. Their olive color was no longer ocher green but a dull gray. The concrete floor felt warm under his bare feet. He hopped over loaded magazines in the belts of machine gun ammunition, yellowed with dirt. He could see sleeping bodies behind the mosquito gauze nets, the rifles and submachine guns stood on their ends, propped against the wall between cots.

Pow. A dry, crackling sound. The familiar gunshot sound.

Bodies in the cots stirred. Now they swung their legs out of the nets, rubbing their eyes.

"What the fuck?"

"Who shot?"

"Go check it out!"

From the next hooch Ian heard the commotion. He stepped into the hooch's dimness, the heat breathed dry, rank on his face. He looked at several men standing in their boxers outside Sergeant Sunu's quarters. Across the length of his room hung two woolen army blankets. Dangling before them was a sign scribbled with a black-inked handwriting: *He crushes.* You could see through the parted blankets his bed draped with the mosquito net, a small table with a black metal chair on which sat an electric fan humming as it turned. Sarge was standing in his shorts, his bare torso glistening with sweat, his hand holding a Colt-45. A body lay on the floor at his feet. He lit a cigarette and waved out the match.

"Take the body out of my sight," he said, laying the gun on the table.

"Yessir," one man said and motioned with his head to another fellow.

Everyone stepped back. The dead was a Viet woman. She lay flat on her back, her chest looking messy, her white blouse doused with blood. The two men hoisted her up and carried her out of Sarge's quarters. Ian could see her head lolling, her eyes half open, her black hair wrapped inside a polka-dot red-and-white kerchief. He remembered her face. A maid hired by the men in some of the hooches. Young-looking, with a dimpled smile, she always bowed to the men who paid for her service. As the men carried her out of the hooch, Ian said, "Sarge, what happened?"

Sarge held him in his unblinking gaze. "Gook stole my Zippo," he said.

Ian shook his head in disbelief.

Someone said, "Damn."

Ian took a step up. "What?" he said. "My Zippo? One I lost to you?"

"Got that right," Sarge said.

"Damn, Sarge. For Chrissake!"

He looked to the table. The Zippo wasn't there. Just the gun.

That whole day he thought about the shooting. He couldn't stop thinking about it. Every time he heard a lighter's click, he flinched. He slept that night hearing the clicking of Zippos in his head. *Jesus. For a lousy Zippo.*

He went on patrols and stayed out for a week without making contact with the enemy, seeing not even one of them. The morning after they came back he walked from the base to the blind colony in the morning heat. Through the embrasure of a corner guard bunker he could see the muzzle of an M-60 machine gun. In that rat hole, three hours from now, he would be sitting hunched up, staring out through that gun slit. Two-hour guard duty. As he walked bareheaded in the heat, something was gnawing at his stomach. It had been gnawing at him since that morning when Sarge shot the Viet maid. A rare breeze came fanning across the land and there was a stench of human waste in the air. It came from the giant pit outside the base where the men would cart the fifty-five-gallon barrels of excrement, to burn it. It was still dry season and the dirt beneath the howitzer emplacements had hardened and gone yellow. Dirt clods would fly like grenade fragments and the ground would quake each time they fired the guns. Yellow dirt clung to his boots as he walked. He thought of paying one of the Viet maids to clean them, a chore he had always done himself, but quickly discarded that notion after what Sarge had done.

There was no sight of Little Mouse outside the refreshment shack. Ian sat in the shack, facing the dirt road. The table was low, the metal chair too, so he sat with his knees bumping the table's edge. Across the room a Viet man sat with one leg drawn up on the chair, smoking a cigarette. The woman owner brought Ian a bottle of beer, a glass half filled with ice cubes. As Ian poured himself a glass, the man called to the woman. "You said you got no ice. Eh?"

"So?" The woman turned her round face, angry, her nostrils flaring.

"What kind of attitude is that?"

"Low on ice, that's that." She jerked her thumb toward Ian. "Can't tell these GIs: Drink your beer warm. Easier to tell you than him."

"Those *Meey* better than me?"

"You can drink warm beer. They can't."

The man dropped his cigarette butt in his glass of beer. Still half full. He got up and, plugging a fresh cigarette in his mouth, walked out.

Ian cupped his hands around his cold glass, pretending he didn't understand the situation. As the woman took the man's glass away, Ian sat gazing out through the gaps of the plastic strips. A yellow DeSoto bus came to a stop farther down the dirt road and people got out. Slowly it turned around, grunting, and sped up in a haze of red dust. Ian gazed at the plywood wall and rolled the chilled wall of his glass on the side of his face. Cutout pictures from magazines pinned on the wall held his gaze for a moment. Actors, actresses. American, French. He recognized the faces. He was far from home now.

He startled when the radio in the shack suddenly blared out. Static noises. Then music came. A Viet woman singing. The owner turned down the volume. Ian closed his eyes. The air hung still.

"GI, wan some fun?"

He opened his eyes.

"Wan girl?" the woman said, standing now by the table.

"Girl?" he said, raising his brows.

"She new. You like?"

"Who? Oh." He leaned back. "All right."

Seeing him nod, the woman grabbed him by the wrist. "Okay," she said, pulling him. "She young. New. Numbah one. Okay?"

He followed her through the back doorway curtained with plastic strips. Crates of beer and beverages crowded the tiny dim aisle. Then padded containers filled with sawdust for ice. He tiptoed through. The woman pushed open a door. He peered in. There was a mattress in one corner covered with a white sheet and in another corner a brass pan filled with water. A girl sat on the edge of the mattress, looking at the floor. Like a statue put there.

"No see. She no see." The woman looked up at him, her fingers pointed to her own eyes.

"No see?"

"No see."

"*Dui?*" Ian said in Vietnamese, poking at his eyes.

"Okay. Okay." The woman grinned. Her gold tooth flashed. She pulled out a condom packet and tried to put it in Ian's hand.

He received it, but his mind went blank. When he felt it in his palm, the woman had already backed out and closed the door behind her. The girl kept her head down. She wore a short-sleeved blue blouse and polka-dot blue-and-white pantaloons. Her hair hung past her shoulders, hiding her face. He felt like someone was watching him. He knew he was just nervous. It passed. He could hear the radio from the front room, the woman's voice greeting somebody entering the shack. He went to the mattress and sat down beside her.

"Hello," he said.

She turned her head toward him. He could see her eyes gazing emptily. She had a small nose and her plain-looking face was honey-colored.

"How old are you?" he asked.

She shook her head.

"No English?" he asked.

Again she shook her head. He repeated in Vietnamese. This time she said, "Sixteen." She turned her face partially to him, the tenseness seemingly gone. At least, speaking Vietnamese, he didn't sound alien to her. The stuffy room brought out the odor of his sweat through his fatigues. He felt embarrassed. He had imagined she would reek of perfume, but he smelled nothing. A plain little girl. With his knees jacked up to his chest, he looked down at his boots. Yellow dirt hazed their vamps and ankles. He pressed down on the condom packet with his thumb, making a crackling sound, and then stopped.

"You new here?" he said.

She nodded.

"Where's the . . . the regular?" he asked, working on his accent.

"Died." She was rubbing her fingertips against each other.

He drew a sharp breath. "Your . . . first day here?"

"Couple days here."

"Any customer?"

"Not yet."

"I'm the first?"

She nodded.

He held his breath, then swallowed hard. He looked down at her. He followed her empty gaze, always looking at something invisible in front of her.

"You . . . born blind?" he asked.

She shook her head.

"How long blind?" he asked.

"Six months." She raised her hands, one open, the other with index finger raised.

"Accident?"

"Onions," she said. "Cutting onions."

"From . . . cutting onions?"

She nodded. "Many, many onions. Every day." She rubbed her eyes with one hand, pointing at the gesture with her other hand.

His mouth fell open. *Sweet Jesus.* "How . . . ?" He looked down at her face, serene and simple, at her chest, almost flat with her small breasts pointing at the front of her blouse. She dropped her hand to her lap, her elbow brushing his arm. He flinched. He felt so big beside her he tried to keep still so he wouldn't overwhelm her. He felt the condom packet held between his thumb and finger, then tucked it in his palm and closed his hand. He remembered seeing the Lambretta minibus once. Saw the Viet women take deliveries of fresh onions from the Viet negro. He thought of Little Mouse. At least the kid didn't have to cut onions for a living. But from cutting onions to this—this. So far gone, unimaginable.

"You here . . . every day?" He spoke slowly.

She nodded; her empty eyes blinked.

He ran his tongue along the inside of his lips, trying to find words. "What if the . . . regular were still here? You still work?"

She raised her face toward him, pursing her lips. "Mmm . . . but she died."

"Died . . . of what?"

"GI . . ." she said, using the American word. "Killed her in there."

"On our base?"

"Shot her dead." She nodded several times.

He lifted his face, took a sharp breath. Something hit him. "You know the boy . . . red-haired boy . . . always standing outside this place . . . ?"

"Mao?" She raised her voice, still a small voice but loud enough.

"Yes. Mao." He almost forgot Little Mouse's real name. Like *Mao Tse-Tung*.

"I know him." She nodded repeatedly. "She was his mother."

His mother. *Lord Jesus. She don't know*, Little Mouse had said, *She don't know*. She'd seen it in Sarge's sleeping quarters.

"Where is he now?"

"With someone," she said in her thin voice. "Friend of his mother."

Ian stretched his legs, and she shifted to give him room. The air was warm. All he smelled was the odor of his sweat. If she had put on some perfume, he'd be glad sharing such closeness and would forget his own big awkwardness. This closeness he had kept with him like some treasure. Being with her, sitting next to her. Now he could hear the radio. Someone laughing. He felt her waiting for him. He drew air through his mouth quietly and then slowly let it out.

"I'm going," he said, putting his hand on top of hers.

She lifted her face, her lips slightly opened. "Going? Where?"

"Back to base." He patted her hand. "I'll pay. Pay the woman."

"You come back?" Her empty gaze raised, following his motion of getting up.

"Sure," he said, then on second thought: "I don't know."

In the front room a Viet man was sitting at the table where the other one had sat. He was drinking beer with no ice. He didn't seem to mind. Sipping, puffing a cigarette, and reading a letter. Ian paid the woman.

"Like her?" she asked, smoothing out the bills, and flashing her gold tooth with a friendly smile.

"Yeah."

"Good? Boom-boom good?"

"Yeah."

"She new. Okay? GI like new."

"Sure."

He turned to walk out, then stopped. Across the dirt road he saw Little Mouse standing in the sun. A GI was coming from the base and Little Mouse was looking at him, waiting. It was Sarge. He looked like a bear moving slowly and deliberately with brisk steps. He stopped when he came near and looked down to the ground. A gray mouse scurrying around. Ian could see the string that was tied around the mouse's neck. Sarge watched the mouse trying to get free. Running left then right, forward and backward. Little Mouse, holding the string, pulled out an onion from his shorts pocket. Reddish papery covering. Sarge stared at the onion, didn't even touch it. He looked down watching the mouse darting around, then took a cigarette out of the pack from his shirt pocket. Sarge lit his cigarette with a match. He blew a stream of smoke and Ian could see him talking to Little Mouse.

From inside the shack, Ian waited until Sarge moved on with those bear-like deliberate brisk steps. Ian sighed.

If he hadn't met Little Mouse, if he hadn't sat in that card game, if he hadn't pawned that Zippo . . .

Good thing Sarge didn't use his Zippo. Good thing Little Mouse didn't see it.

Talk about snakes and mosquitoes and leeches. Monsoon rain and heat. Mama, the Nam sun is deadly. I've got freckles like Rice Krispies on my face and my arms and we all get darker, the whites, the Hispanics, only the blacks stay where they are.

Outside the Quonset infirmary hut we stand in the early morning heat—Sergeant Sunukkuhkau and I—each with a yellow malaria pill. I never liked medicine, and I'm fixed to swallow these bitter pills once a day, so I won't sweat and shake like so many of us around here. Sergeant Sunu lights a cigarette and drops the yellow pill into his Blue Diamond matchbox and closes it.

"What'd you do that for?" I look at his brown face, pockmarked like orange peel.

"Saving 'em, Lieutenant."

"That's news."

"I'm like the Chinamen. They don't get malaria."

"I didn't know that."

"They boil their water, add tea to it, they never forget soaking their feet and scraping their tongues with a wooden stick before they go to bed."

"What has all that to do with malaria? And who told you this?"

"My grandpa. Said in Sacramento back in the old days the mosquitoes would swarm you in droves at night up and down the San Joaquin River. Terrible malaria in those days. Ranchers just leased their land to the Chinamen and went off to live someplace else."

"You bathe your feet at night?"

Sarge shakes his head.

"Don't tell me you drink tea in boiled water."

He flicks his eyes at me. "Tea means whiskey, Lieutenant?"

He has the eyes of a snake: dull, beady, unblinking. I never look long enough into those coal-black eyes to see if his pupils are vertical.

"You take those malaria pills long enough," he says, wrinkling his hawk nose, "your dick will hang like a rice noodle when you call on it. I scrape my tongue every night."

"With what?"

"A stainless-steel tongue scraper." He turns his head toward me, his eyes not moving. "Something won't change, once it becomes a habit. White men sleep with blankies covering their feet and their heads out. I sleep with my head covered. All the time."

"All Indians do that?"

"Full-blooded Indians like me."

Sarge is half Algonquin, half Sioux. This is his second tour of duty.

"My grandma never let any white men come near her with a camera," he says. "Except once. She was in town with her baby and this white man came out of nowhere and took a picture of her and her papoose. Soon after that the baby died. Grandpa went to town looking for that man to kill him."

"Did he?"

"Did not. If it was me, I'd track that sonofabitch wherever he goes and slit his throat."

"Just because he took a picture?"

"White men know full well not to do that. They can do harm to our souls if they get hold of our pictures. That's our belief. But our beliefs mean jack to them."

Trucks are bringing in the Viet laborers. Truckloads of them. It's barely past seven in the morning and the heat is rising quickly. Beyond the hundred-yard-wide defense perimeter around the base, the trucks unload them on the red-dirt field. They are small as children. The trucks pick them up in the U Minh forest's buffer zone where they live, some living deep in the forest, and the trucks will bring them back late in the afternoon. Before they leave they'll visit our garbage dump. They ransack it to find things they can bring home. Cardboard boxes, beer cans they flatten to build huts. Food cans they treat like gems.

Sarge slaps his python-sized biceps and flicks off a squashed mosquito. On his upper arm is the red-devil tattoo. He points with his cigarette pinched between his fingers. "Bet you a cigarette, Lieutenant, one out of ten gooks is a Charlie."

"I don't doubt that."

"You have any feel for them, Lieutenant?"

"Them whom? The Viets or Charlie?"

"You're telling me they're different?"

"They're people. Like us."

"Jesus H. Christ! I don't consider them Viets people when I say people."

We know that. They are either gooks or commies. That's how most of us see them, Mama. And we want to think that way so if we have to shoot them, we're not shooting human beings. But there were times I couldn't help sympathizing with those garbage pickers.

Now the soldiers give them axes, machetes, spades, and hoes and take them in groups to work the field. Sarge squints his beady eyes. "There must be plenty of commies in that bunch. Getting paid to spy on us."

"How'd you figure that?"

"Must be figuring how to cut through 'em rolls of barbed wire—after the last time."

From where we stand I can see the barbed wire catching the morning sun with steel-white glints. The last time—also the first time—five weeks ago, our base came under attack by the Viet Cong 306th Battalion. They hit us before midnight with 122-mm rockets while their sappers crawled their way through coils of concertina wire. Explosions shattered every light bulb in our shacks and the whines of rockets had us praying to Jesus Christ to make them go away. The attack stopped shortly after midnight. During the night I could hear the rats and the wild hogs jerking and tearing the flesh of bodies that got hung up on the razor wire. I could hear the hogs grunt, the rats squeak, and the wire shake.

Three days later Alpha Company trucks through the red-dirt countryside. We are moving on the heels of Dog Company into the U Minh forest.

In the swirling dust appears a man standing on the roadside. Up close I see his face. The old geezer must have caught sight of our convoy and came out of his hut, and now stands on the edge of the dirt road in his ragged army coat. It must be an old French army coat. In his hand he holds a French tricolor flag and keeps waving at us like he was a road construction crew member. Or maybe he thinks we are French, coming back after all these years. Like those Japanese soldiers who remained in the Burmese jungle long after World War II had ended. Down here in IV Corps, Mama, we don't see many traces of the French colonization.

The colonel said up on the highlands in II Corps, you see a whole lot of rubber and tea plantations and those white colonial mansions lived in by rich French citizens. He said the French capitalists pay both sides—meaning the Viet Cong and the Saigon government—big money to stay out of their plantations. He said they even charge the US government for each tea bush or rubber tree that we ruin during our operations. He said he saw the French dames walking naked around the swimming pool in those mansions when he was riding down the road in his Jeep. Here we haven't seen anything like that. I mean, women, Mama. Each day back home is a month long in Nam, they say.

It has rained every day for three days now and the forest shivers with winds and rain. Rain patters on the dense canopy of tree crowns, rain drips from tangles of boughs in a baseless cadence. Everywhere we turn we hear the tattoo of rain on the leaves. The peat swamp is mushy underfoot and it's wet and damp and the dampness crawls into your skin and brings out mosquitoes from the inky-black harbors of tangled fern and leeches crawling down the snakelike climbers. We button our shirt cuffs and collars at night and in the shivering dampness we sleep. Sometimes in the night we hear a scream that pierces the sound of rain. Someone in his sleep must have had a leech crawl into his ear.

On the evening of the fourth day, Dog radios us while gunfire roars in the background. "We need reinforcement, fast." We slosh through the pouring rain for a long time until we hear Spooky overhead. Suddenly the sky glows a hazy yellow, and the yellow illumination lights up the rain-glistening leaves long enough that we can see raindrops on them and on our faces. When the flares dim, a long shadow drags across the forest floor and now we smell the rain-wet gunpowder. Someone stumbles ahead of the column. "Oh,

Jesus!" There is a commotion. The sky glows again, like a yellow shawl trembling in the wind. "Motherfucker! Hey, Sarge! There's dead gooks all over the place!" Then Sergeant Sunu's shrill voice: "Shuddup! They're Dog men."

Mama, after all these years, with the war now long over, I can still smell the odor of the dead. I can still smell the stinging whiff of a crushed leaf, its green goo I daubed on my nostrils. I can still smell the leaf's odor on my fingertips. The stench of the dead doesn't go away.

That one time, when the dinks took our Alpha Company and Dog Company by surprise with the sheer size of their regiment, after the dust had settled, there were no more than three dozen of us left. Night came. We could hear our artillery coming over the forest and the trees snap each time a shell exploded. We could hear our jets hunting for targets above the impenetrable tree canopies and hear the sounds of rockets and bombs and the bright fire they lit up in the bowels of the forest. All night long the flare ship droned above us, dropping flares until it ran dry just before dawn, and then we heard a sound like a train bearing down on us and two jets came over the top.

Mama, I can still see the errant jet that came roaring over us. The canisters fell tumbling above us, these cigar-shaped olive-colored cylinders. They hit our foxholes. I turned my head just as a blinding light fell on my eyelids. The earth heaved with an explosion that tore my eardrums. I went deaf in both ears. Just plain deaf. Until I finally heard some-one scream, *Call it off! Call it off!* The grasses curled up. The air blistered and crackled and then there was no more air and I gasped and the men in the foxholes danced in the liquid fire like flaming marionettes. Then came screams that could pierce ten thousand miles of black smoke. My throat and tongue were sand-dry. We ran. Carrying the burned bodies with us. The man I helped carry by the feet had lost all his clothes and was burned through his flesh. He had no hair on his head. He died while we carried him, for he had breathed the fire into his lungs. When we laid him down, his boots came apart and with them the flesh.

When morning came it brought the early summer heat, and if you came upon us at that time, Mama, you wouldn't have recognized us for the mud that covered us. Midday when the dinks had pulled out, we began looking for our dead. It was like walking on the ground of a butcher shop. Blood and mud had the same color. There were people, or what looked like them, hung dangling on the tree branches. The work of the errant napalm bombs. I found a man from our company. He was sitting against a tree. He looked like he had just crawled up through a mine shaft, a burning one. His clothes had fallen off like crumbs, his skin blackened except for the unsightly burns, red and raw-looking. Centipedes and black ants crawled freely on his arms and legs. He wasn't dead, Mama. "I can't see too well," he said. And that was all he said when I gave him a cigarette. He didn't know he had gone blind.

Later they sent in two Chinooks, and we hauled in first the whole bodies, then the parts in rubber ponchos. In silence we hauled the dead until our hands were red and slick and our fatigues were so darkened with sweat and blood they had the color of plum. When we could no longer pile the bodies from floor to ceiling, we saw blood leaking through the hinges. The choppers lifted. The wind ripped through the open doors and then came a steady splat of rain on the windshields, but it wasn't rain and soon I saw the inside of windshields turn red.

Of our platoon, counting me and Sergeant Sunu, we were eleven men total. They'd captured a Viet Cong. They were holding him, squatting before a tree stump, shorn white and split like someone had tried to wedge it. Toppled trees crisscrossed the charred ground, their roots entwined like a mound of knotted snakes. The heat swelled with a stench of rot.

The prisoner was bareheaded. His head, flat in the back like a catfish, drew your eyes to his profuse wiry black hair, which came down on his low brow in a sharp wedge. He looked to be in his forties, but it was difficult to tell how old the Viets actually are. I stopped a few feet from him. I think something in his stare made me do that. He raised his face up to me and grinned. He had sharp cheekbones, a swarthy complexion, deep grooves around his mouth, skin as dark as Sergeant Sunu's. His hands were not tied behind his back. One hand was missing. The stump's end at the wrist was rounded. They rested on his knees. You could see a cross-stitched scar, like two embedded pieces of thread. I dropped my gaze. His ankles were tied with a string. Red ants darted around his bare feet. He sat stock-still, looking at me with the grin on his face. I stared down into his eyes. The sun was full in his face, yet he didn't squint. Just sat grinning. Stained teeth, chapped lips. Not a mindless grin. I felt irked. His white shirt, opened at the neck, was yellowed with dust. My armpits felt damp. There were no sweat stains on his shirt. We locked eyes until I felt sweat drip down the side of my face. I wiped it and jabbed my rifle at his chest.

"Quit grinning, you moron," I said.

His wide grin changed something in me. I felt wounded. The hollow inside turned to hatred. I leveled my rifle at his face.

"Quit that grin!"

He didn't blink. He grinned into the rifle's muzzle, his eyes fixed on me. He knew we didn't shoot prisoners. I kicked him with the heel of my boot full in his chest. He fell backward against the tree stump. Quickly he pushed himself back up on his haunches. He looked down between his knees, watching the ants zigzag on his feet, red ants and now winged ants. Slowly he raised his face to me and grinned.

"Where's Sarge?" I called out to the men lounging under the shades of cajeput trees, those still standing.

"He's off somewhere taking a crap."

"Hey, here he comes, Lieutenant."

I turned. Sarge already stood at my elbow. He was naked to his waist and his brown skin from his face to his chest glistened with sweat. "You talk to him yet, Lieutenant?" Sarge asked with a cigarette dangling between his lips.

"How?" I glared at him. "You gonna teach me some Vietnamese?"

"*Chao eng mon joy*," Sarge said to the prisoner, bending slightly to get the words across.

The prisoner's eyes narrowed at Sarge. Instantly I felt that he was human. Those words, whatever they were, must have triggered some familiar feeling in him.

"Are you proposing to him?" I asked.

"Means how are you, brother." Sarge shook his head. "That's about all I've learned from 'em Viets."

"From?"

"A Viet kid. He's got red hair and blue eyes. I kid you not, Lieutenant. He was walking this little mouse on a string outside one of 'em shacks you see from our base. Where Viet hookers do their business."

I glanced back at the prisoner. He was watching us, his face grimy, his lips curling up at the corner. Something wry, something smug about that grin.

"What's with the grinning, Sarge?"

"We'll find out. He got Mikey good, right in the chest."

"Mike Nale?" I sized up the prisoner. "With one hand?"

"I speculate that much, Lieutenant. Must've set his ay-kay fifty on his stumpy arm."

"He looks wily enough. Wonder how he lost his hand."

"Must be from the other war. Look at him. He's no teen."

"You mean the Indochina War?"

"That. Or maybe stole something from the Legionnaires and they chopped his hand off." Sarge spat into the dirt. "He's no amateur, Lieutenant. They've got guys like him who've seen just about everything from the wars and we've got cherries like Mikey. We've got guys who're about to get a good grip on how to fight Charlie and guess what? They go home. After one year. Then you've got Fucking New Guys coming in shitting their pants in the bush. Aw Christ, fucking newbies get homesick."

The prisoner had that smug grin. Does he understand us?

Sarge fixed his beady, unblinking stare on the prisoner. "You think it's funny?" Sarge asked him, taking the cigarette out of his mouth. The prisoner eyed the tattoo on Sarge's biceps. His grin got wider. "Let's see wat-you-got," said Sarge, yanking down the prisoner's shirt. Buttons flew. Sarge examined the man's arms, left then right. "You ain't one o'em, eh?"

"What're you doing?"

"He ain't got no tattoos like those young commies. All of them have the same tattoo on their arms. *Born North Die South.* You know what I mean, Lieutenant."

"No, I don't."

"Like I told you, Lieutenant, he's the fox of all the foxes. He don't need no tattoos. Probably speaks French and English. Make us look like fools."

The prisoner pulled up his shirt with one hand. He looked composed. Winged ants and fire ants ran wildly across his legs as if they smelled something palatable. Sarge stepped back, and the prisoner's gaze followed him, studying Sarge's little red devil. He flashed his grin, the same devil grin on Sarge's arm.

"You sure wanna play with my nerves," said Sarge.

"He just plays dumb," I said.

"Will you excuse us, Lieutenant." Sarge turned to me, his nose twitching. "Lemme have a moment with him."

"All right."

I stepped back and the prisoner peered up at me. He squinted, the way a hunter sights game in the crosshairs.

Something gnawed at me while I gathered information from the radio man. I sipped from my canteen, standing in the sun, while the survivors of the carnage lay in the grass, helmets over their faces, boots pointing skyward. Most of them had battle dressings on the arms, the legs. One man, lying with his head on a trunk of a felled cajeput, was wrapped with a dressing around his stomach. The tail of the dressing's olive drab dangled on his side and I could see his intestine bulging out in gray. I turned and walked back to our area.

Sarge came around a toppled tree lying crosswise on the ground. A cigarette, unlit, hung loosely between his lips. He saw me and walked past. There was blood on his lips.

"What happened to you?"

"Lieutenant?" he asked, his lips barely moving.

"You cut yourself?" I pointed at my lips.

His touched his cigarette, one bloodstained finger on the lower lip. "Ain't cut myself. I need water. Guys from Dog have some."

He hurried off. The strange look on his face made me turn and follow him with my gaze. Had he scuffled with the prisoner? Our area was baking in the sun. The shade had shrunk. On the dirt lay the prisoner. He lay flat on his back, his legs splayed at the knees, ankles still tied. His good arm rested against the tree stump, the amputated arm on his stomach, bare, bloody, his shirt ripped on the front and soaked through with blood. The stumped arm rested on a gaping cut below the diaphragm. Wide enough to slip in your fingers.

I looked down at him. The prisoner glared. His eyes were open still. His mouth was open too. Like screaming a silent scream when someone plucked out your liver and ate it. Or maybe he was trying to grin one last time.

1987
Le Giang

"Let me take your mother around the town," I say to Chi Lan. "You can go off with your camera. We'll meet back at the car."

"I'll be back here, *Chú*," Chi Lan says.

Mrs. Rossi couldn't go to the forest this morning because Ông Ba's boat had a problem with its Kohler motor. He said it'd be repaired today.

Barges clutter the waterway and fishing nets throw silhouettes across the fiery water. Her head tilted back, Mrs. Rossi breathes in the metallic tang of fish, the wetly sweet smell of rot timbers and waterlogged wooden stilts. Overhead crows circle, cawing noisily. Some come down flapping their wings in front of the slaughterhouse that sits back from the street. The birds waddle, preening themselves, waiting for throwaways of guts that butchers toss out.

Mrs. Rossi's face radiates with a liveliness. The Main Street clangs with noises and sounds. Little shops of Chinese and Indians sit among local stores. She watches porters, gaunt and barefooted, bent under bales of garments. Men, half naked, oxblood skin perspiring, are pulling

two-wheeled carts on their cranelike legs. On a corner of the
street, grimy children are blowing soap bubbles, laughing.

The street is narrow and jammed with huge baskets
sitting on wooden trestles. Women vendors gawk at Mrs.
Rossi, talking among themselves after we walk past. An
American middle-aged man, wearing an olive visor cap,
nods at her. "Hello there," he says. "Hello," she greets him.

We pass a woman vendor who stands behind a trestle,
under the straw canopy propped by a spindly stick. Slabs
of brown sugar are piled up in the baskets. I stop and Mrs.
Rossi turns toward me. "You like brown sugar, Giang?"

I explain to her that the locals sell no refined sugar; the
white sugar they sell has small crystals and looks like coarse
white sand.

I point at a slab and tell the woman I want to taste it.
She chips a piece off the slab with a short-handled knife
and hands it to me. Mrs. Rossi watches me lick the mud-col-
ored chunk. Amused, she shakes her head, perhaps at my
unusual taste. I pay for three slabs and the woman wraps
them up in a sheet of coarse paper.

We pass stalls selling delicacies and confections. Mrs.
Rossi lingers. She had some fruits this morning before we
left the inn. Maybe she should eat something. Now the
sights of confections, stacked up against the loam-packed
wall of a hut, tempt her. A little girl comes out of nowhere
carrying a child astride her hip. The child's nose is smeared
with snot, her dark velvety eyes rheumy. They gaze at Mrs.
Rossi whose face is shadowed by a wide-brimmed straw
hat. Then their gaze drops at the assortment of preserved
fruits on wooden trays: tangerines, plums, dates, tamarinds.

Mrs. Rossi says to the girl, "What do you like?" and the
girl looks up at her, surprised, and puts her finger between
her lips. I tell her what Mrs. Rossi said. The girl points at a
tray lined with round barley caramel, each sandwiched by
round rice papers the size of a fig.

"I see," Mrs. Rossi says and then to the confectioner, "five, please."

After my translation, Mrs. Rossi pays. She watches the girl take the parcel and hold it as if it wasn't hers.

"Eat," Mrs. Rossi says, pinching an imaginary confection and putting it into her mouth. The confectioner grins as we watch the girl open the paper, pick one candy, and let the child lick it.

As we leave, I bring my bag of brown sugar to my nose and inhale deeply. Mrs. Rossi chuckles. "Giang, please get yourself something. You haven't eaten anything since we left the inn."

"Ma'am, what about you? Is there anything here that you like?"

She looks at my bag. Then she smiles. "Maybe I can share a piece of brown sugar with you."

"Do you mean that?"

"My stomach is growling."

I open my bag and crack a piece of brown sugar with my hand. I offer her the piece, watching her sample it. I know it has a peculiar smell, like burnt brick with a dark honey odor. She says that her stomach now has calmed down.

Sunlight has become harsh and shadows gradually disappear on the street and across the water. When we go back up the street, a crowd of people is gathering on the sidewalk. People turn their heads to gaze at the two of us and then step back to give us a view.

Mrs. Rossi looks down at the American man lying on his back, his face beet-red, the olive visor cap sitting cock-eyed on top of his head.

"He ain't dead," a woman says, and someone repeats, "No, he ain't dead, just drunk out of his skull."

I look around for his bottle. "Drunk?"

A woman spits red saliva of betel chew and wipes her swollen lips with the back of her hand. "Drank *chum-chum* over there. I saw him. Came out here talking to himself . . . looked like a madman." Her gaze lingers on the man lying still at her feet, drooling like a baby.

"He'll die," Mrs. Rossi says. "Call the authorities."

"Ma'am," I say, "he'll be all right. These fools ruin themselves because they've heard of this chum-chum's notoriety. It could pass for poison, this rice liquor the locals brew. All sorts of impurities are let through during distillation. But cheap."

Mrs. Rossi takes one last look at the man, his mouth still foaming. As we walk away toward the pier, she turns to me. "I guess these men don't have families here."

"Yes, ma'am. It adds up when you're alone."

Mrs. Rossi seems to know that feeling—alone in a strange place away from home.

Mrs. Rossi, after having looked at my drawings, asked me earlier this evening as we sat on the veranda if I had only one story to tell, what would that be? Before I could gather my thoughts, she said it was always the sound of acorns falling on the roof that took her back to the night when she heard the news of her son. In Nicola's old room she turned on the desk lamp and sat down in the chair. On the wall above the desk was a Christmas card Nicola had drawn when he was eight. Two figures, one taller than the other, wearing black top hats and holding hands at the foot of a hill. The scene of green pines dotted with white flakes framed his handwriting:

> Dear Mama and Papa
> Merry Christmas and Happy New Year!
> Nicola

Other than the card, the walls were bare. The desk, too, was bare, except for a rectangular tin box in one corner. It could have been a box of chocolates stripped of its wrapping. She opened it. Inside were stamps of different shapes and sizes arranged neatly in cotton padded layers. His boyhood collection. She looked for one from Vietnam but found none. She turned off the light, went to the window, and sat looking out. Raindrops veined the glass, clinging with a tenacious viscosity that defied wind. The street was dark. A single streetlamp cast a shining white glow in the night. As she looked at the solitary light she thought of a children's story she told Nicola when he was a child. The story of a boy who lived in a house on a hilltop. One snowy night his mother became very sick, so his father had to go to town to fetch a doctor. Outside snow fell so thick it looked like white rain. The boy lit a lamp and left it at the window where he knelt and prayed. *Have faith in angels and they will come to your aid.* That was what the storybook said to do when a child needed help. His father returned through the storm, bringing with him the town doctor. The doctor gave the mother injections and then he came to the boy and patted him on the head. The doctor told him that the road was impassable. They had to leave the car and walk. The blinding snow caused them to drift in the dark until they saw the light on the hill. Without the light, they wouldn't have come in time to save his mother.

Mrs. Rossi said that night she gazed at the white streetlight until her eyes teared. Nobody came back.

I told Mrs. Rossi that the bright yellow of false jasmine always gave me pause. She said, "Why?" "Because," I said, "it has to do with the one story if I had only one to tell."

There was a man who lived in my district and this man had gone South to fight the Americans and when he came back a year and a half later he had no arms, no legs, and he was blind.

I called him Uncle, like we youngsters would address our seniors. Uncle Chung was thirty-one when he returned home. A blind war veteran. I was eighteen and about to be drafted to join those destined for the South. When I saw Uncle Chung for the first time I knew why many boys my age grew alarmed at being drafted into the army. Uncle Chung used to work as a machinist. He was once a big man but now limbless. His image came back to me years later in the South when I saw a freak, a country boy burned by napalm, so far gone he looked like a glowworm at night, and his father would charge each neighborhood kid ten xu to come into the house to look at him, a mutant.

I saw Uncle Chung on a day Huan's father, the herbalist, sent me over to the man's house with the medicine. The medicine. Always the medicine. And the wife. Each time Uncle Chung's wife came to the shop to consult with the herbalist, I would hang back, so I could listen to her melodious voice and steal glances at her while trying to look busy in the shop. She was in her mid-twenties, but she looked older, the way she rolled her hair up and tucked it into a bun, so when she turned her head you could see the long nape of her neck. She always wore a white or pale blue blouse. Just white or pale blue. And always the first customer when the shop opened. The early morning light would cast a pallor on her face, and her ink-black eyebrows only made her face seem paler. Yet despite the white of the undernourished, the unwell look, she was beautiful. The city was full of women her age and older. Now and then you saw men—many had gone South and most of them never returned.

One rainy morning I went to their house with the medicine. Down an alley through the standing water, floating with trash, to a stucco-yellow matchbox dwelling in a housing project. Its green door was left ajar. Stepping in, I heard a man singing:

> *If I were a dove*
> *I'd be a snow-white dove.*
> *Spring and then summer.*
> *The flowers, the flowers, the flowers.*
> *You say aren't they pretty*
> *And I say*
> *Aren't they really.*

I looked down at the man sitting on the pallet. The gruff voice stopped, the man turned his face toward the door. His skin, his eyeballs were yellow, the mucus yellow. I couldn't tell if he was blind, but his eyes had the look of fake eyes you put in stuffed animals. His song about the pretty flowers struck me. What could he see now but his own memories? He kept nodding—I wasn't sure if he had any control of it—and he had a large head matted with tousled black hair that covered his ears and the collar of his shirt. The old olive-colored army shirt, with its long sleeves cut off, revealed the stumpy ends of his severed arms. You could see the rotten-wood brown of the flesh—what was left of his upper arms.

I told him I brought him the medicine and as I spoke I looked at his full wiry beard. If his wife refused to shave it for him, I thought, it would one day hang down past his neck. He must have been a big man; aside from his large head, the only part left of him, his torso, filled out his army shirt. His chest was as thick as a boar. He wiggled on his rump. "Make me a pipe," he said as if he knew me, or I were someone he used to boss around.

I stood eyeing him, a squat hunk of meat sitting on two slabs of flesh. What looked like his shorts were a pair of army trousers shorn at the knees.

"Don't stand there!" he snapped at me, his voice viscous, as if spoken through a mouthful of glutinous rice.

"I brought your medicine, Uncle," I said and bent to put the herb packet next to a water pipe that sat before him. It was a long bamboo pipe. Near the bowl the yellow had become stained with black smoke. The pipe stood on an angle, harnessed by a wide bamboo strip that went around the pipe's trunk and came down to rest on the ground like a mortar tube on its bipod.

"Make the pipe," he said. "Then you can go."

I just shook my head.

"Don't you know how to light a pipe? Boy?"

"I do, Uncle."

"Then light my damned pipe. And get out!"

Light your own pipe! But I stopped short of ridiculing him. I didn't pity him. At first sight, he struck me as freakish. An overbearing freak. Then I thought I'd better set the tone for myself.

"You'll see a lot of me, Uncle," I said to him politely, "as long as you need Chinese medicine. And I don't take orders. Not from strangers."

"You a prince?" His voice twanged. "Some sort of a pampered shit?"

"If I were, Uncle, I wouldn't be here bringing you this medicine."

"Did your Pa teach you manners? Or is he too busy making drugs?"

"My Ma and Pa died a long time ago."

"So you're an orphan. No wonder."

"I can behave, Uncle."

My calm voice had him lost for a moment. He rotated his jaw, then asked, "How old are you?"

"Eighteen, Uncle."

"You be joining the army soon, eh?"

"Right. The way things are."

"You know what I did for a living before the war?"

"What did you do, Uncle?"

"I was a foreman in a machine shop."

I pictured lathes and mills. Those shops must be busy during wartime. Hearing nothing from me, he leaned his head to one side as if to determine where I was. "In the army I was a senior sergeant," he said. That fit him, I thought. Some were domineering by nature. He went on, "Used to do all the things myself. My woman didn't need to lift a finger. Now, now, the world's turned upside down. Man has to beg from a woman's hand. When you're down and out, you're worse than a mutt. I can't even piss or shit unless she lets me."

His voice was flat, but I sensed no self-pity. Like he was telling me about the weather. I thought of walking out, but I changed my mind. I could see the pipe's bowl had no tobacco. "Where's your set, Uncle?" I asked.

"Look around," he said tonelessly. "Set shaped like a persimmon."

The bare room had two metal chairs. Under one chair sat a lidded pot. It looked like his toilet pot. The only piece of furniture was a black-wood cupboard. The ornate flowers embossed on the cupboard's doors gave it a vintage feel. It must have belonged to his once-proud past, before the war ruined him.

"Can't find it?" he asked, keeping his head still as if to listen for a sign of my presence. "Used to have things every-where around here. But she's sold most of them. Now you can hear the echo of your voice."

Through a thin flowered curtain that sectioned off the interior of the house, I saw a bamboo cot draped with a mosquito net. The net hadn't been rolled up. I went through the curtain looking around. A gas stove sat against the yellow-painted wall next to a stand-alone narrow cabinet, its black-wood glass doors opaque with smoke and dust. On the wall were hung rattan baskets dyed plum red and peach yellow. A wooden table sat in the center of the room, and on the table I saw the persimmon-shaped caddy painted coal black. The caddy made of fruitwood had a keyhole. I brought it to him. It was locked. I told him.

"Damn woman," he said.

"She keeps the key?"

"Damn, she did."

"She forgot?"

"That woman? Never. Never forgets anything."

"Well, Uncle," I chuckled. "What's with the key anyway? Even if she left it for you, I mean."

"I've got help." He jerked his chin toward the entrance. "Door's always open."

"Your neighbors?"

"Them louts. Sit at the door every day. Gawking and giggling."

"Ah, kids. They help you, Uncle?"

"Some do. Some I have to bribe."

I wondered what he bribed them with. "Where is she now?"

"Out. Business."

I shook the herb packet for him to hear. "What's this medicine for, Uncle?"

"Stabilize the *yin* and *yang* in my body. That's what your Pa, eh, the herbalist said."

"Your *yin* and *yang*?"

"This body," he said, pressing his chin to his chest to make a point, "still has a piece of shrapnel in a lung. The metal junk messes up the balance of *yin* and *yang*. So I heard."

"How's that?"

"I puke blood whenever it gets bone chilly."

"They didn't take it out of your lung?"

"If they could, it wouldn't be in my lung now, eh?"

I ignored his remark and looked around. The slatted side door opened into a common garden. I knelt on one knee, looked at the water pipe, then at him. "You smoke often, Uncle?"

"Often as she lets me." He grinned, then yawned.

I could smell his rancid breath. I tapped the caddy until he cocked his head to listen to the noise. "I can make a pipe for you, Uncle," I said. "But I'd have to pry the lock open."

"I don't give a damn about the lock. But I know what she'll do if the lock is busted."

"What then?"

He nodded again, like he was following his thoughts. "Once I lay here in my piss and shit the whole damn day till she decided to clean me up. Otherwise the house would stink and that'd ruin her dinner."

"What started it?"

"Like I told you. I only piss or shit when she lets me."

"So she wanted to condition you, didn't she?"

"You're wrong, boy." He frowned. "I mean, young man, she was talking business with this man in the alley. Talk. Talk. I yelled to her. Damn did I yell. Then everything burst out of me. When she came back in I doubt she bothered to look at me. Then when the smell couldn't be ignored for heaven's sake, she just left the house."

Listening, I recalled her, that beautiful woman, and couldn't reconcile what I just heard with what I'd carried inside me ever since I first saw her. He wiggled on his rump and the nylon sheet that covered the pallet squished. "If I can have me a drink," he said. "Hell, if I can have me some rice liquor."

"Where does she keep it, Uncle?"

"That woman won't waste money on that kind of stuff." He wrinkled his nose, snorting a few times to clear it. "We'd been drinking, me and some old friends. They brought a bottle with them and after they left I began having chills and shaking like a dog. She came in and saw the mess of cigarette butts and ashes and unwashed cups and started yelling at me. I cursed her, so she sat me up and screamed in my face, and it was then I threw up. I believe I just let it gush out all over her blouse."

"You vomited on her? Why?"

"To spite her? I'm not sure. She emptied the bottle into the drain. That's far worse than hearing her curse me or let me rot on my own."

"I'll get you some liquor the next time, Uncle."

"I have no money. To pay you."

"I know."

"I'd appreciate it, young man. You drink?"

"A little."

"That won't hurt. You going into the army soon. I used to get high while we stayed for months in the jungles. Ever heard of dog roses?"

"They told me. Wild roses that crave blood to bloom?"

"Hogwash." He blew his nose with a loud snort. "But the wild roses have a subdued fragrance, not as strong as garden roses. And their leaves when crushed have a delicious smell. We cut up their fruits too and add them to the tobacco. The rose hips give an added authentic kick when you're high."

His mouth hung open with an amused smile as he stared into space. Those eyes made me think of yellow marbles. Quietly I looked at his limbless torso, the wiry beard that covered half of his face, and a thought hit me: How would I carry on if I became like him? This man seemed to survive the way a creeper did, by latching on to living things nearby. He wanted to live.

I went back to Uncle Chung's house a few days later. This time the herb packet I brought contained finely cut leaves of yellow false jasmine. When Huan's father wrapped them up, I asked him what they were for. "For hemorrhoids," he said. "For external swelling and pain. But never take them orally," he said. "It's fatal." I asked if the wife knew about it and he nodded. "She didn't want the ointment," he said. "She wanted the leaves and the seed pods." Much later when I was fighting in the South, I would occasionally come upon this vine in the jungles. At first glance you could mistake it for honeysuckle. Then I found out that the vine—any part of it from its root to its leaves and flowers and fruits—was also toxic if taken by the mouth. I also learned the words the Americans called it: *heartbreak grass*.

I bought a half liter of rice liquor in a bottle. Uncle Chung was lying on the pallet, sleeping on his side like a big baby. I woke him and helped him sit up. He kept squirming.

"Hemorrhoids bothering you, Uncle?" I asked him.

"Like hangnails," he said. "Just a nuisance. You said you've got the spirits?"

"I bought half a liter."

"Let me smell it."

I opened the bottle and held it under his nose. He leaned forward to have a full whiff of it and nearly toppled. I held him up. He grunted, his face contorted into a painful scowl. The hemorrhoid must be bad enough, I thought.

"You want to lie down, Uncle?"

"What for? Wish I had arms to hug this bottle here. Eh?"

I found a cup and poured him some of the clear-colored spirit and brought the rim of the cup to his lips. He sniffed, then inhaled deeply, his nostrils flaring. Then he thrust his head toward the cup, and said, "Give me." He made a loud sucking sound, lifting his chin in a great effort to imbibe the liquor.

"A smoke, Uncle?"

"Got no key to that caddy." He burped. "You know that."

"I got you cigarettes. Here."

As I lit and puffed on a cigarette for him, he sniffed like a mouse. "You're a prince, young man," he said, and his lips curled up into a wide grin. "If I die tonight, I won't regret a damn bit."

I plugged the cigarette between his lips and let him drag on it. When the ash curled and broke, I caught it in my palm and went to the door and let the rain wash it from my hand.

"We need some sun." I sat back down. "To air things out."

"Rainy day like this, you just want to sit and sip liquor and cuddle up with a pipe. Eh?" He tilted his torso to one side and I could tell that he wanted to ease the pressure on his hemorrhoids.

"This stuff for your hemorrhoids," I said as I jiggled the herb packet, "has it helped?"

"What?" His dead-fish eyes looked blindly at me.

I gave him another shot of rice liquor. Then huffing he said, "Opium might help."

"Opium? You can't afford it, Uncle."

"My woman gets it at the border."

I lit another cigarette and put it between his lips. "You said it helps? Against pain?"

"Kills pain. When I was all busted up by a *mìn cóc*, they gave me opium. Damn. It worked."

"What's a *mìn cóc*?"

He described it. Leaping Frog mine. Gruesome destruction. The kind of mine that jumps up when triggered and explodes two, three feet above the ground. Severs your legs and, worst of all, maims your genitals. Bouncing Betty. That was the name I later learned from the Americans.

I asked him if he lost his limbs from a Bouncing Betty, and he said yes, nodding and snorting. He asked me, "Which would you rather lose: both of your legs or your penis?" I said I would never ask myself such a question, for it was a warped sense of humor that should have no place in a sane mind. He chewed on the cigarette butt leisurely and said, "Soon you'll ask yourself such when you start having fears of losing body parts." I told him I never treated one part of my body more favorably than another. If it happened, I'd live with it. One older guy in the army said the same thing to me, years later when I was in the South, that your body parts are like your children and you don't favor one over another. Now, out of curiosity, I asked if he still had his penis and he laughed, spitting out the cigarette, and the ash scattered on the nylon sheet. I brushed off the ash and waited until he stopped cackling and put the cigarette back between his lips. He shook his head, so I took the cigarette out and he said, chortling, "Still with me, young man. My treasure. So I don't have to pee through a tube. And am still a man. Don't ask me about my woman though. I don't blame her." I mused on his remark as he asked for another sip. Afterward he said there was this thing called "crotch cup," which had gained popularity in the South among men in his unit and others. It started out when this guy custom-made a triangle cup-shaped piece that he cut out of an artillery shell, and through its three sides, he drilled holes to run three twines and looped them around his torso to hold the piece in place against his crotch. He became the butt of every joke told among fellow soldiers. Then when more and more men fell victim to Bouncing Betty mines, many having been cut below the waist, their genitals pulverized, blown and stuck to their faces in pieces of skin and hair, they grew so paranoid they started finding ways to protect their manhood—and their lineage. The crotch cup became their holy answer. I tried to absorb the horror of the war, twinged with the knowledge that I, too, would soon be a part of that reality. Then, snickering, he said some fellows in his unit at one point decided to take a break from wearing the crotch cups, and the next thing, they hit Bouncing Betty mines. What he never could forget were the crotch pieces of the army trousers all shredded and glued to fragments of white bones, unrecognizable lumps of the genitals found on the ground, some still with skin, some with hair. Without sight now, he said, he imagined those scenes day and night. I listened and decided to take a sip of liquor. I wasn't afraid, but the gloomy picture he painted affected my mood.

I hadn't visited Uncle Chung for more than a month and I hadn't seen his wife coming to the herbal store for prescriptions. One late morning when the weather cleared up, I went to his house. The door was closed but not locked. Inside the house, dim and cool, there was a moistness in the air. It was tinged with a fermented sourness of liquor that had been spilled. On the pallet scattered with clumps of cooked rice, Uncle Chung was lying facedown, the seat of his cutoffs damp-looking. Just as I sat down on my heels, his voice came up, "That you, young man?"

"You awake, Uncle?"

"No. I never sleep," he said with a deep-throated chuckle. "Just airing out my rump."

"Wet your shorts?" I peered through the curtain. "Where is she?"

"Be back in the afternoon. She closed the door, didn't she? Should have left it open for fresh air."

"It smells in here, Uncle. Want me to open it?"

"Well, don't chance it. She closed it for a reason."

"What?"

"Bunch of those kids were coming here this morning. Some were new, I could tell. So she yelled at them, 'You want to peep at him? Do you? How about pay him? That's right. Pay him and I'll let you ogle at him, pet him. Long as you like.' They just broke off and ran."

I eyed the stain on his buttocks. "She meant it, didn't she?"

"It came out of her mouth. So."

I thought of her. The pretty face. The pleasant voice. "Want to sit up, Uncle?"

He twisted his head toward my side. "My back. Can you scratch it?"

I pushed up his army shirt, paused, and brushed off pellets of rice stuck to his back. A warm, sweaty smell rose from his body, and for one brief moment I stared at his back, its bare flesh speckled with black moles like someone had sprinkled raisins on it. His voice drifted sleepily, "She kept telling me . . . those black moles I was born with were flies . . . flies . . . crushed into my skin."

As I scratched him, he squirmed. His stomach groaned. I wondered if he had eaten since the night before. "Get a towel in there . . ." he said. "Check the kettle. Might have some hot water in it. That'll take the itch away."

I found a dish towel hung between the rattan baskets. I reheated the water in the kettle and wet the towel and wrung

it as steam wafted up. I saw a bowl with some cooked rice
left in it, sitting on the table. A few cubes of fermented tofu
lay on top of the rice. Next to the bowl was a glass with
some water. But it wasn't water when I sniffed it. Liquor. I
took the bowl and the glass with me and came back out. The
hot towel seemed to help him feel better against the itch. I
scrubbed his back until it turned raw red.

"That damn monkey meat," he slurred.

"What monkey meat?"

"She brought back some monkey meat yesterday. I ate
some."

He tried to turn onto his back. With my help he rolled
over. His left cheek had a cut and several scratches. Red,
raw, they looked fresh. Since I last saw him he had lost much
weight. I could tell from the hollowness in his cheeks and
from the slackness given by his shirt. "Let me sit you up,"
I said. An ammoniac smell hung about his face. I winced.
"Your face, Uncle," I said, "smells of piss." His nostrils
twitched. "Yeah. From my head to my butt, eh?" His beard,
longer now, felt like a woolly wad when I wiped his face.
"Woman's piss," he said and shook his head.

"What?"

"She pissed on me." He grinned as if amused. I felt dis-
gusted. "I had a seizure last night. That came after I ate that
monkey meat. Good thing I didn't die. I woke up and she
was sitting on my face and watered me with her holy water.
For heaven's sake I felt cold sober after that."

I told him perhaps her quick thinking might have bailed
him out of danger. He nodded. For the first time I noticed in
his jet-black hair the gray hair had started showing through
here and there. I could hear his stomach growl again. "I
brought you leftovers—rice and liquor," I said. He asked
me to dump the leftover liquor into the rice. Obliging him,
I stirred the concoction, a tart smell of stale liquor and tofu.
I spoon-fed him. He slurped and swallowed. He didn't even

chew. I asked him how he could eat anything like this, and he spat out some rice and said, "There comes a time when you'd eat anything given you. In the South once we had no salt for weeks so we ate ash. Not a bad substitute." He hiccuped. "Be adaptable, young man."

"Where'd she get the monkey meat from?" I asked him.

"From a baby monkey, fallen off a tree and drowned in a flood. Well, she and this guy were up across the Viet-Sino border on opium runs. They got caught in a flood and had to eat bamboo rats."

I recalled the man he mentioned coming to the alley and talking with her. "What if she gets caught by the border police?"

"I'd know when that day comes."

He told me she gave him the black pellets of opium whenever he had a bout of pain—the hemorrhoids, the lungs. The pain would go away. Since then the seizures had come more than once. If she was home, she would give him liquor and that seemed to blunt the fit and, sometimes with much liquor, he would fall asleep.

"I cursed her for giving me the monkey meat," he said. "She yelled at me, 'You're a dunghill. A dunghill for me to risk my life just to earn some cash to keep all your perverted sicknesses at bay.' That woman has a sharp tongue. But she spoke the truth. Said, 'Who's going to make all your pains disappear? Doctors? Your crummy pension? That? That goes out the window in no time just to pay the helpers to clean up your filth and buy you liquor so your opium fits won't kill you. Monkey meat, *hanh*? Last time you crashed, was it monkey meat? Or was it opium? I'm an expert now on how to kill your obscene pains when you convulse on the floor like a leech, your eyeballs roll into your head, your mouth foams like baking soda. And next time when you bang your head, find a sharp corner. *Hanh*?'"

It dawned on me about his facial cuts. "You banged your head? During a seizure?"

"Broke her cactus pot and got their spines all over my face."

As I put the empty bowl away, the fermented sourness made my nose twitch. He cleared his throat, his sticky voice becoming raspy as he told me he had done his part around the house, and yet she never appreciated it. When it did not rain for days, he twice managed to crawl out to her vegetable patch and urinate among the spinach, the purslane, the fish mint. He could tell by their smells. And she could tell what he had done sometimes by the sight of the cigarette butts lying among the patch. The fish mint leaves would smell repugnant when she chewed them, then she would spit them out and daub the paste on his forehead. He would curse, shake, to get rid of the slimy gob and she would say, "You get what's coming to you. It smells like your piss, doesn't it?" She loved her garden patch. Nights when it rained, the air moist and cool, he could hear raindrops pinging on the cement steps and the moistness in the air seeped through his skin. He liked the rain, for he knew rain would soak the soil in the vegetable patches. At first light the soup mint's downy hair would spark red, the crab's claw herb would glisten, the thyme, the basil would be gorged with moisture. He could tell that one of her pet plants, the yellow jasmine vine, was coming out in clusters. She'd watered it every morning from the time she brought home the seeds, allowing the pods to dry first before breaking them open, and nursed the seeds with much watering until one morning he could smell something fragrant and that was the first time it flowered. He might hear her cheerful voice, for a change, when she plucked them at dawn.

I didn't visit Uncle Chung until one morning I saw his wife coming into the herbal store. She was wearing a white blouse and a red scarf around her neck, and the red was redder than hibiscus. She asked for a cough prescription. Huan's father asked if Uncle Chung was having a cold or flu and if he had a whooping cough. She smiled, said it was for a sore throat. I could hear someone coughing outside the store. A man was smoking a cigarette, standing on the sidewalk with his hands in his pants pockets. Lean, dark-skinned, he was about Uncle Chung's age. His slicked-back hair was shiny with pomade. He glanced toward the store, coughed, and spat. When she met his gaze, she smiled. She had that fresh smile that showed her white glistening teeth.

I thought of that smile when I went to see Uncle Chung afterward. He wasn't on the pallet. Seeing him sitting or lying on that pallet had become a fixture in my mind. So his absence gave me pause. I went through the curtain and saw him crawling like a caterpillar toward a corner of the room where the bathing quarter stood behind accordion panels. He bumped a chair, stopped, wiggling his head as if to get his bearings. I called out to him.

"Young man?" He cocked his head back, his hair so long now it looked like a black mane.

"Why are you in here?" I went to him.

"Water."

"Where?"

"Where she bathes."

There were no pails, not even a cup, in there. Her black pantaloons were the only item hanging on a string from wall to wall. I could see water still dripping from the pantaloons' legs. Before I said anything to him, he gave a dry chuckle. "That's my water." I pictured him worming his way to where he could catch the dripping water with his mouth.

It took a while before I could move him back out onto his pallet. Though he said he hated water, he drank some from the kettle, which I poured directly into his mouth. He asked for a cigarette. I told him I was out of cigarettes and promised him when I got money I'd buy him a pack and some liquor. I brought the black caddy to the pallet.

"I'll make you a pipe, Uncle," I said, tapping the caddy.

"It's locked. You know it."

"I'm going to break the lock." I thought of the way she'd smiled at the man, feeling resentment.

"Go ahead." He grinned.

Surprised by his encouragement, I twisted the blade of my pocketknife inside the keyhole until I felt the lock snap. "I saw her at the store," I told him casually, folding the pocketknife.

"She breezed out of here this morning and I swear I could smell perfume." He tried to clear his throat, for his voice suddenly sounded strained. "Make the pipe. I need it."

Inside the caddy a jackfruit leaf lay on top of the tobacco. The leaf was no longer fresh, the blade having gone a dark yellow. He listened to my movements and mumbled something about the leaf left in there to keep the tobacco fresh. Without it, when you smoke, he said, the tobacco lacking moisture would burn dry in the throat. He asked me what she was wearing. I told him. Then remembering her red scarf I told him that too. "Damn," he said. He brought his lips to the pipe, paused, and said, "I remember her wearing that scarf, that red scarf, only once in her life. On the day we got married." He took a heavy drag, the water in the pipe singing merrily, and then he tipped up his face and blew a cloud of smoke toward the ceiling. "Wish I had eyes to see that scarf on her this morning. Damn it. Was she with somebody?" I told him she was, adding that he must be her business partner. Uncle Chung grunted with a twisted grin. I could sense his muted pain and at the same time my still simmering displeasure toward her. "But my woman. Oh, my woman. Whenever she bathes in there, I still feel that urge to caress her full calves. Know what they remind me of, young man? The wax gourds. Those fleshy ripened gourds to sink your teeth in." He stopped snickering and drew a healthy drag, kept the smoke in his mouth as long as he could, and his eyes became slits in his bliss. I repacked fresh tobacco in the bowl, thinking wishfully of a rice liquor bottle, because I wanted to get drunk, very drunk, with him. I took one big drag with the fresh tobacco, my head buoyed, tingling, as he slurred his words, "Know something else, young man? In the South when they amputated my limbs, they said, 'Don't cry now, Sarge.' You know why? We got no anesthesia. So I had someone press her picture on my eyes and I imagined her in that red scarf and I sucked in the pain until her picture shrank with the pain and I passed out." He nodded his head up and down like on a spring and said he understood her and even felt grateful to her still being with him. He told me the night before a female cat was yowling in heat as it wandered off the garden and into their house and his wife left her cot to come out, turned on the light, and saw the cat push its bottom against his stumped leg, rubbing and purring, and his wife said, "Look at it, oh, will you look at it," and he said, "She's horny. Aren't women like that when the moon is full?" and the cat just howled, and she said, "How can I sleep with its obscene squealing? Now, now will you look at its obscene way of showing itself?" He said, "How obscene?" She told him that the cat was lying down, twitching its tail and then flinging it to the side and there it was: the slit of its genitalia, pink and swollen. Before going back to her cot, she said she was going to stuff the cat's mouth with *lá ngón*, the yellow jasmine leaves, if it didn't stop yowling. He made a snorting sound as he laughed, said it took a long time before things got quieted down, the cat now gone, but the sound of her cot creaking beyond the curtain kept him awake into the night.

I saw a pot on the doorsill, a tall wooden stake rising from its bottom, and around the stake twined the false jasmine vine. Uncle Chung's wife's pet plant. I could tell by its pretty yellow flowers.

The next morning a boy from Uncle Chung's alley ran into our store and asked Huan's father to come quickly to Uncle Chung's house. Huan's father was like a doctor in our district, where western medicine and its physicians weren't considered trustworthy. I went with him, the boy running ahead of us before we could ask him. Inside the house I saw Uncle Chung lying facedown by the back door where the pot of yellow jasmine sat. It took me but one look to see that he had plucked nearly all the fresh leaves of the vine, and some of them were in his mouth still and some of them lay scattered over the doorsill. White foam coated his mouth and his head full of long black hair lolled to one side and in the morning light I could see the gash and the scratches on his cheek.

I knelt down, looking at his eyes, still open. I ran my hand over them, but they stayed open. Like dolls' eyes.

I wondered if he ever cried, and if he did, would there be tears?

Rain. Falling on the inn's red-tiled roof, which slants sharply over the veranda, and falls like a white-water curtain.

It's noon and it hasn't let up all day. Water started rising on the roads on my way back from the town. On a day like this, Mrs. Rossi usually stays home; but today she has gone with me into town to shop for groceries.

Near home I slow the car to a stop. A duck is waddling across the road, then turning around. I sit, watching, and here comes the duck again, followed by six ducklings, each a fuzzy yellow ball. The mother duck hops onto the curb. But it isn't so easy for the ducklings, and they all fall down when they try to jump onto the curb.

I get out of the car and walk to the ducklings. They make peep-peep-peep sounds as their mother looks down. I pick up each little fuzzy ball and put it down on the curb with its mother.

Mrs. Rossi shakes her head repeatedly as I get back in the car. "I'm sorry, ma'am."

"You know what, Giang?" she asks softly.

"Yes, ma'am?"

"You just did what Nicola did on a day we went grocery shopping together for the last time. I remember he stopped the car and car horns were blaring behind us. He got out and did what you've just done. Oh, sweet Lord."

"He must be a kind soul."

"A gentle, caring boy when he grew up."

"What was he like, ma'am?"

"He was very attached to me. He would run to me when I came to pick him up at a daycare center in the afternoon, jumping into my arms to receive my kisses. He would snuggle against me, just clinging onto me. He slept in his own room. But sometimes I woke up in the night and found him sleeping at the foot of my bed—he was afraid to wake me up."

"Where was his father then?"

"We slept in separate bedrooms. I was drinking so I could sleep because of insomnia." Mrs. Rossi rubs her eyes. "Nicola was a peaceful boy, but he always tried to measure up to his father's and grandfather's image. He came home from school one day and his feet were all bloody. I had to go to a local drugstore to buy a bottle of iodine, then came home and washed the cuts on the soles of his feet. I asked him what happened. He said he raced barefoot with his friends on a graveled slope. They took off their shoes and socks, rolled up their pants, and ran up and down the slope until somebody quit. He won. I said to him, 'That's foolish.' And he said, 'I wanted to be tough like grandfather.'"

"He was a soldier?"

"In World War I. His grandpa died when his company tried to stop the Germans from advancing to Paris."

"Was there a girl in your son's life before he went to Vietnam?"

"Not that I know of. I think that might've been the Lord's blessing for him, because when you're in love, you dream of a home and someone might end up with a broken heart, a broken dream."

"Wouldn't it have been a joy if your son and Chi Lan met?"

"Oh, stop it, Giang." Mrs. Rossi laughs, a scratchy laugh.

1967
Nicola Rossi

Mama, we were staying in the base camp that was once a French fort during the Indochina War. From the rear of the base looking west, you could see the U Minh forest beyond the perimeter of barbed wire. The leaves of the forest green at first light turned a dusty green during the day because of the heat haze. But the forest was always beautiful in the early morning when trees flowered white, and soon the flowers would wither and fall in the heat and then in the monsoon rain. From the base looking east past its gate you could see the little Viet town—the blind colony—the red-dirt road that ran through the town and the spreading crown of the chinaberry that shaded the refreshment shack.

Beyond the town the river glinted like a mirror. The River of White Water Lilies. That's what the Viets called it. The river took us north on our patrol until it bisected the U Minh forest into Upper and Lower U Minh, where we would stay out for a week at times guarding the villages that lay hidden in the banana and bamboo groves along the river, and one of them sat beyond the riverbank and back into the forest so that on a quiet evening you could hear from inside the village the sound of waves coming from the western sea.

That village was a Catholic village, which we protected against the enemy. The villagers were northerners who had escaped the communist terror in 1954 when Vietnam was divided by the Geneva Accords into North and South. They were anti-communist and would kill any communists without remorse. We were friendly with them, and they liked us. The mamas and grandmas would bake dumplings and steamed buns and we'd eat them and thank God that we wouldn't have to eat our ham and lima beans and in return we gave them our C-ration cans. The village militia had lookouts in the forest and along the river and they communicated with one another using Morse code through their handheld radios. They had M1 Garand and carbine rifles, and though underarmed and undertrained, they had no fear of the communists. We gave them M-16 rifles and mortars and they were quick to put them to use. One night their scouts spotted the Viet Cong's movement toward their village and sent their men the coordinates through Morse code. They fired their mortars. Mama, they got the Viet Cong just as they were crossing the river. When it was over, canteens, rubber shoes, and bodies floated on the river. In the morning the river had carried away the blood, but the blood had soaked the mud along the riverbank and the fish now fought one another for the human flesh caught between the battered-looking paling.

In this village Ian Vaughn met a girl. We were stationed on the riverbank and he would go into the village during the day, the free time he got before his night guard duty. Sometimes he had the girl up on the ten-ton thunder truck, sitting on its bed mounted with a quad-fifty machine gun. The kids would wave and smile at the truck as it rolled through the village and the adults stood in muted admiration at the sight of the quad fifty draped with an American flag in red, white, and blue. Late afternoons sometimes the men would test the fire range through an exercise, and Ian would sit with the girl on the bank while the quads roared like thunder, and the twilight glowed with myriad streaks of red tracers, and every living Viet in the village would come out of their hooches, watching the fireworks in awe. He told the girl, who was the village schoolteacher and spoke good English, that it always pinched his gut when the quads went into action. She asked why, and he said that it meant some souls in the bush were in trouble. She said he had a good heart and he told her he always carried the Bible with him, even when he was out on patrol. Being a Catholic herself, she studied the Bible with him. He helped her with her English and she taught him Vietnamese. When he felt confident enough to speak Vietnamese to her, he asked her if he could teach English to her students. She was happy to hear that. The children would perk up at the sight of the red-haired American who stood hunched in the low-ceilinged classroom, speaking words in English to them and hearing them repeat the words in chorus. The lanky young American made them laugh with his sometimes off-tone pronunciation of tricky Vietnamese words and their teacher, the girl, would cover her mouth, giggling. Say *khúc khuy. Mazy.* Say *ngoan ngèo. Zigzag.* The children guffawed. Ian laughed too. Those were words he found impossible to pronounce. "Your jaws must relax," she'd say. "Let your lips form the sounds."

"Tough words," he said. "How about saying that backward?"

She cocked her head. "Mr. Ian," she said, "if you have an iron will."

"I'll count on that," he said. "My father used to drill me on spelling and multiplication when I was a kid. The only child, so it was pretty hard not to get my parents' attention."

"So was I, the only child."

"Did you grow up a Catholic?"

"Yes. My parents' whole village was Catholic in the North. And what are you?"

"Presbyterian."

"*Giám Lý?*"

Ian laughed. "I haven't the foggiest idea what that is."

"That's where I get confused," she said. "I heard that the sects in America are split into black congregations and white congregations."

"We have Presbyterians, Episcopalians, Baptists, Methodists, lots of others. Of course, the Baptists are divided into sects of their own. We have Shakers, Quakers, Mormons, Lutherans, and only God knows how many more."

"Stop!" She giggled, touching her brow. "I've already forgotten all those names."

Sometimes after school he would follow a kid's parent home and, sitting on a rush mat on the packed dirt floor, eat their food. First he worked his feet out of his heavy boots so he could sit like they did with his legs cross-folded painfully into each other. Over time his limbs began to adopt such posture with less pain and his tongue acquired a taste for boiled vegetables, poached fish, and rice. They ate a lot of fish, cabbage, and sweet potatoes, and every meal there was a crockpot of *canh*, their soup, with pumpkin and baby shrimps. With *canh* was *nuoc mam*, their fish sauce, the pungent smell soon becoming inseparable from the food he ate. A few times he ate with them before it got dark and, the river now rising with the moon, he could hear the deep-throated cuckoo-cuckoo of the birds echoing mournfully across the water and the swamp, shrubs, and trees. Every dwelling was built of cajeput wood and thatched with nipa palm fronds. Evenings they would burn cajeput leaves and the bitter-smelling smoke made his eyes teary; yet it kept away the mosquitos. There were chickens roaming and feeding happily in every garden, and the bright red of a rooster's comb was the red he'd see in his mind when he thought of the village; the clucking of hens and the calls of cuckoos would bring him a peaceful feeling. Sometimes he'd bring C-rations and he would show the kids how to open the cans with his P-38 can opener. Then he would sit and watch the kids eat ham and lima beans with rice, and most of them would pause when they first took a mouthful of spaghetti and meatballs and some would spit them out and some would swallow with such difficulty it made him laugh. He made her try the franks and beans. She took the hot dogs, cut them up and fried them with onions and ate them with the white rice. It tasted much better that way when they shared a meal, and the beans were cooked with the porridge, steeped in chicken broth, and afterward it didn't taste like C-rations anymore. The first time he went to her house, upon her invitation, he remembered what she told him and removed his boots before entering the anteroom. Her father was the village chief, a cultured white-haired man who came from a mandarin family in the North. The man sat in the chair with his feet planted on the floor, his hands resting on his thighs. He never crossed his legs. Ian considered himself fortunate that he sat like they did, for later she told him that one of the Viet protocols of mutual respect was never to cross your legs with your foot pointing toward your guest. "Do not sit like a cowboy," she said. "And do not touch their heads." The head. He had rubbed many Viet kids' heads, he told her. "That was all right," she said. "But you are considered uncouth if you pat an elder on the back or rub his head." Ian gradually opened up to their culture and began to realize that once he put away his biases, he no longer felt alien around them. Nothing they did, nothing they had to offer in his daily contact with them, would take him aback. Once she asked him after the class what "full of piss and vinegar" meant, pointing to

an editorial in the *Stars and Stripes* that he had brought with
him. "In Vietnam," he read, "poor bastards have been at war
for fifteen years. And here we come, full of piss and vinegar,
wanting to win the war in six months." He explained that
it meant "full of youthful energy," and she, not satisfied by
the explanation, asked, "Why can't they use some refined
words instead of crude ones to express the same thing?"
He wanted to tell her that his culture *was* unrefined, that
the cowboy tongue usually got the better of him before he
could rephrase his thoughts. But it was too much to try to
explain that to her, so he just laughed, and she joined him
in laughing at the peculiar expression. And if you ask me,
Mama, was there anything about this people that might
have shocked him? Well, probably the sight of their black-
lacquered teeth. It shocked me too, the first time I saw one
of their elders smile. Then I learned that the older Vietnamese generation had dyed their teeth because they believed
the lacquer protected against decay. It shocked most of
our men, especially the West Pointers. Those with brilliant
minds in physics, mathematics, who understood how the
B-52s' all-metal skin worked, how the wrinkled appearance
of the fuselages' forward sections expanded and became
smooth when the aircraft gained altitude. Those who knew
Samuel Huntington's credo on how to defeat a people who
struggled against foreign intervention: "Dry up the ocean
so that the fish don't have any water." What would these
educated men think when they first met a Viet whose teeth
were all black? But, Mama, Ian understood these people. He
ate their rice, rice that we burned so the Viet Cong wouldn't
feast on it, rice soiled with buffalo dung that they brought
home and sifted through with care because rice was the
staple of their livelihood, rice that grew in paddies where
we killed the Viets sometimes indiscriminately and later the
farmers would bury the bodies and harvest the rice and by

then the bloodstains on the rice stalks had turned to the color of paddy dirt.

One night the Viet Cong attacked our platoon outside the village. It was half past three in the morning. We held our position, but when dawn broke we could hear gunfire in the village and we knew that the Viet Cong had punched through the village by holding us at bay long enough on the riverbank. At first light a pair of jetfighters showed up, dropping low, nearly skimming the treetops still wet with dew. They spotted the Viet Cong in the canal, the long canal that flanked the village and flowed into the Trem River, and released napalm bombs on them. From the river we saw flames and smoke and soon the wind brought a foul smell of petroleum. We could hear guns roaring each time the jetfighters came swooping down, drawing enemy fire, and we could hear the trees burn, popping loud, and the air felt hot on our faces, the downwind fumes reeking so bad we had to cover our noses with our hankies. The jetfighters repelled the attack and now, with the mist having burned off, we moved into the village.

We came upon a long line of men and women frantically digging a trench between the side of the village and the canal. The wind was fanning the fire that licked the brush on the canal bank, and people started cutting down cajeput trees to prevent the fire from spreading. Ian found the schoolteacher. He had prayed that he would see her again and when he saw her, spade in hand, dirt-smeared face hardened with the muted pain he saw so often on the Viets' faces, he crossed himself and took out his entrenching tool and joined them. They chopped and hacked away climbing fern and tree roots, and the severed roots of milkwood trees that dangled white and dripped sap like leaky faucets. They dumped dirt from the trench into the raging fire, the peat soil so porous it was easy to dig. An elder told her to dig quickly but not to swing her arms too high, so she wouldn't tire out too soon, and she told Ian that too. The fire roared past the canal bank and trees shivered and crackled, and Ian could see the shimmering water and knew why they didn't use it against the fire, for water only helped the napalm fire gain strength. Through the smoke he could see her back and the backs of the people ahead of him. The heat grew, the air soaked with a gasoline smell. The trench grew longer, deeper, and wider until the fire came upon them and its heat breathed a murderously hot air on their faces. Some slow-footed women and kids got burned and people had to pull them, and as they pulled they brushed the skin, the clothes with their hands and the jellied petroleum stuck to their skin and they and the victims all screamed in agony.

By evening the fire had stopped at the trench. The sky was a hazy yellow from the smoky treetops, and the heat of the fire had waned. She stood leaning on her spade, her face blackened from dirt and soot, her blouse stained with sweat. As she gazed at the ruins, Ian took out his canteen and gave it to her. "Drink," he said. "Things will get back to normal." She took a sip, coughed, and said, "This is the worst I have seen." Her voice was soft. Around her people stood contemplating the charred landscape, their eyes glassy, their figures soon darkening into silhouettes as dusk came. They followed the canal home, walking in tandem, some wrapping their heads with an elephant-ear taro leaf for heat relief, and the last glimmer of sun cast a glow on the water, and there were bodies lying in all sorts of positions in the water, on the banks, where they got caught under the felled trees. Along the bank she picked up a tortoise, as it tried to crawl away from the heat still simmering on the ground. She patted its dome-shaped shell. "Poor thing," she said to Ian. "Let's find a cool place for him." When they reached a grove of cajeput, she placed the tortoise in the grass and they heard the frantic calls of storks and herons deep in the harbor of tree crowns. Wings beat on and on and the harsh calls didn't stop. As he looked up into the inky black vault where the birds were marionette shades of pale white, he could see them hovering like hummingbirds and none touched down. He heard her exclaim, "Heavens!" The birds had lost their roosts; the petroleum heat from napalm bombs had made their colony uninhabitable.

It took two months for the village to rebuild. He often helped when he could. One day before he went on a seven-day leave to Singapore, he brought her a gift. A paint box and a notebook with handwritten poems. The paint box was enameled white with two deep mixing wells. The notebook, pressed together by two faded brown cardboards, had drawings and poems written neatly in Vietnamese on the ruled-line sheets. She asked him where he had gotten them and he told her from a dead NVA soldier's rucksack. He said he couldn't throw them away after he saw that the notebook was filled with love poems. Each was illustrated with drawings of flowering twigs and solitary blossoms, of floating clouds and a full moon. He couldn't imagine that soldiers like him would have a mind to write down their thoughts and feelings in poetry and pictures. The notebook no longer had an owner. It was like smelling a dead flower. What he said moved her. "You have the mind of a poet," she said. "These are love poems written by a soldier yearning for home and his sweetheart." "Where does it say that?" he asked. She put her finger under two words, "*Yêu em.*" Love you. He mouthed the words. Loud enough for her to hear. That made her blush and she broke out laughing. "You silly silly silly oh silly you," she said, still laughing and he, too, laughed. Like two children.

In Singapore on his Recreation and Recuperation leave, Ian bought himself a three-piece suit for fifty dollars and a long sapphire-blue silk scarf. He settled on the scarf because he didn't know what else she would like. She always wore indigo or sapphire blouses. He imagined her wearing the silk scarf. He imagined its translucent hue, its intense blue. He wrote the words *"Yêu em"* on the back of a card and put it in the gift-wrapped box.

When he came back to the base camp, his platoon was still out in the bush. But it wasn't guarding the Catholic village. They had pulled out right after he left on his R&R, and the following night the Viet Cong overwhelmed the village defense and walked every villager to the Trem River where they shot each of them in the head and kicked the bodies into the river. Those who hid away survived and were later taken to the New-Life Hamlet, a free-fire zone. He found out that fewer than twenty had made it to that place and she wasn't one of them.

When he left the ruins of the village and rode back on the ten-ton thunder truck mounted with a quad-fifty machine gun, the truck went up along the Trem River. In the bright morning the deep green of cajeput was breathtaking, the river white with water lilies along the edge of the riverbank, and the scents of water lily flowers perfumed the air. He watched the river go by and couldn't make sense of what had happened. It did not add up. He watched the storks taking flight from the river, going, going until they reached their roosts in a cajeput grove beyond, and he thought of a home with her.

1987
Le Giang

After Tet, our NVA's First Division was decimated. We stayed deep in the jungle. To reach us, it would take two full days on foot from the Mekong Delta. We hacked away brush and vines and bamboo thickets and leveled the fern-covered ground to build our camp. Above us rose giant trees, one rising above another so that they formed foliaged crowns so thick that when it rained mere drops sluiced down the curves of the vault. When the sun reached its zenith at midday, it looked like twilight below.

The American prisoners were quartered in a thatched hut, low lying with three mud-and-bamboo laced sides. Its open side faced a guard shack outside the bamboo enclosure. I could see them moving around, drooped, heads bent. The hut was built that way so that, to move around, the prisoners had to lower their heads all the time. That adopted posture would eventually affect their psyches. Outside the fence, along its base where the earth was thick with creepers, a line of bamboo stakes was planted underground. None of the prisoners would try to escape, because the booby traps might not kill them but the wilderness beyond would.

He was one of the first American prisoners of war I saw. He could speak Vietnamese and, except in long statements, he had only a slight accent. I heard his prison mates call him Ian. Later I heard that he had been with us for six months. They captured him before his friends could get to him. They had to carry him. His legs were messed up from one of our handmade mines. A piece of metal from the mine was still lodged in his head. He said our doctors told him they couldn't remove it, not that they didn't want to try, but they didn't want to risk his life by doing so. He only slept on the side of his head opposite the wound. He said it gave him a numbing headache if he slept on the other side. It was his bad karma, he said, that he had stepped on the mine. He said it in Vietnamese and we all laughed at the word he used. *Nghiep*. Smart man. Said the mine was made from a howitzer shell. American artillery shell, he said. Then he winked at us as we sensed the irony.

When the mine went off, he screamed, then blacked out. Upon waking, he felt like he'd been hit on the side of the head with a blackjack. *O death, where is your victory? O death, where is your sting?* He said the Bible words in his head. He saw faces looking down at him. Crowned by oyster-colored pith helmets. He said—without even opening his mouth—*Làmon!*

He had a frail frame, his red-haired head always lolling to one side. I said to him in English, "No one wants to die."

"To die is gain," he said. Then he quickly added, "That's from the Bible. You Catholic?"

"No." I shook my head.

"Buddhist?"

"No."

"No religion?"

"None."

He eyed me, his lips puckered. He looked so gaunt, so malnourished, his cheekbones cut sharp like Vietnamese cheekbones.

"I'm surprised they didn't kill you back there," I said.

"They didn't," he said, this time in Vietnamese. "But the people in the next village almost did."

"What did they do?"

"This woman came running to me," he said. "She had a hoe in her hands. I was in a litter. The guards didn't see her. I raised one arm to avert the blow. I grabbed a guard by his shirt with my other arm. He grabbed the hoe and shoved her back."

His words came out slowly. His Vietnamese accent was neutral, neither northern nor southern. He must have picked up the language from all sorts of speakers. He said short statements in Vietnamese, but when he talked at length, he would throw in English words. Likewise, I'd fall back on Vietnamese when I talked with him in English. And we understood each other very well.

He paused to regain his breath. His eyes were serene. Hazel eyes. They never darted while he spoke to you. Never a second thought fleeting in them. I liked him.

He asked for a Vietnamese word. Cinders. Then another. Mortar. He said, "I saw many huts burned to cinders on our way through. Half the village was gone. People gathered along the dirt road. They pointed toward me on the litter and yelled, *Meey! Meey!* I was the main attraction. We went past a graveyard. There were a number of fresh graves, I could tell by the color of fresh dirt. In front of a grave I saw three mortar shells laid out in a row. Iron-rust color. They were duds."

He said the word "duds" in English. I said I knew what it meant. He said, "I'm sure they'll be used as booby traps on us. Then a guard spoke to me in his broken English, 'See that man?' I tried to follow his hand pointing toward the crowd. 'See that woman? That boy?' Then he pointed toward the fresh graves and kept nodding at me. I took that to mean that one of those fresh graves had been part of the woman's family."

Ian asked me for the word "blowfly." He remembered the *ruoi xanh*. The flies had been following him for three days. By then his legs began to smell. He could see white eggs in his wounds. "You pick them and leave them in the sun and they will hatch in three hours," he said. "I saw it myself." Some hatched in his wounds. They turned purplish blue. But he never let the wounds bother him. The pain throbbed, horribly at times. The smell had grown stronger. He tried to rise to salute the camp commander. A guard yelled at him. "Bow!" He steadied himself and lowered his head at the commander. Then he slumped to the cot. White maggots dropped from his wounds to the dirt floor. The commander winced. Later in the day a nurse came in. Before she did, a guard told him of her arrival. From what the guard said—"Americans number ten"—he gathered that she hated him and his kind. The girl was young. Clear-eyed, perky. Yet she wore a glum look about her as she poured alcohol on his legs. The wounds smarted. He felt ashamed when she pinched her nose, then donned a mask and worked on a pair of surgical gloves. As she squeezed the pus out of the wounds, he looked down at her gentle face. He held still, not even breathing, while she swabbed the wounds with a cotton-tipped hemostat. He watched her bandage his wounds deftly, neatly, and he could smell the fresh gauze, the stinging antiseptic. As she handed him a small bottle of antibiotic, he said in English, "What's your name, Miss?" She looked into his eyes in silence. No English, he thought, and then tried to put together a couple of Vietnamese words. She looked at his bandaged head. "Do you have much headache?" she said in English. "Yes," he said. "I can't sleep." She motioned for him to sit up and then unwrapped the gauze and checked the gash. She changed the gauze. "Our doctor will look at this," she said. He felt comforted by her soft voice. She turned to leave and he called to her, "You didn't tell me your name, Miss." She answered without turning her head, "You don't need to know."

A few days after the young nurse cleaned and wrapped his leg wounds, Ian had a fever. The pain returned to his legs. He ate very little from his meager meals and lay the rest of the day shivering on the rickety cot. He couldn't walk, so every day an interrogator came to his cot. The interrogator spoke hardly any English and was accompanied by an interpreter. Ian told them what he knew. He'd thought about the interrogation before they came. He knew he must tell whatever they asked, not to lie but at the same time not to risk the lives of his fellow soldiers with what he told them. He'd memorized the Code of Conduct. He also knew how much he should say under the Geneva Convention for the treatment of the prisoners of war. But all that vanished when the interrogator said, "You are a criminal of war and you will be treated accordingly." At that, Ian gave them only his name, rank, and date of birth. When pressed, he gave them his service number and unit. He kept silent on the military questions. The interrogator glanced at Ian's legs and gave them a quick tap with his metal ruler. He mouthed his words in Vietnamese and when he stopped, the interpreter said, "We will treat your legs if you cooperate. If you do not, you will eventually lose your legs to amputation because of unavoidable abscesses." Ian said, "I will tell you what I know. Radio frequency? No, I am not a radioman. How many M-79s in the company? No, I am a rifleman, I only know what's in my squad. Other weapons carried by the company? No, I am in a rifle squad, my knowledge of weapons is limited to my squad." The interrogator asked, "How did you get to Vietnam?" Surprised, Ian said nothing. It must be a trick question. At the interrogator's silence, he said, "By airplane. Twenty hours by airplane." The interrogator turned to the interpreter. "*Hai muoi gio à?*" The interpreter nodded. Twenty hours. The interrogator said, "*Ôi!*" His baffled exclamation had Ian nodding to confirm what he'd just said. "Very far," Ian said. They both shook their heads in bewilderment. "Give us your family's address in America," the interrogator said. Ian felt perplexed. "What for?" he asked. "Just give," the interrogator said. Ian heard in his head the ugly threat about his legs. He thought of the distance between shores. He told them his family's address. Unsettled, he felt cross. The interrogator said something incomprehensible in English. The interpreter then said to Ian, "What is your father's profession?" Ian studied the men, then said, "He is dead." "What was his profession when he was alive?" "He was a . . . civilian," Ian said. "Who did he work for?" "He was a car mechanic." The interrogator winced and asked the interpreter, who asked Ian, "He repair automobiles?" Ian nodded. The interrogator mused, then said something to the interpreter, who asked, "Where did he die?" "At home." "What did he die of?" Ian looked down at the floor. "Cirrhosis of the liver," he admitted. "What?" the interrogator asked. "He died of sickness," Ian said. But the interrogation went on for two more days until the interrogator felt satisfied with the consistency of Ian's answers. By then, biting down the pain in his legs, Ian began to grit his teeth. But only momentarily. Evil pain. Horrible pain. He knew now why people killed themselves when pain became unbearable. Then a doctor came. The doctor felt his calves, probing with his fingers. Each probe made Ian swallow his moans. The doctor shot his legs with novocaine and proceeded to clean out the wounds with a hemostat, the way the nurse did. Then he picked the metal splinters out of the wounds. It took a long time. After the last sliver was removed, he shot Ian's legs with penicillin. His thick glasses fogged when he was done bandaging Ian's legs. He clapped shut his medical satchel. "You are gud," he said. "Tomorrow I give you more penicillin and I luk at your head."

There came more American prisoners now, a dozen more, since I saw him that first time. By now Ian's legs had healed but his head wound still gave him a constant headache. He'd never smoked before he had the headache. Now he chain-smoked. He knew how to roll cigarettes like us, his captors. Thumbs, middle fingers twirling and coaxing the tobacco-packed paper into a tight, stubby cylinder, the paper edge quickly licked to seal it. He took a drag, sitting on his haunches just like a Vietnamese, his arms flopping over his knees, the cigarette hanging between his lips the way Vietnamese smoked their hand-rolled joints. On a nearby cot sat a blond American, thin as a reed, with the hairiest eyebrows like caterpillars, who shook his head at Ian. "Doesn't he look like a gook, eh?" Some of the prisoners had begun to squat like gooks. They also rolled up their trouser legs past their knees like gooks. From their cigarette ration that he had pooled together, Ian bribed a guard with two dozen cigarettes in exchange for a small bottle of *Nhi Thiên Duong*, the pungent, comfort-soothing eucalyptus oil the Vietnamese would daub on their nostrils and temples when sick. Squatting on his heels, Ian smeared his palm with a streak of the blue-gum oil and then rolled his cigarette back and forth over the streak. He passed the bottle to a next guy among the smokers. "Conserve it," he said. "That's precious as gold." He lit his cigarette, sucked on it deeply and closed his eyes. The acrid smell of hand-rolled cigarettes momentarily distracted them from the rotten odor in the hut. It wasn't from the kitchen—an aperture in the ground lined with rocks with a long bamboo tube that carried the cooking smoke and dispersed it out of sight of the American spotter planes. The odor came from outside, ten feet away in the rear of the hut, where the open-air latrine was—a hole in the ground covered with a wooden plank. Blowflies would drop eggs in the hole whenever someone forgot to lid it, and soon the pit was alive with maggots and the air was humming with metallic blue, green flies. Sometimes a hen or rooster would come and stick its head in the hole to peck away the maggots among the muck. When I came by his hut I'd stay outside, for a permanent stench pervaded it when the breeze blew and on a hot day the god-awful smell would give everyone a headache.

It rained all night. In the morning the distant mountain lay shrouded in a fog burning slowly off as another wall of fog would come rolling in, thinned by the sun and drifting away like a hallucination.

Outside the prisoners' hut I saw Ian sitting on his haunches, swathed in a burlap bag. It was what we gave the prisoners for a blanket. We took the US Agency for International Development rice bags—stamped on the outside with a clasped-hands logo above the line *Donated by the People of the United States of America*—cut them open and sewed them together to the size of a small blanket. It was chilly. Ian peered up at me, his hands palming a tin cup. It must have been hot tea, for steam was curling up from the cup. They received a tea ration but never coffee, and by now most of them had probably forgotten what coffee tasted like.

I drew deeply on my cigarette, and his gaze followed my hand motion as I exhaled a plume of smoke. I could tell he craved a cigarette. Yet I couldn't offer him one, because the guard in the lookout shack behind me was probably watching. "Tea is good on a morning like this," I said to him in English.

"This isn't tea," he said, dropping his gaze to the cup. *"Sua ngot."*

He extended the cup. The condensed milk looked like chalk water. He sipped, holding it in his mouth as if to savor something precious. As he swallowed, he sucked in his cheeks. Gaunt and anemic looking, his face had a fuzzy line along the jaw. His beard wasn't growing anymore, his red hair was thinning out because of malnutrition. He clasped his hands around the cup, shivering.

"Where are your sandals?" I asked, looking down at his bare feet. Hunched up, with the burlap bag draping his back, he looked like a pelican at rest.

"Saving them," he said, eyeing my black-rubber sandals. "Wearing them only when I go picking greens."

They would go with the guards deeper in the forest to pick wild greens and the guards would tell them which plants they should avoid if they wanted to live another day—most of the greens were inedible and some poisonous. Often they brought back wild banana flowers and then peeled away the tough outer layers until they reached the tender-looking, finger-length buds, yellow and lithe. They would cook them in watered-down *nuoc mam* and eat them with cooked rice. They craved fish sauce, which was rationed, so Ian told me they added water to the fish sauce and boiled it. The heated *nuoc mam* would taste much saltier that way.

Sipping his watered-down milk, he told me they received a can of condensed milk the other day to share among themselves. Each one got a spoonful to add to his cup of hot water and the diluted milk was so thin it barely tasted sweet anymore. He said the trick was to drink it hot to intensify the sweetness. He said he hoped to receive another can of condensed milk soon, because fresh supplies had just arrived. At my quizzical look, he grinned and pointed toward the trail beyond the lookout shack and said he saw women carrying USAID burlap bags into camp the prior evening. I nodded, remembering one time he asked me why the women porters had large banana fronds covering their backs beneath the bags, and I explained to him that the fronds helped keep their sweat from soaking into the rice bags. "Ingenious," he said. "Just common sense," I said. He shook his head. "No, I mean the way they took our AID bags and turned them into backpacks with straps sewn on them for carrying things."

Like most prisoners, he cherished rice. Between rice and boiled manioc, they would beg for rice and *nuoc mam*, which they treasured for the scarcity of salt. Once I saw him sitting outside under the sun with the rice pot between his knees. "Rat shit," he said. I could see black clumps among the shiny rice grains. Whenever they forgot to lid their rice pot, as they would with their latrine, rats would get in the pot in the night and eat the grains. Mornings they would have to wash the rice grains to get rid of rat feces which, at times, were so clumped up with the grains they could not be separated.

The next day I gave Ian a handful of black seeds and told him to soak them in water overnight and then plant them. "*Mong toi*," I told him. "Red-stem spinach. Very nutritious."

The following day I saw him behind the hut, burying seeds in the soil. "Some kind of seeds," he said to me and showed me the can in which he'd soaked them. The color of the water was wine-red. I explained to him that the red-stem spinach would grow as tall as an average Viet man and he said, "I'll build a teepee for it." "What's a teepee?" I asked.

"Wait till you see it," he said and started splitting bamboo. He drove the strips into the ground and tied the splits with the *choai* strings—the vines from a swamp fern plant that we would soak in water and use as ropes. The conical-shaped support he built became a home for the climbing spinach. Monsoon rains that soaked the forest for days helped the seeds sprout quickly. In two weeks, scarlet stems began pushing up and twining around the teepee, and pale green leaves shot out from the stems that now lost their baby red and turned into a deep-wine red. After I showed him how to cook the spinach, he went around collecting more than two dozen cigarettes and traded them with the guards for two chicken eggs. He cooked the spinach in the two pots they had—the rice pot and the pot for boiling water—and borrowed from the guards another pot to cook their rice. He had his mates crush a handful of red peppers that they grew behind their hut and mixed them with the diluted *nuoc mam* in a wooden bowl. He cut up the two boiled eggs and dropped them into the bowl. It was the first time I saw the prisoners eat together, sitting on their haunches in a circle, the pots in the center on the dirt floor, arms flying, chopsticks clacking, shoveling rice into their mouths, dipping clumps of spinach into the egg-and-red-pepper *nuoc mam*, inhaling their food and all forgetting the latrine-nauseating stink that made the air blister.

Summer drew to a close and that year the cicadas hung on stubbornly in the trees. You could hear them ringing and shrilling across the air, deep in the tangles of cajeput and bamboo groves. Ian and his mates had seen the guards hunt baby cicadas at night, and the sight of flickering lanterns around the bases of trees had become familiar around the camp. They looked for newly hatched cicadas. The cicadas peeked through the earth, crawled up tree trunks, and shed their skins. Their wings were pale. Before the nymphs' new skins could harden—their wings would fill with fluid to turn themselves into adults—the guards would pick them, one by one off the tree trunks. They would drop those nymphs into a salt-water pot, so the nymphs' wings would stop stiffening, and then they would boil them. In a wok they stir-fried them with granulated salt and you could smell a mouth-watering aroma coming out of the camp kitchen.

At noon when I walked by the prisoners' hut, I heard Ian call out from inside: "Giang!" He was sitting on the dirt floor with five of his mates, the lidded rice pot on the floor among them. Inside the hut the terrible smell from the latrine made me hold my breath. I saw what they had cooked for lunch. To go with their rice, they had boiled corn, which they grated and doused with *nuoc mam* mixed with crushed hot peppers. "You want *ve*?" Ian asked me, holding the rice bowl in midair.

"*Ve*?" I said. "Cicada?"

He nodded, shushing me with a finger to his lips. I looked toward the guard's hut and turned back. "You caught the baby cicadas," I said, curious. The prisoners were forbidden to go outside their hut at night, except to use the latrine in the full view of the guard. One of his mates lifted the lid on the rice pot and inside, piled up above the cooked rice, were stir-fried baby cicadas. Ian picked one up. "Try it," he said. The cicada had a smoky smell when I sank my teeth into it. It popped with a *plup* sound. A fatty flavor rich with raw salt bit my tongue. "This is good," I said to him, licking my lips, feeling all my taste buds rise up. "You caught them?"

"Late last night," he said. Popping sounds came from the rice pot and the lid was quickly put back on. They all grinned happily, like children on the Lunar New Year.

We had a late-summer storm. Most of the roofs suffered damage and we had a shortage of drinking water. The storm and heavy rains had roiled the creek nearby, from which we ran a long bamboo channel to our kitchen and from the kitchen the prisoners were to carry water to their own hut in hard-rubber containers. Mud was everywhere. Red mud left footprints on the dirt floors, the footpaths, on cots and hammocks.

For days the rain came and went. During the lulls the heat beat down on the forest and the forest floor steamed. While we lay the footpaths with wooden planks, the prisoners were taken to a distant grassland to cut buffalo grass and elephant grass, bundle them and carry them back to camp to thatch the roofs. I saw them hauling back large bundles of it. It was a sweltering day and the forest vapors hazed the air. I saw Ian sit down on his heels by the trail to take a breather. He was naked to the waist, his back striped with cuts from grass blades. They smarted with their toothy blades, and their coarse undersides caused skin rash. You would scratch yourself until your skin chafed. The guards ordered him to move on, and I could see the heat was taking its toll on him. His legs looked rubbery, his head hung to one side.

We worked long days into nights until our camp was restored. At night it turned cold. I had to put on another shirt and, wrapped tightly in my blanket, I still shivered. I thought of the prisoners and their burlap blankets. Each of them had only one shirt and one pair of pants. I had seen them join their cots so they could draw heat from each other, each sleeping balled up in the fetal position to keep warm. A few days later Ian came down with dysentery. They said he had drunk unboiled water that the prisoners carried back to their hut from our kitchen, unclean water from the nearby creek. I understood that the prisoners had neglected boiling their own drinking water because they were taken every day to the grassland to cut buffalo grass, a long trek. From dehydration to bone-chilling cold at night, something had to give. Some prisoners suffered diarrhea. One of them walked around with no pants in the hut. The guards told him to put his pants back on and the next thing they saw was watery discharge running down his legs. I went into the hut to check on Ian a few times and he wasn't doing well. He could hardly sit because his testicles had swollen to the size of a tomato. His legs and his stomach puffed grotesquely. At night sometimes the urge to release was so sudden and great, he would let it gush out of his body onto his cot. The guards would make them clean the floor every day to get rid of the excrement.

Within days summer was over. One morning we heard the sound of airplanes and the next day too, then several days after. The droning of the planes soon became familiar in the early days of that autumn. Nobody knew what the lumbering planes were doing, except that everyone would feel like they had just walked out into a drizzle and felt a dampness on their faces. Everywhere it was damp. The thatch roofs were wet, the hammocks were wet, and leaves began to fall, suddenly browned and withered, not the brown or red of autumnal leaves, and the grass yellowed like in drought. Then we learned about those C-123 planes and the chemicals they sprayed on the forest. The spray fell like mist, wetting the leaves, and the air smelled tart. On the morning we woke and saw a giant canopy of the forest cleared away; the mountain showed through as if the forest had moved overnight toward it. On that day Ian's red-stem spinach died.

That afternoon I visited Ian in his hut. I brought him a can of condensed milk. He looked so pale and his face so misshapen that he shocked me with his smile. "*Cám on*," he said, holding the can tightly in his hand.

"You are welcome," I said, standing by his cot and holding my breath. His teeth were clattering. I took out a

Gauloises Caporals cigarette pack and placed it in his other hand.

"This-thing-is-strong," he said, slurring.

"Help me cut down," I said with a grin.

He held up the blue-colored pack, gazing at the winged helmet logo, while I let out my breath slowly. I could see dark blotches on the fly of his pants and on the inside of his pants legs. The legs had swollen noticeably.

"Our treasure plant died," he said, raising his voice with an effort.

"The spinach in the back?"

He nodded.

I told him about the chemicals the two-engine Caribous had sprayed on our forest. He said nothing for a while, then, "So they can see you. That's bad."

"Bad for all of us," I said, thinking of him and his sick mates if we had to move.

That evening, after supper, Ian lapsed into a coma and died before midnight. They said he craved sweet so he drank half the can of condensed milk without eating his evening meal. Our doctor said that so much condensed milk could be fatal for a dysentery victim. In the morning we gave them a coffin to bury Ian, and his mates carried the coffin to the camp's graveyard and dug a grave. They were digging when we heard the plane and soon we saw a spotter coming over the forest. The prisoners stopped and lowered the casket. It was a shallow grave. They said the Lord's Prayer in the droning of the plane as it disappeared over the mountain.

Sometime in the afternoon the sky buzzed and throbbed with the sounds of helicopters. The gongs alerted us to aerial attack and many of us, including the prisoners, were forced into the bomb shelters. From underground we heard the gunships firing rockets and the roaring of their miniguns and we heard our antiaircraft in concealed locations around the camp. The tremors went through the earth and we could feel it shake in our bunkers.

It was dusk when we left the bomb shelters. Most of the huts were destroyed, our kitchen and the prisoners' hut too. The graveyard was hit with rockets and large holes in the ground gaped. We could see old coffins upheaved, many burst open, flung about. We could see the fresh graves gutted and there wasn't anything left in them.

As I walked away from the graveyard I remembered I'd once told Ian I had no religion. Something clawed at my throat. Had I faith, what solace could it give me now?

1967
Nicola Rossi

Mama, I'm glad that you kept my oak bed. The little girl you brought home has slept on one side of the bed since she was five. Did she tell you the bed was too large? Now she's no longer a child. And the bed fits her just right. Chi Lan. I can say her name with ease. But many Viet names are harder to say. I can't help thinking about the time I was two when you put me in that bed, first with Papa, then by myself. Papa told me he missed the closeness between father and son. So every night he would tuck me in, turn off the light, and lie down beside me. In the dark, Papa would tell me stories about growing up in Georgetown, a few alleys away from a black neighborhood named Cherry Hill. People there had no indoor electricity or plumbing.

"The reason I'm telling you this," Papa said, "is so you'll remember that there's poverty in the world. There are people not nearly so fortunate as we are. I don't want you to take anything for granted. Your grandma worked sixty hours a week and took home a dozen shirts to sew on Sunday and earned a pittance. And the sweatshop owner still threatened to fire her and her friends and bring in the Chinese. The Chinese were willing to work for thirty dollars a month. She raised me, put me through college. A cup of coffee and a loaf of bread was all she ate the whole day, and she ate that every day of her working life."

"Why didn't she live with you and Mama?" I asked.

"Would've been too far for her. She thought she needed to work. Grandma was only fifty when she died."

"Did Grandma tell you stories at night when you were a child?"

"She was too tired by the time she got home."

"What happened to Grandpa?"

"He was a soldier. Then in June 1918, when I was just born, his outfit attacked the Germans in Belleau Wood to stop them from taking Paris, and he was killed."

One night I kept tossing and turning. Papa said, "What's wrong?"

"Why can't I sleep with Mama?"

"Mama goes to bed late."

"I don't mind."

Papa sighed. "She has insomnia. She needs rest."

"What's insomnia?"

"Can't sleep. You count sheep, but it doesn't help."

"Can anyone help her? Can I help her?"

"The doctors treat her. Yes, they help her."

When I was a first grader, you and Papa wanted to put me in second grade. But that school system didn't accommodate advanced students. The principal convinced you that the child still needed to learn and develop his social skills, because intelligence and maturity went hand in hand. The principal said she was pleased to have me in her school. Then, noting my bony legs, she mentioned the school's outstanding physical education program.

I rode the school bus every day. One evening Papa came home and found a note from the bus driver. He said I pushed a girl in the back on the bus steps. She scraped her knees and hands when she fell. She was the principal's daughter. Papa sat me down on the couch after dinner and asked me about the incident. I said the girl called me "stupid."

"You must've done something to her," Papa said. "She wouldn't call you names for no reason."

"I didn't give her the seat she always sat in," I said. "She said it was her seat."

Papa squeezed my hand. "You don't push anyone in the back like that. It's uncalled for, it's dangerous."

"But I didn't push her. A kid behind me did."

"Nicola!" Papa glared at me. "Don't lie!"

"You don't trust me."

"I do trust you, Nicola."

Papa scribbled a note and put it in my hand. "I want you to give this to the bus driver. I want you to apologize to that girl, you hear?"

Papa hated disorderly conduct. He thought everything would be all right once I said I was sorry.

In the afternoon I came home with a note from the bus driver.

Papa dropped the note and bent down to my face. "I'm ashamed of what you did, Nicola. Why didn't you tell her you were sorry?"

"I didn't do anything wrong! I didn't push her."

"Enough!" He grabbed me by the shoulder. "Say you're sorry and go up to your room."

"I won't say it."

"Go to the basement and stay down there until you do."

I went to the basement and shut the door. Papa made himself a sandwich and brewed a fresh pot of coffee. It was getting dark. After eating the sandwich Papa came down to the basement. I was sitting in the dark, cradling my head between my jacked-up knees.

"Stand up!" he said.

I tried, but my legs were gone under me. Papa grabbed me by the collar, yanked me up. "Have you come to your senses?"

I didn't answer him.

"I want to hear it."

I stood, tucking my chin against my chest.

"You know what I'm down here for," Papa said. "You know why you're down here, so let's hear it."

In a small voice I said, "I think I wet my pants."

Papa felt the seat of my pants. "Say you're sorry, then go up and change."

"I can't say I'm sorry. I didn't do it."

Then I sat back down, covering my head with my hands.

"Go upstairs! Wash up!"

I went upstairs, washed, and ate my dinner. That night in my sleep I saw Papa stand in the doorway like a blanched photograph. I cried, "Papa, I didn't do anything wrong!" When I woke I heard the piano downstairs.

I climbed out of bed, padded barefoot downstairs, and stood quietly at the foot of the stairs. A night-light as dim and soft as a low-burning candle lit the living room. At the piano, you were singing, *Go to sleep, baby child, Hush-a-bye, don't you cry. When you wake, you will have, All the pretty little horses.* When you stopped, I went to you. Half turned, you saw me and pulled me to your bosom.

"What happened, baby?" you asked hoarsely.

"Nothing," I said, pressing my cheek against your warm chest.

"Did Mama wake you?"

"Why don't you go to bed?"

"I'm not sleepy, hon."

You kissed me on the cheek, and on your breath, I smelled the sweet odor of brandy. I put my arms around you and closed my eyes. I felt not sleepy but dreamy in your softness and warmth.

"Can I sleep with you?"

"I go to bed very late, hon."

"I'll wait for you."

"You know you have to get up for school early in the morning, don't you?"

I peeked at you with one eye. "You won't wake me up when you come in. Papa never wakes me up. So can I?"

"I'm used to sleeping alone, hon." Then you looked down at me and gently laid my head in your lap. "I need a drink or two," you said, "before I go to bed. That helps me sleep."

"Will you ever be cured?"

"Listen, it's late. Go on back to bed." Then you glided your fingers across the keyboard. The sound rippled merrily.

"Can I stay here with you?"

You knitted your brows. "What for?"

"I just want to be with you."

"I don't want you to be tired in the morning."

You lifted my head from your lap, and I knew I shouldn't insist. You'd get upset.

I went back to my bed and soon I slept to the sound of the piano. When I woke in the dark, I sat up in bed, look-ing at the blurred white of the bedroom door, beyond it the hallway and your bedroom. As quietly as I could, I gathered my pillow in my arms and crawled out of bed. The floor creaked as I tiptoed from the room. The smell of brandy hung in the air in your bedroom. Light from the front porch gleamed on the white curtains. The breeze carried in the earth-dry smell of grass. Afraid to wake you, I lay down at the foot of the bed next to your feet under the bedcover. I watched the curtains rise and fall in the breeze, listened to the dry sounds of autumn leaves on the lawn, and no longer feeling the tugging at my heart, I slept.

Mama, I saw her in a white dress sitting by a canal in the Plain of Reeds. She was as cute as a hamster. I know she could only speak English and not many words in Vietnamese since you adopted her as a child. But I heard her voice, Mama. Her voice was Vietnamese. We went into this swamp by amtracs and rubber rafts. We scorched Charlie with flamethrowers and the smells of their charred flesh and burned vegetation were carried downwind to the next village. We brought in gunships and they came roaring over the flooded plain. They skimmed the water, shooting at stilt houses, firing rockets into the water where Charlie submerged themselves with a stalk of reed in their mouths. So many had died in there. A killing ground, Mama. She saw me and said, "Why doesn't Charlie fly gunships and jets?" And I said, "It'd be a long war if he did."

The first time I learned how to skin a deer was the night I went riding with Papa in his pickup. On a country road west of Maryland near home, he hit a deer. He got out and took the long rope in the pickup bed and dragged the deer to where we parked, and we lifted it onto the truck bed. We pulled up on our driveway at midnight and I helped him lug the deer up to the steel metal hook on the side of our garage door. He got out a handsaw and a skinner knife and showed me how to flay the skin.

He gave me his shotgun the next year, when I was thirteen. He showed me how to load and shoot. On Christmas Eve I was in the woods in the back of our house. Near the creek with a footbridge I shot a raccoon in its black-masked ugly face. It sat down, baring its teeth, and I shot it again through its mouth. I wanted its fur but didn't know how to skin it, so I kicked it into the creek.

I have to speak to you about everything I have done. I've closed the slit in my throat with one hand, caught the dripping blood with the other. I can hear my voice, Mama.

1987
Le Giang

Yesterday I took Mrs. Rossi to Ông Doc town to see a doctor. She was running a fever. Both mother and daughter were in the doctor's office and I was there with them as an interpreter. It could be the sun, or insect bite, the doctor said. The forest can be a scourge.

I translated what the old doctor said. He administered an intravenous antibiotic and Mrs. Rossi rested for a while. When we came out on the street, the forenoon sun was so strong she stood back on the curbside and donned her straw hat. She looked darker now, but not because her face was shaded. She'd gotten peasants' skin from riding day after day in the sampan and going into the forest. Her crow's feet showed in deep grooves when she squinted to watch a wedding procession going down the street. Standing hunched, hand locked in Chi Lan's, Mrs. Rossi still had that quiet, determined look. I wondered how much longer before those soft blue eyes would lose their dogged expression.

Water was receding on the street after a hard rain, and a wind-born stink came from the waterfront where fish were being sun-dried. Chi Lan pointed toward the procession.

"Mom, look!" The bride in her long white dress stood before a large puddle of water. The procession stopped. Then the bridegroom and the best man hoisted her up and carried her across the street, not even rolling up their pants legs. The rest followed, sloshing through the water. You could hear everyone laughing.

Mrs. Rossi smiled. She looked tired but relaxed. Perhaps being here with her daughter, instead of the forest, brought her enjoyment. We walked back to where I parked the Peugeot, and the noise the swiftlets made in the bird colonies made her cock her head. Chi Lan explained to her about the chirpings as she held her mother's hand, both finding their steps on the rough parts of the incline of the street, where broken pavement was patched with hewed logs of mangrove and date palm. We stopped at the café, also a brothel, and I bought them each a *café sua da*, the Vietnamese iced coffee with a dash of condensed milk. I knew Chi Lan had told her about the upstairs rooms with red-bulb wreathed window shutters in pink, because Mrs. Rossi kept looking back.

The port was empty of the fishing boats. "Where have they gone?" Mrs. Rossi asked. I told her that after the full moon, all the boats would head out to sea for days. "Why after the full moon?" she asked. Before that time, I told her, the water was moonlit and fish wouldn't bite the bait, so all the fishermen stayed in town getting drunk day and night and the brothel was as busy as a soup kitchen. Then when the moon became a waning crescent, the boats were unmoored, and one by one they left the river port, taking with them the owl's eyes painted on both sides of the bow, those wakeful eyes day and night having longed for the return to the sea.

Back at the inn, I hung a hammock on the veranda for Mrs. Rossi to take her siesta. I gave her a glass of iced lemonade. She stayed the swing with her bare feet and took a healthy swig. With one leg stretched out, she pulled up her pants leg. "Giang, look," she said. "Your tobacco water is a wonderful remedy. I wore socks I soaked in that water and no leeches have bothered me since."

I was glad to see no fresh bite marks on her ankles. I asked her if she felt any better from the fever and she nodded, pressing the chilled glass against the side of her face, flushed from the afternoon heat.

Chi Lan came out with two glasses of lemonade. She handed me one and sat down on the floor, knees drawn to her chest. The heat glimmered above the road and the air quivered. You could hear the cicadas singing in the tree tops, pulsing across the air, in the tangles of hummingbird trees, sea almond trees, and palm trees. The ethereal cadence at times died down, then suddenly flared up. I asked if they had ever seen bamboo flowering, and Chi Lan, gazing at the grove, asked, "Is it true that soon after they flower they will die?"

"Yes," I said. "Some species flower every one hundred years, and those of the same kind flower simultaneously all over the world. I saw the bamboo flower one day in the forest when I was your age."

"The massive flowering?" she asked.

"Yes," I said, "the once-in-a-lifetime phenomenon." I told them about the moment the greenish-yellow pods opened, and the petals unfurled, mauve and trembling, and every clump of golden bamboo turned pale purple.

Mrs. Rossi shook her head, smiling. "I won't live long enough to see such a wonder."

In the evening we sat on the veranda, the air now cool, and the breeze brought a scent of mud from a canal across the land. Mrs. Rossi reclined in the hammock, her loose shirt untucked, hanging down to her thighs, its whiteness a pale luster in the dark. Chi Lan and I sat in the metal folding chairs, looking toward the road. Mrs. Rossi said she was thinking of Maggie and her husband. She really liked Maggie, whom she called "a barrel of fun." The Irish couple had left that morning. Before leaving, Maggie held Mrs. Rossi's face in her hands and said, "This is awful. Ya should quit going into de forest and see de trees. Dat's right, love. At your age ya should rest. Ya should drink plenty tamah-toe juice and take plenty vihtamin. I wish ya find what ya lookin for over dere."

I told Mrs. Rossi I would miss the sound of Maggie's laugh. Chi Lan reminded me that I forgot to cook a dish of snake meat for them. She looked toward the road. A street peddler was pushing his cart and a boy, silhouetted against the glowing lantern hung behind him on the cart, was walking and striking his bamboo clappers. The *tok-tok-tok* kept cadence with his steps. I said, "You must try that man's noodle soup."

"*Pho*?" Chi Lan said.

"No, *hu tieu*. Chinese-style noodle soup."

"I'd love to try it," Chi Lan said. "Mom?"

"Sure, dear," Mrs. Rossi said. "Anything."

The man pushed the cart to the veranda. I asked for three bowls. The boy sat down on his haunches, gazing up at Chi Lan, who clicked her camera while the man prepared the dishes. He sliced the pork belly into thin cuts, pinched a handful of egg noodles, and dropped them into the boiling iron pot, then quickly strained them and placed them into a bowl. His hands deftly garnished the bowl with the meat, bean sprouts, sautéed garlic, and shallots. He wiped his hands on the rag hung on the handlebar and arranged three wontons on top of the bowl and squeezed a lemon wedge on it. Ceremoniously he ladled the pork-based broth, his head tilted watching the ladle hover and empty itself. Steam rose from the bowl in the wavering lantern light. A pungent fragrance wafted up to the veranda. The man fitted the bowl with a pair of chopsticks and a spoon and the boy carried the dish up. I told him to give the first bowl to Mrs. Rossi.

"Do you want to sit at his cart and eat?" I asked her.

"Sure," she said. "I want to try that."

She walked barefoot down the steps to the cart and the man pulled out a folding wooden chair for her. She placed the bowl on the metal ledge and motioned for us to join her. We sat at the cart, watching the man prepare each bowl, the air warm and wet with the noodle odor.

After we were done eating and the noodle cart left, the *tok-tok-tok* of the bamboo clappers fading into the distance, I made *café sua da* for each of us and we sat in the dark, sipping coffee. Above the creaking of her hammock, Mrs. Rossi said, "It's so beautiful here. Sometimes it makes me wonder why life is so complicated."

"You mean this rural life?" I asked.

"Yes." She put her glass on the veranda floor. "My son told me about this river. Around here somewhere. Said it was covered with white water lilies and full of fragrance. I wish I could see it the way he saw it. Just once. So help me God."

"Can we take her there when she's well again?" Chi Lan asked me.

"Certainly," I said. To Mrs. Rossi, I added, "You cross that river just about every day when Ông Ba takes you to the forest in his sampan."

Mrs. Rossi sat up, lifted her glass. "That river we came in from the canal? That's the same river my son told me about?"

"Ma'am," I said, "that's the Trem River. You'll see the stretch with water lilies farther up toward Upper U Minh.

They used to grow so wild they covered the river with only a narrow passage for boats, and when the flowers are in full bloom you could smell their scents way upriver and downriver."

"It must look like a painting," Mrs. Rossi said, "the way he described."

"I'm sure he must have had an artistic eye."

Mrs. Rossi sipped her iced coffee and, palming her glass in her lap, gazed into the night. "Look at that!"

In the bamboo grove a blue light glowed, drifting knee high above the ground. The night was so dark the incandescent blue looked eerie, hovering in that stillness.

"What is that?" Chi Lan asked.

"The blue-ghost fireflies," I said. "It's their mating season."

"Fireflies?" Mrs. Rossi asked. "Why aren't they blinking?"

"They are not the ordinary fireflies," I said. "Not the flashing ones. They only glow. The males."

"Those lights are from the males?"

"Well, the females glow too. But they don't have wings. They stay on the ground. They need much moisture and ground cover. During the day both males and females hide under the leaves on the ground. I used to see them when I was deep in the forest."

"So if you destroy the ground and the forest," Mrs. Rossi said, "like the war did, then you destroy them too. Am I right?"

"Especially the females," I said. "They can't fly."

"Especially the females," Mrs. Rossi said. "The source of life."

"They're beautiful," Chi Lan said.

She picked up her camera on her chair and knelt on one knee on the top step, clicking off several shots, and the flashlights made quick bright bursts. "They're like winged ghosts," Chi Lan said.

I coughed into my hand as Chi Lan turned to look at me. I had refrained from smoking whenever I was with her. Mrs. Rossi returned to her hammock, swinging it side to side.

"Yesterday," she said, "Mr. Lung and I encountered something very bizarre in the forest. We saw under a tree a heap of dirt shaped like a sitting human. Mr. Lung explained that it was a termite mound. I said, 'What's inside?' He tapped it with his spade and the dirt mound started to fall apart, and Holy Jesus, it's a human skeleton. A sitting skeleton carrying a rucksack. The rucksack, too, was encased completely in dirt." She held up her hand. "Giang, I know what you're about to ask. It was a North Vietnamese soldier, from what Mr. Lung saw in the rucksack. But there was nothing to indicate his name or where he had lived."

Mrs. Rossi said she felt devastated when she thought of the dead soldier's family, who might still be searching for him, or waiting for him to come home. She wondered where all the souls of the dead have gone. I told her perhaps the ghosts needed a medium to show themselves to the living, and the fireflies' blue lights were that medium, just like earth, water, fire, and air made up the medium of living human beings. Mrs. Rossi said she had never believed in ghosts, but after going into the U Minh forest she wasn't so certain anymore. She said once in the forest, in a damp, shaded place she had sensed somebody's presence. She got goose bumps. She said she believed the woman inn owner's story about the sound of human crying in the forest on rainy nights following a muggy day that made the air thick like vapors rising from the bogs, and the vaporous air was the right medium for otherworldly manifestation. I told them the story of five hundred French paratroopers who were dropped into the U Minh forest in 1952. All of them disappeared in the mangrove swamps forever. "One night recently," I said, "I was standing at the window of

my room smoking a cigarette and the night was full of the
sawing of crickets, the clicking of bats, the harsh squawking
of night herons up in their tree colony. As I listened mindlessly to them I heard a thump, then another. There I saw
two clods of dirt resting on the window ledge. How they
landed precisely side by side I did not know. Neither did
I know where they came from. The following night it happened again. I had to tell the woman inn owner about the
incidents. She said, 'They want to be fed.' 'Who?' I asked.
'The dead people,' she said. So she put on the rear veranda
a bowl of cooked rice, a plate of boiled chicken, a bundle of
bananas, lidded with a dome cover. After that there were no
more clods of dirt."

Mrs. Rossi said she believed that through the praying and worshipping we keep in touch with the spirits of
those who are gone. She said she saw many shrines in the
land and understood that they remind us of things beyond
us. But she said God will hear you only if you are sincere
in your praying, because faith is something not seen, not
touched, therefore not explicable to mortals.

It was the first time I saw her cry.

It's late in the afternoon when the funeral procession shows up on the road that goes past Old Lung's dwelling. Standing outside his abode and watching the cortege move along slowly, the coffin bearers shaded by the setting sun, I remember years before watching men carrying new caskets to the front, time and again, shouldering the palls as they climbed the hill, the long line of soldiers bearing the coffins silhouetted against sunset, moving slowly up the hill slope that grew wild with passion flowers like yellow daubs of fresh paint.

"Must be the hour," I say, "this late."

"Must be," Old Lung says, brushing off the cigarette ash that fell on the front of his shirt. "These folks surely believe in the right hour to bury someone."

It's one of those new coffins that Old Lung made for families of the deceased in the buffer zone. He made this one on a day he stayed home while Mrs. Rossi was recuperating. He asks me when she'd need him again and, knowing Mrs. Rossi, I tell him I wouldn't be surprised if she would be back into the forest before she was fully well. Old Lung says nothing. But moments later he says, shaking his head, "Poor old lady." He strokes his gray tuft of goatee. "You know that I done whatever she asked me to. But it just makes no damn sense at all. This whole business. Few times I wanted to tell her that. Like . . ."

I look at him quickly. "Like she's gone out of her mind?"

Old Lung snorts a yeah.

The procession passes by. Silent. Solemn. The coffin bearers step slowly, keeping the poles level so as not to jolt the miniature altar, the candles, the flower vases, sitting atop the pall.

"Let's give 'em a shoulder," Old Lung says, tossing away his cigarette stub.

Reluctantly I follow him. He always lends them a shoulder when they pass by his house, because all of them are his clients. We each put our shoulder to a pole, walking parallel. The rock-heavy weight sinks through the pole into my shoulder. I wonder who the dead might be to weigh this much. Old Lung says, low-voiced, "Relax, don't strain yourself." He walks easily in step with the bearers and we move slowly in the dying sunlight, and the air is full of chirps the bush crickets make in the undergrowth and roadside weeds. A canal appears in sight, and if you follow its course due east for a fair distance, you will reach the cemetery below a commune.

Halfway down the road, Old Lung detaches himself from the pole. "We get off here," he says to me.

I stand back, watching the line move on in the trilled *kr-r-r-ek* the tree frogs chorus from the water. Old Lung heads for a dwelling that sits back from the road behind a banana grove and hummingbird trees. He disappears in the twilight and I wonder what he's up to. Frogs are calling from the water and mosquitos whine in my ears. It's their feeding time.

Old Lung comes out of the darkening trees. He's lugging a sampan that makes a dry scraping sound as he drags it to the water.

"You borrow it?" I ask him. "What's the idea, old man?"

"Let's go get drunk," he says, pulling the sampan. It's a flat-bottomed boat powered by a shrimp-tail motor.

"Where to?" I'm stopped by a sudden cough.

"To see a buddy of mine," he says.

The boat hits the water and slides in with a splash. Old Lung starts the motor with one quick yank of the cord. The motor roars, echoing across the still water.

In the twilight we go past a logging camp, then the district town flickering with gas lamps from the thatch-roofed dwellings on the northern bank of Cái Tàu River. I have been on this canal, among others, where the sunlit water during the day glitters with gourami, translucent blue and red-striped. We are on the river, wide and eddying and gurgling over deep-bottomed drops, where it flows fast before entering the sea. The boat goes down a creek and in the dusky light you can see the land, bare and brown, and hear the sound of waves coming from the sea.

Mr. Rum is a fisherman. Old Lung introduces me to him in the twilight outside his place. By the door sit two pots of cycads, their woody trunks crowned with stiff leaves. As we enter his dwelling, we can hear the seaward wind humming under the aluminum roof. A dark smell of tobacco and burned wood hangs about the house, lit by a gas lamp that sits on a square table in the center of the room. The yellow light casts a fan-shaped glow on the rafters. Hung from a rafter is a bamboo cage. A bluish-gray, red-beaked parrot stirs at our sight, clucking its tongue. *Tak-tak-tak.*

"Guests coming! Guests coming!" it squawks.

"Don't you know me by now?" Old Lung shakes the cage gently and the bird bobs its head nervously.

"He's not a dog, mind you," Mr. Rum says, his bass voice drawling in a southern accent.

He's half a head taller than I am, about Old Lung's age. His closely cropped hair is cloud white. His skin is amber dark, like fish-sauce color, more red than brown. In his white undershirt his sinewy arms are tattooed with a tiger's head on one upper arm and a whale on the other. He yanks off his undershirt and drapes it over the bird cage. We can hear the parrot purring and clucking in its cloaked world.

"Keeps him quiet for a while," Mr. Rum says.

A shiny gash runs from the middle of his chest to his abdomen. You can't help thinking that, at one time, someone tried to cleave him open with a butcher knife.

"Sit down," he says, "sit down."

Old Lung sits on a rush mat in the center of the room next to a tall hardwood, coal-black column. In one corner, atop an aging armoire, sits a small altar. A black-wood tray holds a tea set in white ceramic, the teapot decorated with a hand-painted bright red dragon. In a corner of the tray is a Bastos cigarette pack. I step forward to look at the brass-framed black-and-white picture propped behind a candle-holder, its white candle just a stub. A young-looking girl, her hair wrapped in a polka-dot head scarf, carries a boy astride her hip, smiling happily at the camera. A charming girl with beautiful white teeth. Hung on the wood-paneled wall behind the altar are three stingray tails, leathery looking and blackish. You can still see the barbed stings on them. I wonder if he ever dusted the altar, for cobwebs hang across the corner, filmy and gleaming in the gaslight.

Mr. Rum goes out the back door to the veranda. On the top step stands a metal barrel. He lights a fire with his cigarette lighter and the barrel roars, the fire growing brighter and brighter, and though it burns on the windward side, the fire's insect-repelling smoke of cajeput twigs and leaves drifts, warm and rank, into the room. In this season, mosquitos swarm the land and feed on cattle and people until they are so swollen with blood they eventually land somewhere, anywhere, to rest.

Mr. Rum brings in an iron brazier and a clear plastic bag bulging with blood cockles. Old Lung is building a fire in the brazier while Mr. Rum hovers over a horseshoe-shaped bench in a corner that frames a brick hearth. Steam puffs in gray wisps from a pot that sits on a wrought-iron tripod. He comes to the mat and puts down a tray—bowls and spoons and short glasses and salt-and-pepper shakers, three oyster knives, a thin wooden rod that pierces through six fresh lemons. In the center of the tray stands a bottle of pale yellow liquid.

Old Lung uncorks the bottle, passing it back and forth under his nose. "Devil you," he says, grinning. "Devil wine."

"From friendly neighbors," Mr. Rum says, sitting down to inspect the hissing cockles on the smoldering brazier.

"What neighbors?" I ask.

"The Khmers," he says, sitting back, legs crossed over each other. "Over the border. They grow unbelievable crops of glutinous rice over there. Cook this rice and the fragrance is so rich it brings down sparrows from the sky. They let it ferment in copper stills and then steam it inside banana leaves." He arranges the three short glasses and watches Old Lung pour the wine into each glass.

We toast one another. I sniff. A bursting bouquet of baby rice kernels, buttery smelling, baked-bread dark. The wine spreads in my mouth, numbing my tongue with a mellow sting. Momentarily I feel a small fire warming my stomach and I feel as if I have known Mr. Rum for a long time and I appreciate his company.

He swirls his glass and, holding it out in front of us, says, "Look at those streaks. Only devilish wine has 'em."

Clinging to the side of his glass are silky- and oily-look-ing long legs. Old Lung slaps me on the thigh. "Told you," he says, his eyes twinkling. "Brother Rum knows more than just fish."

Mr. Rum simply nods. His eyes are red, the opaque red from sand and seawater that permanently stamps a mark on fishermen and seaside dwellers. He pulls two lemons out from the rod and, with his pocketknife, slices each of them into several thin wedges. I mix salt and pepper in each smaller bowl while Old Lung blows at the brazier. The coals glow red, the cockles sizzle and bubble along the shell mar-gins. When the shells open, we pick them up by hand, feel the smoking heat cut through our fingertips, and drop them into our bowls. I squeeze a wedge of lemon into a shell, pry the meat loose with an oyster knife and touch the meat, pinched between my fingers, in the salt-pepper mix in the smaller bowl. The heat stings my tongue, then a seawater taste sets in. Chewing, I raise my glass. The chewy meat tastes sweet, tangy with a whiff of cucumber like when you just slice a knife into it. I down my glass. Instantly my eyes water. I exhale a buttery-dough scent through my nose and reach for the bottle.

"I'm gonna visit you more often, *Ông* Rum," I say to him.

He lets me fill half his glass, asking me where I came from originally. I tell him between sips. In the clanking of shells, the smacking of lips sucking the cockle's juice, he says, "Ahh!" while grinning like a devil. "You're like me," he says, raising his glass to mine. "I was a Viet Minh fighter, say, before you were born. Have lived here in the Mekong Delta all my life . . ." He spreads more cockles on the bra-zier, the red-hot coals hissing and smoking from the spilled juice of those cockles already eaten, and tells me there are many old Viet Minh fighters like him in the region, and I think about Ông Ba who took Mrs. Rossi to the forest every day until she fell ill. "Then the French left," Mr. Rum says in his deep voice, "and the Americans came. I was married and we had a son. Had a piece of land up near Trem River and Ra Ghe Creek. One day their helicopters flew in and spirited away just about everyone in my village. I came back from the field and my-oh-my I was all alone, like an alien. The ARVN quarantined all of my people in a barbed-wire camp in the town district until every living man from our village showed up to claim his family—men they believed were either Viet Cong or deserters. They got me and set my family free. They ran a check on my background and though they found out I was a civilian, they knew I was a Viet Minh during the Indochina War. So they said to me, 'You've been dodging our national obligations during war-time. Now serve the country or stay behind bars.' What did I do? I became an ARVN soldier." Mr. Rum pours the bag onto the brazier, the cockles rolling around like stones, and empties our bowls filled with shells into the bag. He lifts the bottle, almost gone now, and refills our glasses, except his. "You can say that I was a South Vietnamese soldier, but I had no desire or intention to kill for them. I missed my family. Months went by and still they granted me no leave. Then the day came when they said I could go on leave. I remember someone laughed. I saw a smirk on their faces and it was then they told me that my village wasn't there anymore. They played with me while I asked, 'Relocation?' One man slapped me on the back, said, 'New-Life Hamlet woulda been too good for 'em. Your whole village was a Viet Cong village. Tell ya this: they fired at our patrol from inside the village, and guess what? We relocated all of 'em to hell.' No one survived, they said. I felt my life explode right in front of me. I told them I quit. They threw me into a cell and asked me three days later if I changed my mind. I told them I wanted to die and they laughed. 'Let's have some fun before that happens,' they said. So they tied me to a river craft and sped it down a river and I was bouncing up and down on the water holding on to the rope for my dear life, and they changed the speeds so that one minute I sank, drinking a belly full of water, and the next minute my body was flung about like a rag. They turned into this swamp and the muddy water was so thick I took a mouthful and knew this was where they wanted me to die. They sped up the boat and something sharp in the mud cut me lengthwise, cut loose the rope, and I sank into the stinking mud, my mind was half gone, but my body still had enough strength left and I managed to move on foot in that shallow water, keeping my head under as I heard them doubling back, the engine noise, the men cursing, and I had in my mouth a long reed stalk and I breathed through it as long as I could till I heard 'em no more. Know what I did after they were gone?" Mr. Rum checks me, squinting. "Put mud on this wound here and lay in the reeds till nightfall and then found my way out of that town." Mr. Rum peers down at his naked torso, oxblood dark, at the gash that seems to bisect his trunk. An ugly looking cut. "Before long I joined the Viet Cong's regional forces. I might not be as educated as those from the main force and not likely to become a Party member, but I never gave a hoot about that. I was a full-time soldier again."

I lift my gaze toward the altar. "That your wife and son?"

"Yeah." Mr. Rum taps his fingers on the empty bottle, musing as he looks at it. "He was four in that picture."

"And how old was he when they wiped out your village?"

"Seven." Mr. Rum rises and goes to the hearth. He carries back the pot still bubbling with steam and places it on the brazier. As he lifts the lid, a rich smell of onions wafts up. My mouth waters. Old Lung clucks his tongue and dips his head to sniff the aroma. Inside the pot is creamy rice porridge, flecked with fried onions in brown. Meaty looking fillets of fish float about.

"What you got in there, Brother?" Old Lung asks, lining up three bowls alongside the brazier.

"Sea bass." Mr. Rum ladles the porridge into Old Lung's bowl. "Caught it today at sunrise."

"You got nothing else to do at that hour?" Old Lung grins at Mr. Rum.

"Just me and the bass." Mr. Rum dips the ladle in the pot and fills my bowl.

I sprinkle black pepper on the porridge while Old Lung slurps it from his spoon. I hold the broth's dark peppery taste in my mouth until my nose breathes out warm, wet air. I break a small chunk of fish and chew. Its firm texture flakes in my mouth and melts with a smoky flavor. I glance up at Mr. Rum, who is blowing steam off the bowl.

"You catch stingrays too?" I ask.

"Stingrays?" he asks, gulping. "No. Have no use for 'em."

"I saw their tails on the wall over there."

"Ah." He draws in a sharp breath, his gaze lingering on the wall. "Reminders of something I'm not too proud of." His hand holding the spoon stops in midair. "Used to discipline my son with those—the tails. You can say I was a bad-tempered man. Used to beat him till his mother threw herself on top of him to make me stop. She used to salve his cuts from the lashes and made him sleep facedown to ease the pain. You see, I'd lived my life with rules. Couldn't tolerate anything that broke the rules. Until one day I was out fishing and got whipped in the face by a stingray and it stung like hell. So bad I had to go ashore and find some liniment to take the pain away. From that day on I never touched a stingray tail again—as a whip. Ever. But memories. Ah. They never die, right?"

Old Lung nods, smacking his lips. I say a soft yeah. Mr. Rum's voice, empty of emotion, and his face, devoid of expression, make me feel the pain for him. He says, "See the cycad pots when you walked in? Well, she used to have them around. She had some sort of affection for 'em palms. Strange species. Grow slowly and live very long. She said some live to a thousand years." He gives a soft chuckle. "I guess I grew them to keep the memory of her around. Maybe something that outlasts all of us like those palms allows us the illusion to hang our memories onto it." He shrugs. "To keep our memories alive. Wouldn't you say?"

"Well," I say, "if you really love someone and the person dies, will the love die in you after that?"

"No," Mr. Rum says. "I think of them every day."

I muse briefly. "So you don't need the cycads."

"I guess not." Mr. Rum grins, a rare grin. "Maybe to spice up my life, that's why, eh?"

Old Lung yawns, shaking his head. Mr. Rum reaches out and slaps him on the shoulder. "Don't fall asleep on me now. Bring your glass with you outside."

The fire in the metal barrel has died down, now smoldering, and the air smells bitter. We arrange three folding metal chairs along the wall on the rear veranda. Mr. Rum puts out the gas lamp and removes his undershirt from the birdcage. In the sudden dark the parrot croaks, *Tak-tak-tak, chào Ông Rum!* And Mr. Rum says, *Chào con.* Hello, son. He has his white undershirt flung over his shoulder. In his hand is a fresh bottle of rice wine. It's pitch-dark and a steady breeze coming from the sea drives the faint leaf-burned smoke toward the land in the back of the house. Mr. Rum lights his pipe, a long curving one, and the darkness smells sweet.

The land lies bare, stretching until your eyes can see a grove of trees, dark and dense, screening off the horizon. I ask Mr. Rum if the trees are cajeput and he says yes, for reforestation. After a brief silence, he says, "Bad land. Bad

soil. Just black or brown acidic soil. Can't grow any vegetables. Any time I crave vegetables I have to go off into the
cajeput grove and look for climbing fern—those that thrive
only in cajeput forest. Here people eat the fern's sprouts as
salads."

He refills our glasses and we sit sipping our rice wine
and slowly the cockles' seawater taste is gone from my
tongue. I pop a cigarette into my mouth, drawing deeply
on it without lighting it. I think of Chi Lan, hearing her soft
chiding words each time she sees me reach for my cigarette pack. I feel a sudden urge to cough and fight it. Eyes
closed, I let my mind go blank. I can hear the stillness. Then
a bellow sounds across the air. Deep, spiraling, mournful.
Like the sound of a bugle on the battlefield. A chorus of
it fills the sky. It breaks the peaceful quiet and I hear Old
Lung curse. Mr. Rum raises his voice, "I know, people hate
that sound. It'll be gone soon."

"It sure plays with my nerves," Old Lung says.

"Sounds like a whole lot of bugles blowing, eh," Mr.
Rum says. "From those fluted clamshells they blow on.
Have that queer sound, quite irritating. But it drives off the
bats from feeding on their fish let out to dry."

Old Lung chortles. "You got me there, brother. The bats
can hear those sounds?"

"Certainly. Go down to the fishing hamlet and take a
look. What you see are dead bats all over the shore. Like
they were shot down when the horns get going with all
those terrible sounds."

"*Aya*," Old Lung says, smacking his lips.

"Those bats came one day," Mr. Rum says, "when they
saw fish laid out to dry. They just dropped down and
feasted on the fish and before folks could react, everything
was gone before their eyes. Bat plague, they called it. Went
on and on, the worst nightmare to fishermen's families. For

years, mind you. After they'd tried this and that and nothing worked, they tried the fluted clamshells. The shells are big, biggest one I saw was forty centimeters long."

Old Lung flicks off his cigarette butt and scratches his cheek. "Who coulda thought of that?"

Mr. Rum pours some more wine for Old Lung. I close my eyes, steadying my nerves. The irritation in my throat begins to recede. "When they blew on the shells," Mr. Rum says, "those bats went berserk. Many flew off, many dropped like rocks, many died. They'd come back though. And the sounds of fluted shells would drop 'em again and again. Then one day the bats stopped coming."

"*Aya*," Old Lung says again. "True story, brother?"

Mr. Rum laughs, then drops his voice, "Told to me though."

They say nothing for a while and both must have thought that I dozed off, for I can hear Old Lung say in a low voice, "Who was the genius who came up with the fluted clamshells?"

"This young fisherman," Mr. Rum replies. "They said when they were still chasing those bats away with sticks and oars, they caught a big one. Wingspread's a meter wide. This fellow was playing with his fluted clamshell nearby and every time he blew on it, the bat seemed to struggle in confusion. Or pain. He stopped blowing and the bat seemed to be its own self again. He blew and blew and the bat went berserk and then lay dead. It was then folks found out that the bat could hear the sound the fluted clamshell made. Lethal sound."

"All this happened before you came?"

"Way before. Our hero would be one hundred years old now."

Old Lung snorts. Then Mr. Rum's voice: "Know what happened to that fellow?" His bass voice drops even lower.

"He was working for this man who owned a big fishing boat and one night the man caught him screwing his wife on the boat."

"Musta been a night with a full moon, eh?" Old Lung laughs in spurts.

"You got that right," Mr. Rum says, clearing his throat. "They said his boss saw fish jumping and thrashing on the deck. Said a whole container of live fish musta been knocked over when those two lovers wrestled each other on the deck. And that's how our hero met his end."

"Boss killed him?"

"With an oar."

"From hero to villain over a woman, eh?"

I hang my head back, stretching my neck. The fluted clam horns have stopped, and in the stillness drifts the sound of waves. I breathe slowly, emptying my thoughts, and I can feel myself float in air. Old Lung's whisper comes across. "Look, here it comes."

"I see it," Mr. Rum replies.

I open my eyes a slit and see the blue-ghost fireflies massing a short distance down the length of the land. A soft stationary blue orb hovering above the ground.

"You think he'll come?" Old Lung says. "Likely," Mr. Rum says.

"Last time it took a while."

"I remember."

I sit up, fixing my gaze on the blue sphere. It moves slowly, at times keeping still, at times whirling. "You talking about a ghost?"

Both of them turn their heads toward me.

"An old ghost," Mr. Rum says.

"Yeah," Old Lung says. "Just keep your eyes open."

I raise my glass to my lips. "Hey, old man. Can I see this ghost without putting lime on my toes and fingertips?"

"Don't have to," Old Lung says, lowering his voice. "Once you break the barrier between you and them—and you did at my place—you won't need lime again."

"I'll keep quiet this time," I say, resting the glass of wine in my lap. Mr. Rum's voice drones on in the quiet, saying that when there are not many living souls on the land, the yin force overwhelms the yang, that Buddhas and Bodhisattvas are too far away, and demons and ghosts are at your door every night. Across the land katydids call from the cajeput grove, a rattled *ch-ch-ch* chorus pulsating endlessly. The orb glows bluer and brighter, and as we watch in silence a human figure suddenly manifests in the center of the bluish sphere. A soldier. He wears the American army combat uniform and it looks wet. His hair, too, matted wetly in strands on his brow. He stands in one place, his hand clutching his throat, his other hand holding the clutching hand's wrist. He looks lost, turning his head left then right, as if to take his bearings in the night. Then he moves toward the cajeput grove, the blue orb following him, and somewhere before the woods the blue light disperses into the night and he too disappears.

I lean back, hard, in my chair. The chair's legs scrape the cement floor. "Ông Rum," I say to him, "how often do you see him?"

"Once in a while," Mr. Rum says. "He's harmless. Every now and then I put out food to pacify him."

"This region's full of them," Old Lung says and lights another cigarette.

"He just shows up like that?" I ask. "Out of nowhere?"

"Nah." Mr. Rum puffs on his pipe, the red pinhead glows then dims. "He's got a place over there on my land. I buried him."

"How?" I lean forward. "How'd he get there?"

Mr. Rum exhales with a great effort. "You know, over the years I've buried a few people here on my land. Dead.

Unclaimed. Drowned in the ocean and drifted ashore. I remember one time during the war the Americans dropped shallow-water mines along the seacoast and not a day went by without seeing a corpse come floating in. Most of the time you can't make out the faces. No, sir. Not after birds and fish have made a meal for themselves. Personal effects, I kept. Got a marine wristwatch that you can read the dial at night. Got a pair of heavy-duty binoculars. Got a French beret. Hope they don't mind me keeping 'em." He stretches his legs, turns toward me. "This fellow who shows up occasionally on my land is one of 'em. Wasn't drowned though. Just drifted in from somewhere and got caught in my fish trap."

Mr. Rum lifts the bottle and motions to me for a refill, but I shake my head. He pours some wine for Old Lung and himself. "That morning about sunrise I went down to the creek, where you came in earlier, to where I set my fish trap overnight just before the ocean. I usually got out there earlier but that morning I skipped one tide cycle and was sure there'd be plenty more fish. Was plenty of 'em all right by the time I got there. Low tide and my fish trap just shook with giant sea perch and threadfins and sea bass and prawns. They jumped and smacked, and I reached in with my hand net and felt the waves push something against my fish trap under the water. Thought it must be a giant grouper so I lifted my hand net to let the fish go into the trap. I couldn't see its shape. Huge, though. It went sideways, blocked the trap's mouth. I dipped my hand into the water and felt something other than a fish. I grabbed a handful of hair. Felt like a handful of kelp. Felt around and seized a part of a shirt and pulled the thing up. Damn if I didn't try. But I finally got it to float up with my oar as a lever. Quite a sight. A soldier. American soldier. He was wearing a rain poncho. His boots were so soaked through they felt soft. He didn't smell. Musta died the night before by looking at his poncho and remembering the hard rain we got the previous night. By the time I got him onto the boat with fish jumping around him it was first light. Just misty all around. But I could make out his face. And what I saw was a hole in his throat. Another hole in the back of his neck. He musta been shot there and the bullet went through his neck.

"His hands. I couldn't straighten their fingers. They were bent like crabs' claws. So I just let them be and rowed home."

I lift my face. "When was all of this?"

Mr. Rum rubs his nose a few times. "When? Hmm. Nineteen sixty-seven."

"Remember the month, don't you?"

"August." Mr. Rum shakes his head. "The ninth. Was my birthday, that day."

I take a quick sip. "He have any personal effects on him?"

Mr. Rum nods. "Wallet, dog tag, a plain old wristwatch. I kept 'em."

I lean forward to see him better. "Ông Rum," I say, "can I see his personal effects?"

Mr. Rum tilts his head back. "His stuff? Yeah. Why?"

"Just let me see them. You mind?"

"Not at all. Lemme get 'em."

Old Lung turns in his chair, pats me on my shoulder. "What's the idea?"

"Curious."

Mr. Rum comes back out, holding up the gas lamp and carrying in the other arm a burlap sandbag in faded green. Without saying a word, he holds the lamp while I pull out the poncho, ripped in places. It comes out of the sandbag, like it emerges back into the world, shaking off a horribly musty smell. Mr. Rum lowers the lamp as I empty the poncho's contents onto my lap. A plastic-wrapped packet. Inside is a paper-wrapped packet and inside it are a wristwatch, a leather wallet, and a dog tag. The stainless-steel dog tag shines in the light as I lift its long ball chain to read its stamped letters, numbers in five lines: Rossi, Nicola, followed by a line of numbers, then "O," Catholic.

I feel a rush of blood to my head. I could never forget the date. Everything from that night comes back. As if it moves around on the shiny dog tag. Time suddenly shrinks. Twenty years is merely a blink of an eye.

"He was a lieutenant, wasn't he?" I ask Mr. Rum without looking at him.

"I think he was," Mr. Rum says. "Heaven knows how many times I looked at his uniform before I buried him."

I stare at the dog tag. *Nicola Rossi.*

"But what are you looking for?" Mr. Rum asks as I open the wallet.

The photographs' colors in the plastic sleeves aren't sharp any longer. I look at Nicola Rossi, youthful, sandy-blond-haired, standing in a white shirt outside a house. I look at another photograph. Mrs. Rossi, I can tell. Reddish-blond hair, in her forties. A man, handsome, dark-eyed, wearing a white shirt with a red tie. Nicola Rossi looks more like his mother than his father. Solemn-looking in the picture.

Holding the opened wallet in my hands, I tell Mr. Rum about Mrs. Rossi who came to look for the remains of her son, a lieutenant who went missing-in-action during the Vietnam War. Old Lung listens, says *Aya* repeatedly, thanking heaven and the Buddhas who finally cast their merciful eyes earthward and put a stop to Mrs. Rossi's ordeal. Mr. Rum sets the lamp on the floor and, stroking his stubbled chin, says, "Did she tell you the date her son went missing?"

"No." I fold up the wallet. "I don't think she was aware of it. It probably means nothing to her."

"Then why'd you ask me about it?"

"Because that night," I say, "August the ninth, we over-ran his base before daybreak and we killed every survivor and then we pursued those who got away and he was one of them. Me and my men got into the forest chasing him in the torrential rain until we spotted him near a creek. He was unarmed. We shot him. I did. I shot him. Just as he turned around facing us. Got him in the throat. We kicked his body into the water and left." My throat feels sand-dry. "We'll bring her the news tomorrow. Can I take his stuff with me?"

Old Lung smacks his lips, scratching his head like he had lice. "You gonna bring her peace or you gonna bring her hell?"

There isn't a soul on the moonlit road that goes by the inn as I return from Mr. Rum's place. I carry the burlap bag in the crook of my arm. Nearing midnight the moon hovers directly overhead, a beautiful round disk in a cloudless sky, and the road glows softly in a pale light. You can see along the road the cajeput flowers white as milk and you can smell their scent light as the lotus's.

The road bends and, ahead of me after the curve, a peddler's cart is moving along, the *tok-tok-tok* of a bamboo block sounding like the Buddhist wooden percussion. A cart selling fresh corn. I walk faster until I come within earshot to hear the portable radio music coming from it. At this hour mother and daughter must be sound asleep. They have never tried the local sweet corn. The woman peddler pushes the cart along with one hand on the handlebar, the other hand tapping the bamboo block with a wooden stick. She passes by here now and then, always late at night, and always there are customers who get hungry around this time. The cart's blue umbrella, on this clear night, is furled around a tall metal pole behind the handlebar.

Past the inn a voice calls out from the veranda. Chi Lan's voice. It startles me. I clutch the bag tighter. I tell the woman peddler that I work at the inn and my late-night guests would like to try her sweet corn. I walk beside the cart through the entrance crowned with bamboo and I can see both mother and daughter standing on the veranda.

"*Chú*," Chi Lan calls to me.

"Giang!" Mrs. Rossi raises her voice. "Are you a street peddler now?"

They both laugh. I smile at them. I feel sad but happy at the same time. Happy to see Mrs. Rossi in good spirits. Happy to see her smile. In her nightgown she stands barefoot, reclasping the hair band behind her ears, her hair and gown startlingly white. Chi Lan walks down the steps. Also barefoot, she wears white shorts and a red T-shirt. She doesn't look sleepy.

"Where've you been, *Chú*?" she asks and drops her gaze to the burlap bag in my arm.

"I was visiting friends."

"Is that a sleeping bag?"

"No." I put my other arm on it. "Just some stuff."

"We got hungry and Mom didn't want to ask the old woman for snacks. They're in bed now."

"I know." I try to smile. "I thought you would both be in bed too."

"Well." Giggling, she looks up to her room and back at me. "You know why I'm still up?"

"Why?"

"There's a bat in our room."

Mrs. Rossi coughs to interrupt her. She says, "Dear, you're holding up the lady."

Chi Lan puts her hand to her mouth. "I'm sorry."

I move to the side of the cart by the gas lamp. "What can they have, sis?" I ask.

"That depends," the woman says as she lays down the stick in her hand. "Do they like boiled corn? Or roasted? With butter and fried onions? Or stir-fried corn?"

I tell Chi Lan the choices.

"What's stir-fried corn?" she asks.

"They break loose the kernels and stir-fry them."

"I'll have one roasted corn."

"I'll try stir-fry," Mrs. Rossi calls down. "I've never tried that."

"What do you have, *Chú*?" Chi Lan asks me.

"I already ate," I say, avoiding her gaze. But I feel hungry again, or perhaps it's the gnawing in my stomach. My throat feels so dry it hurts when I swallow. She stands with me watching the woman lay a corn ear on the coal brazier, fanning it with a hand fan until the coals come to life, burning bright red. While the corn is being roasted, she places a skillet on a portable gas grill, turns up the flame, and quickly pours some cooking oil onto the skillet. She turns the corn ear on the brazier, one side palely browned, and fans the coals, and the warm air smells of burned match-sticks from coal smoke. She empties a plastic container onto the skillet as the oil begins bubbling. The kernels, yellow and wedge-shaped, pop merrily. Chi Lan sweeps her hair back behind her ears and watches the woman cut a thin slice of fresh butter from a stick she stores in an ice box, and the butter melts instantly into a sizzling yellow puddle. She sprinkles some diced onions and adds a pinch of sugar, salt, and powdered red pepper. She stirs the kernels quickly, so the heat only shrinks the onions into curly clumps of light brown, the kernels glistening with butter and red-pepper flecks. She turns the corn on the brazier until the ear browns evenly. She pulls and cuts a large sheet of aluminum foil and, with a brush, smears the foil with melted butter. As we watch, she coats the butter-filmed foil evenly with salt and pepper, picks up the corn by the shank and wraps it tightly in the foil.

We sit on the veranda in the dark after the peddler is gone, each of us having a glass of fresh lemonade that Chi Lan made earlier in the evening. The moon washes the land with a dreamy light, soft as a veil. The buttered smell of corn lingers in the air and I feel the gnawing in my stomach again. Mrs. Rossi, sitting on a chair by the hammock, says the stir-fried corn is delicious. She asks me what I had for dinner. I tell her. Chi Lan chimes in, "I'd love to try blood cockles, but not the liquor." Mrs. Rossi chuckles. "Dear, they go together. At least that's how I remember." Chi Lan explains to me that her mother used to drink. That her drinking became heavier after her son went missing in the war. I ask Mrs. Rossi about her husband. I remember the man in the wallet photograph. After a silence she says that he killed himself. Her tone gives me pause. I touch the burlap bag under my chair with my foot and drag it in closer to me. "Why?" I ask. Mrs. Rossi closes the carton, wipes her lips with the back of her hand. "After the war," she says. "He never really came back."

I sigh. I want to get up and walk out into the night, filling my lungs with fresh air, and I want to walk down the moonlit road like the crazy old man who occasionally takes to the road with nothing on his mind.

Chi Lan wraps up the finished corn in the foil. Its faint rustle breaks the quiet. "You should've tried the roast corn, *Chú*."

"You enjoyed it?"

"So tasty. I'm fascinated with the street peddlers around here."

"I knew you and your mom would love the fresh corn they sell from the cart."

"I love corn. Do you, *Chú*?"

"Yeah. How many kernels on a single ear?"

Chi Lan turns her head toward me. Mrs. Rossi says, "Good question, Giang. I know the answer but let her try first."

"That's a weird question," Chi Lan says, giggling. "Who could've thought of that?"

"Well," I say, "how many?"

"I don't know, *Chú*." She grabs my hand. "You call the woman peddler back. I'll order another corn ear and I'll tell you how many."

"Want me to tell you?"

"Please. I learn new things every day here."

"Eight hundred on a single ear."

Mrs. Rossi weighs in. "A thousand on a healthy ear of corn. How many rows do you think each ear might have, Giang?"

Chi Lan turns to her mother. "Mom!"

"I used to teach, remember, dear?" Mrs. Rossi says, smiling.

"Sixteen, ma'am," I say. "Roughly."

"You're right," Mrs. Rossi says.

"You're good, *Chú*," Chi Lan says, placing the foil-wrapped corn at her feet.

"What did you do today?" I ask her.

"I went out with my camera. You know what I photographed behind the inn?"

"Did you wear a long-sleeved shirt?"

"Yes, *Chú*. I remember the wasp sting." She averts her gaze when she sees me looking steadily at her. "I photographed the red-vine spinach."

"They're the old woman's prize. I put up the poles so they can climb on them."

"They're so beautiful in the sun. Those red-stemmed, red-veined leaves in close-up shots. They're green on the sun-facing side, but I didn't know they were pale purple on the underside."

"They have berries now. Did you see them?"

"Oh, yes. I took a few pictures of those."

I tell her I love the dark-red stains from those berries, an intense purple color, darker than beet juice. I say I would love to see her photographs someday. Maybe her photographs would help keep alive my memory of her, like my memory of the girl on the bridge, so many years ago. I want to preserve those memories, pure as honey, as long as I live.

She seems to want to say something but holds back.

"Did you close the window shutters before you went to bed?" I ask her.

"No, *Chú*. I left them open for fresh air."

"And you saw the bat fly in?"

"No, *Chú*. I saw a black thing on the wall." She laughs lightly. "Now I know why they painted all the walls white. So you can spot centipedes or ants. Or bats. That bat is the size of a lemon. First I thought it was a giant moth. Then up close I saw it wasn't a moth. And that ugly thing was hanging on top of the door frame."

"I'll get it."

"I told my mom, *Chú* can get this ugly thing out of our room, and she said she hasn't seen you all evening."

"It was my day off."

"I couldn't fall asleep," she says. "Good grief. Have you ever listened to those house lizards at night? They make those *tak-tak-tak* sounds. Always three. Then again. *Tak-tak-tak*."

I love listening to her melodious voice. Clear, lilting.

"You know something else, *Chú*," she says. "You won't notice how the hour hand on a clock moves, even if you lie there with your eyes open and try to see if the hour hand moves. I swear to God, it never moved and after a while I got up."

"Were you afraid the bat might drop down on you?"

"No. But the notion of having that hairy creature in my room scares me."

"I had one in my room, a big one, the first night I came here. Back then window shutters were never closed. The old woman just forgot. She didn't tell me where I was supposed to sleep either. So I asked her, 'Where do I sleep tonight?' And she said, 'Where? Here I've got four hectares of land and you can pick any place out there to sleep if you can't find a place in the house.'"

Both Chi Lan and Mrs. Rossi laugh. "She's a little sour most of the time," Chi Lan says.

"She's a good old woman," I say. "If you get to know her. By the way, ma'am, when you feel like visiting places again, I'll take you and Chi Lan to the Trem River near Upper U Minh."

"Where we can see the white water lilies?" Mrs. Rossi asks.

"Yes, ma'am."

"That'd be lovely," Mrs. Rossi says. "Before we go back home."

"Go back home?" I ask with a start.

"Very soon. I'm still tired. So I'll rest for a few more days."

Chi Lan turns to look at me. "My mom doesn't want to go back into the forest anymore. I wanted to tell you that today."

Mrs. Rossi rises and goes to the hammock. Sitting down slowly to find her balance, she says, "But I'd love to go see that river of white water lilies. I really would. Just once."

Her voice is strained. She puts her hand on her forehead, half reclining in the hammock.

I rise from the chair and kneel on one knee by the hammock. "Ma'am," I say.

"Yes, Giang." She peers down at me, her voice scratchy.

I look down at my feet, at the floor, then I look back up at her. "I have something to tell you. I found the remains of your son."

"What?" Her hand drops from her face. "What did you say?"

I feel the presence of Chi Lan over me. "The old man I visited today . . . he buried your son . . . after he found him in a creek the night he died."

"What?" Mrs. Rossi tries to sit up. "Lord Jesus. What are you telling me, Giang?"

"Your son has been laid to rest . . . on that man's land for twenty years now." I rise, pick up the burlap bag, and bring it to the hammock. "In here, ma'am. All his personal effects. Wallet, dog tag, wristwatch, the rain poncho he wore on the night he died."

Mrs. Rossi leans back, as if afraid to touch the bag. Suddenly she shakes her head repeatedly. "What's going on?" Her voice cracks.

Chi Lan bends over her mother, gathers her hands into her own. "Mom!" her voice sounds thick.

Mrs. Rossi brushes her hand across her eyes. She stares at the faded green bag. Heaving, she says, "Can I see what's in it? Can I?"

"Let me get the lamp," I say.

When I come back out, holding the gas lamp chest high, Mrs. Rossi is clutching the burlap bag, pressing her cheek against its rough texture, and Chi Lan is kneeling at her feet.

I set the lamp on the floor. "Ma'am, you want me to take them out for you?"

Mrs. Rossi says nothing. She reluctantly gives the bag over. I pull the poncho out, crinkled and smelly, and she pulls it to her chest, sniffing the dark fabric, stroking it. I hold the dog tag and the opened wallet with her son's picture for her to see in the light. Her lips crimp. She looks at them, then suddenly tears fill her eyes and she sobs. "God. Oh, God. Oh, Lord God."

Her voice choked, she sobs, and Chi Lan cradles her mother's head in her arms and cries with her mother.

I sit looking at my feet, at the lamp casting a yellow oblong on the floor. When Mrs. Rossi finally gathers herself, she reaches out and seizes my hand, and squeezing it, she says, "Bless you, Giang. Bless your heart. Can you take me to his grave tomorrow?"

I nod. "Of course."

"I want to thank the man who had laid my son to rest," Mrs. Rossi says.

"Yes, ma'am," I say softly.

Mrs. Rossi wipes her eyes and her nose with the heel of her hand. "I guess nobody knows what happened to my son. How he ended that way in a creek. Dear God, do I want to know?"

I raise my face to her; my whole being tensed. "Ma'am. I know how he died."

I put her son's wallet in her hands, then the dog tag, then the wristwatch. I explain to her that his base camp was responsible for many of our combat losses and casualties, because it controlled the whole stretch of the Trem River that cuts through the U Minh forest. That night when our battalions attacked his base we were told to leave no survivors. Then I tell her how he met his end. "It was I, ma'am. I shot him. I didn't know until tonight who he was."

"No, Giang. No. This can't be true."

"It was a terrible day, twenty years ago. It pains me now beyond words."

Her hands shaking, Mrs. Rossi weeps, pressing her son's belongings to her chest. I bow my head. I cry. I cry for his youth and mine, lost, wasted. I cry for Huan and Uncle Chung and Ian Vaughn, for mothers like Mrs. Rossi whose lives ebbed and flowed with the hope that their sons would someday be found, what's left of them, so they can hold them again like they did on the day they were born. Tears roll down my face. Crying for lives so broken. I feel Mrs. Rossi's hands touching my head, pulling me to her, and, gently, I rest my head in her lap as if she were the mother I never had. And we hold each other. In that eternity.

Acknowledgments

I would like to acknowledge the following titles as my research sources: *Portrait of the Enemy* by David Chanoff and Doàn Van Toai; *Survivors* by Zalin Grant; *Winter Soldier Investigation* by The Sixties Project; *Quagmire* by David Biggs; *Three Years in Vietnam (1907–1910)* by Gabrielle M. Vassal; *The Red Earth* by Tran Tu Binh; *Dem Thap Muoi* by Le Van Thao; *Huyen Thoai Bien* by Truc Chi; *Di San Cua Noi* by Huynh Man Chi; *Ban Chien Dau* by Doan Dung; *Trong Vuon Truc* by Tran Thanh Giao; *Mua Mua* by Vu Thi Thien Thu; *La Ngon* by Nguyen Binh; *Cau Chuyen Trong Rung Thieng* by Minh Chuyen; *Ngay Ay, Truong Son* by Ha Khanh Linh; *Dat Song* (Bao Moi Daily).

A heartfelt thank-you to The Permanent Press Co-Publishers, Martin and Judith Shepard, whose staunch support for this book from the day they first read its manuscript has brought it to life—Martin for his about-face on the book; Judith for her love and commitment; and to advisor Chris Knopf for championing the book to everyone he met. I wish to say to them, protectors of fine fiction, most modest of communicators, to accept this book as a gift that bears their signatures as it travels in time no matter how far.

I'm grateful to Barbara Anderson for her conscientious efforts in making the manuscript error-free and factually consistent.

A special thank-you to my sister, Ha Le Thuy, who believes in me and has always been an excellent listener over the years.